HELD

CAREY FURZE

HELD

Based on a True Story

S

First published in 2003 by
WriteLight Pty Ltd for Sandstone Publishing
8 Clubb Street, Rozelle NSW 2039
Ph: 9810 2936
Distributed by McMillan Publishing Services

The National Library of Australia Cataloguing-in-Publication data:-

Furze, Carey
Held
ISBN 0 9581934 2 8
1. Girls – Crimes against-Fiction. 2. Prostitution –
Thailand – Fiction. I. Title.

A823.4

Cover design by Tomas Smid (Flammable Design), and Arash Nabi.
Cover photography by Tomas Smid
Text design by lj design

Printed in Australia by McPhersons Printing Group, Victoria

54321   05 04 03

Dedicated to all those families whose children
never returned home.

FIONA

"So where's the money then, ya fuckin' slag?" The thug dropped his bulk down next to Fiona, thrusting his brutal face close to her delicate features. She recoiled, revolted by the stench of decades of tobacco on his breath.

Fiona cowered back into her seat. She was frightened, really frightened. She should never have become indebted to these people, but she had had no choice. She really needed the stuff. It was her medicine.

"I've, I've tried to contact my father and ...", Fiona stammered. She wracked her brain, desperate for an excuse and tried to retreat further back into the booth. The 'Frog and Toad' was noisy, warm and smokey, crowded with the Friday night regulars. No one seemed to be paying any attention to her predicament. Fights and arguments were common in this rough East end area of London. A raised voice barely raised an eyebrow.

"Ya already told me that crap, ya bitch! I know ya don't 'ave a father. Gimme ya purse!" The thug snatched at her bag, his speed belying his muscular build. "No, please don't", Fiona whined, trying to hold the bag behind her back. "I promise I'll pay you some money next Tuesday, a friend is lending me some". Fiona's eyes darted around, trying to find a sympathetic soul to help her. There were none. All eyes were averted, no-one wanted to get involved.

The thug wasn't even listening anymore, he had heard all these lies and excuses before, many times before. Four months ago he had started giving her the stuff on credit. He was surprised the Boss had not kicked up a fuss before now. Every time he had met her and given her more, she had promised to give him the money the next day at the pub, and every day she avoided him and came up with all sorts of reasons why she couldn't pay.

"Typical fuckin' junkie bitch", he muttered. Usually the Boss was smarter, especially with the addicts. Maybe it was because Fiona didn't act or look like a junkie. Sure, she was from a bad family; poor, alcoholic mother, father had run off years ago, too many brothers and sisters all trying to live off the welfare system. The very people who could never afford the habit always seemed to take it up, the only way to escape the drudgery of their miserable lives, he supposed. He had thought that Fiona was different. She was one of the most beautiful girls he had ever seen, in the flesh anyway. He had plenty of beauties under his bed, in the pornographic magazines he regularly bought.

Fiona was only twenty-one years old, above average height, with a fantastic lean body. Real model material. He glared down at her, without a shred of sympathy in his steely eyes. She glanced at him quickly, looking miserable and pathetic.

He remembered when he had first met her he had been unable to tear his eyes away. She had looked so pure and innocent, with her creamy English skin, sparkling blue eyes and the most kissable rosebud lips. Her mane of curly, red hair cascaded down around her shoulders and back, accentuating her silky white cleavage, visible whatever she was wearing. She was mesmerising and he knew that she made him weak, but he had to get the money to his boss. That fear overrode everything else.

He shoved her back with a thick, hairy forearm, grabbed the bag from her feeble grasp and pulled her purse out. She lunged forward trying to snatch it back, but he was too quick and strong, fending her off easily with one arm, as if she were a troublesome toddler. He started to get excited. She was making such an effort to get the purse back from him, maybe she did have the money. He knew she had been paid that day.

"Please, I don't have anything, only enough to buy a pie for dinner. Please, don't take it". Tears clouded her vision, adding to her already wretched look.

Even though she was so beautiful, he was starting to get annoyed with her. Such a whiner! There were only a few pounds in her purse, and he pocketed it. Her grizzling made him screw up his harsh, black stubbled features with irritation.

"Ya'll 'ave to come wiv me to see the Boss, I've 'ad enough of this." The thug grabbed her tightly around the top of her soft white arm and hauled her out of her seat. The people she had been sitting with looked on with concern, but no one was willing to stand up to a guy like Stubby. They all knew who he worked for. It was Fiona's own fault for getting involved with that gang. They had warned her. The noisy mass of patrons parted quickly as Fiona kicked and struggled all the way through the bar and out onto the street. The bouncers took one look at who was involved and stepped back, nodding respectfully to Stubby.

He shoved her roughly into the back of the waiting van and slammed the door. Fiona felt very weary all of a sudden. How had her life got to this point? None of her so called 'friends' had helped her in the bar. They weren't friends, just people she got wasted and drunk with. She was so fed up with her crummy life, no chance of ever getting out. Fiona slumped in the seat and silently cursed Nigel, her ex-boyfriend.

They had been sleeping together for a couple of weeks, when he had invited her for the first time to an 'industry party'. Fiona wasn't sure exactly what Nigel did for a living, but he was always invited to these high profile movie producers' and actors' parties, probably because of his merchandise, because he definitely wasn't an actor. Fiona had been completely out of her depth. She had seen people she would have only ever dreamed of meeting, stars from the movies and TV. She had sat alone on one of the sofas for the first few hours, holding a warming beer, feeling very conspicuous and nervous, as Nigel worked his way around the room, ducking away for a few moments every now and then before reappearing with a huge smile on his face. He winked at her, but she only saw the furtive stares of the other guests, as they stuck close together in their cliques, like packs of dogs wary of any stranger in their midst. Eventually Nigel came back and handed her a fresh beer.

"Why aren't you talking to anyone?" He frowned, looking down quickly at her, then back to the room, so he didn't miss anything, his leg jiggling in time to the thumping music.

Fiona stood up quickly, spilling a little of her drink on her short black skirt. She ignored it, desperately trying to act cool in front of him.

"I'm having a great time, Nigel. Wow, I've seen so many famous people. Did you see ..."

"Be quiet!", Nigel snapped, eyes blazing. "Stop blabbing like a star crazed groupie, they hate that."

Fiona looked down, ashamed. Tears welled up and her throat started to close. She had wanted to impress Nigel so badly, now he thought she was an idiot groupie.

"Sorry, I'm so sorry, Nigel, I didn't mean to ...", she muttered, still looking down at her dirty, scuffed shoes. She felt so embarrassed. She didn't belong in this crowd, they were in a different league from her. Her tears finally broke free and careered down her pale face.

Nigel darted a quick look at her, starting to feel a little sorry. She was just as pretty as the other girls at the party, but her rough clothes and heavy make-up were just not right. It was like wearing a sign saying she was from the wrong side of the tracks. Some of the other people at the party were from the wrong side of the tracks originally themselves, but wore the appropriate costumes now to hide the fact. They were the most snobbish to others from similar backgrounds, trying to distance themselves from their past as much as possible.

"Don't bloody cry here girl, you look daft," Nigel said calmly, still casing the room. Fiona wiped her tears away clumsily with her fingers, not wanting to smudge any of her carefully applied make-up. She desperately needed to blow her nose.

"Where's the toilet?", she mumbled. "I'll take you," Nigel offered and led the way further into the mansion, smiling and nodding to people as they went. Fiona kept her head down and shuffled along behind, feeling as if everyone was looking at her and talking about her. There was a queue for the bathroom and Nigel chatted easily to everyone there, while Fiona felt smaller and smaller, wishing she could just be swallowed up by the blurring shag-pile carpet. Three girls came out of the bathroom giggling crazily and wove their way back to the party. Fiona wished she could be one of those confident, beautiful girls. Nigel pulled her into the bathroom.

"OK, I think you need a little pick-me-up, eh girly?" Nigel pulled a plastic bag from a concealed pocket in his baggy combat pants. He tipped a small pile of lumpy, white powder onto the vanity and started expertly chopping the crystals into a finer powder with his credit card. He divided it carefully into four neat lines. He snorted a line up each nostril then handed her the rolled fifty pound note.

"Here you go, this'll make you feel better." He smiled, eyes watering slightly. Fiona had tried Cocaine a few times before and liked it, but it was too expensive for her to buy and take regularly. She bent over the inviting lines and snorted. She could taste it in the back of her throat immediately, kind of metallic but not unpleasant.

Nigel also pulled out a couple of pills, one white and one yellow. "Take these as well, they'll kick in when the coke wears off." Fiona obediently threw them into her mouth and drank from the tap. She felt so much better now. Nigel was a great guy, being nice and taking care of her. She started kissing him, feeling suddenly horny. "Not yet." Nigel pushed her away. "I have more business to do. I want to sell the whole bag. Let's go back to the party."

Fiona shrugged and quickly went to the toilet and fixed her face, before re-entering the party. This time she felt marvellous. Everyone was smiling at her and looking friendly. What a nice bunch of people. Fiona followed Nigel over to a group of smartly dressed, beautiful people and started chatting to one of the other girls. She was a model from France and was over for a shoot. Fiona was dizzy with excitement that this girl would even consider talking to her. They chatted for a while before more of the girl's friends came over.

"We're going for a quick line, do you wanna come?", the girl whispered into Fiona's ear. She looked around for Nigel, but he had already moved on to another group. "I'd love to." Fiona grinned broadly, feeling honoured to be included. At this point she would have done anything to be part of this 'in' crowd. The girl grabbed her hand, as if they had been friends for years and they staggered off to the bathroom with two other girls, laughing and pushing each other teasingly. "Finally," Fiona thought, heady with the attention, "I'm one of the beautiful people. They have accepted me as one of them."

Since that night Nigel had always been generous with the pills and powders, and Fiona loved them all. Their relationship had been a stormy one, but then, all of Fiona's relationships were either violent or verbally aggressive, usually both. Nigel had never hit her, but she had caught him sleeping with other girls many times. To get back at him, Fiona had slept with a few of his friends. Nigel didn't seem to mind, he even introduced new ones and asked if he could watch. Fiona had obliged a couple of times, when she was wasted, but never felt too good about it afterwards. The pills always helped.

Eventually Nigel stopped coming around and Fiona saw him out with another girl. He wouldn't return her calls or give her any more of her desperately needed medicine. That's when Stubby had offered to help.

Fiona was beyond crying. "I don't care if I live or die", she thought morosely. Stubby and another rough looking character drove her to a very seedy part of town. The van tyres dipped and bounced over the pot-holed, narrow back streets. Factories and warehouses loomed out of the darkness as the headlights briefly illuminated their decrepit corrugated roofs and shanty walls. Fiona stared unseeing out of the window, wondering if they planned to kill her now, or just scare her. No-one would miss her, anyway. She sniffed and rubbed her reddened eyes.

They marched her into one of the dark buildings, and down the back to an office where the Boss was seated, bent over papers, busy writing.

The Boss was not as scary as Fiona had imagined. He was an older guy, with a shaved head, very thick leathery skin, big features and watery blue eyes. She was pushed into a seat in front of his desk. No-one spoke. The Boss looked up every now and then, as if appraising her, but carried on with his paperwork. Fiona squirmed in her seat; the suspense was excruciating. She wondered if this was part of their scare tactics. Finally, he asked if she wanted a drink and something to eat.

"You mean my last supper?", she replied, like a smartarse. He smiled at her humour. "Get us some curry, mate, and two gins," he said to Stubby, continuing to stare intently at Fiona. "Ya like curry and gin, don't ya?"

"Yeah, it's OK." Fiona mumbled her reply and fidgeted under his gaze. All she could think about was having a fix, anything to stop these feelings of fear and anxiety. She crossed and uncrossed her legs, not sure how she was supposed to behave.

"Maybe ya want something else, eh girly?" The Boss seemed to have read her mind.

Fiona looked up quickly. "What do ya mean?" She eyed him warily.

"Maybe you want some dessert first, eh?"

"Why is he offering me some more, when I already owe him so much money?", Fiona wondered, confused, but tempted.

"Yeah, I'd love something, what do ya have?"

The Boss chuckled. "Well, I have a little of everything, darlin'." He opened one of his desk drawers and pulled out a tray filled with all sorts of drug paraphernalia; powders, coloured pills, syringes. "I'll make you up something nice." He expertly prepared a formula and sucked it up into a syringe.

She looked on nervously. "I usually just take pills or coke. I've only shot up a couple of times." She hadn't done it herself, it had always been Nigel's idea.

"That's all right, luv, this stuff's much better. You've never felt ecstasy until you've tried this, I guarantee it." He smiled and his whole face softened. He flicked the syringe with his fingernail and came around to her side and sat on the edge of the desk.

Fiona looked at his honest blue eyes and moaned, "I need something to help get rid of this depression."

"Just hold out your arm, this won't hurt at all, and you'll be feeling fantastic in two seconds."

Fiona really wanted to feel fantastic in two seconds. He put a rubber tie around the top of her arm, found her vein easily, and injected the liquid like a professional nurse. Within moments Fiona slumped back in her seat, a look of calm ecstasy on her face.

"Thanks Boss, it's very good of ya, do appreciate it," Fiona babbled away, feeling completely relaxed and happy.

"Come over to the sofa, luv, and get comfortable." The Boss put a tender hand under her arm and helped her over to the sofa, then sat down cozily next to her.

"Thanks luv." She smiled and looked at him through glazed eyes.

"Now, you owe me quite a bit of money don't you?" The Boss looked at her sternly.

"Yes I do." She smiled back. She was floating in the most wonderfully safe place, not a care in the world.

"I know you have an office job, but it will take you two lifetimes to pay me back, won't it?"

"Yes." She was still smiling, like a crazy person, not having any clue where this conversation was going and not caring either.

"I have a proposition for you," he continued slowly, making sure she was listening. Fiona was finding it hard to concentrate on what the Boss was saying.

"One of my suppliers overseas has a package for me, and I need someone to fly there and bring it back. Someone with a clean passport and a good steady job. You would be perfect."

"Bring something back for you?" Fiona's tongue was thick. It was difficult to talk.

"Yeah, that's right luv. I'll pay for your ticket and accommodation, you have a bit of a holiday, go shopping, take some photos. I'll give you some shopping money and you bring back my package."

"Shopping money?" He smiled, leaned forward and patted her arm reassuringly, "Yes, luv, shopping money."

"Where?" Fiona was trying hard to process all the information.

"Thailand, luv. A beautiful place to go for a holiday."

"Julie went to Thailand last year. Her and Gary loved it. Beautiful beaches. You'd give me shopping money?" He nodded.

"And pay for everything?" Fiona looked at him sceptically, waiting for the 'but' part.

"Yes, of course luv. You'll have a great holiday, meet my business contact and bring back my package and then your debt with me will be wiped."

"And I can go to the beach?" Fiona smiled, imagining herself on a beautiful tropical beach, all for free, even getting shopping money. It was a dream come true.

"Of course you can go to the beach. My contact will take you." He grinned happily, this was a lot easier than the last couple of girls.

"Can I go swimming too? I've never been swimming at the beach before." Fiona suddenly focussed and looked up at the Boss, eyes wide. "I don't have a swim suit!"

"I'll buy you one," the Boss reassured her quickly. "Let's go shopping tomorrow and we can buy whatever you need."

"When do ya want me to go?", she asked, enjoying the euphoric sensation of the drug.

"In one week. That will give me time to organise everything." He was already calculating his profits on the deal.

"Stubby will take you home now." At the mention of his name, the thug walked into the room with the curry in a take-away container.

"I will pick you up from work at 5.30 tomorrow, OK? We'll go shopping and I will brief you on everything. Here's a little present to last you till then." He scooped up a handful of pills and held them out to her.

Her smile was dazzling as she grabbed the pills and stuffed them into her jacket pocket. "I want a red bikini, to go with my hair."

"You can have whatever your heart desires, luv," he smiled. What a successful meeting. Nigel had been right about this one.

All that week Fiona was on cloud nine. Mostly due to the free drugs, but also at the idea of her holiday in Thailand.

"I'm off to Thailand for a lovely holiday next week," she was bragging at the pub to anyone who would listen.

"How can you afford it?", was the jealous, disbelieving reply. They were all surprised to see her back in one piece, without even a mark.

 "I have a wealthy boyfriend taking care of me. He's very generous." She was thoroughly enjoying being the centre of attention.

"We're going to the beaches in Thailand and going to drink cocktails at a bar right on the water's edge." Fiona had picked up a brochure from the travel agent near work.

"How long ya goin' for, Fi?", a girl in her group asked.

"Just a week, that's all we have time for." She had tried to get two weeks from the Boss, but he had outright refused to finance that. He wanted his package as quickly as possible. The manager at her office had not been too pleased with the short notice, or her lack of performance over the past week, so she had been fired and given two weeks' pay as compensation. She was ecstatic. Everything was turning out wonderfully.

She called her mother to show off a little, telling her about the new boyfriend taking her to Thailand for a luxurious holiday. Her mother sounded tired and a little drunk, as usual, even though it was the middle of the day. Fiona could hear crying in the background.

"Is that Jem crying?" Fiona wondered why her baby sister was not at school.

"Yeah, they sent 'er 'ome, bad behavior," her mother mumbled. Fiona could hear her sucking heavily on one of her self rolled cigarettes.

"Really, wad she do?" Fiona smiled at the thought of the wilful seven year old. She had always been naughty and hyperactive.

"She punched 'er teacher in the guts, little bitch," her mother snarled. "Now I 'ave to put up with 'er 'ere at 'ome for three fuckin' days."

Fiona wanted the conversation back on her. "So, I'm goin' to Thailand for a while."

"Where's Thailand, anyway?", her mother asked, only half listening.

"Somewhere in Asia," Fiona responded, not really knowing herself.

"That makes it real clear," her mother retorted, voice full of sarcasm. Suddenly she started one of her coughing fits. Fiona held the receiver away from her ear for a moment, until the spasm had passed and her mother had spat into an ever present hanky.

"So, I won't be back for a while," Fiona continued. She wanted to get out of going round to her mother's depressing, dingy flat every three weeks or so to visit her brothers and sisters. They never appreciated it anyway. All they ever wanted was money.

"Alright, luv. 'ave a good time." Her mother sounded eager to get off the phone. "I got another call comin' in."

"OK, Mum, see ya when I get back. Hi to the kids," Fiona hurriedly replied, before being cut off.

"She probably doesn't even believe I'm going anywhere, she never trusts me." Fiona was hurt by her mother's lack of interest, but quickly turned her mind back to happy thoughts of the fast approaching, exotic holiday.

K A R I N

"You can't do this to me!", Karin screamed down the phone at Stefan, her normally beautiful face screwed up in frustration. She stormed around the lounge of her luxury city apartment in Stockholm, kicking the sofa with one of her perfectly manicured feet, making her sleeping Persian cat jump in fright.

"But, Baby, what choice do I have? Please don't be angry," Stefan pleaded, trying desperately to avoid sending Karin into another one of her tantrums.

Karin slammed the phone down in fury, shouting obscenities at the wall. She stomped over to the picture window. It always calmed her to look out over the city from this height. She was used to getting her way, but it was just not working this time. Karin and her boyfriend, Stefan, had been planning this trip for such a long time, and now he couldn't go! She shouldn't blame him but she was angry and needed to blame someone. His mother had been in a car accident the previous week and was still in hospital. Initially it had been serious, but she was over the worst now and Karin thought it would be OK to carry on with their plans. She had been looking forward to this trip for six months and had worked all through the summer to get this time off in October. They had decided that going to Thailand in the peak summer season would be no fun; everyone from Europe went there in August.

Karin had the typical North European good looks. A tall, long legged slim figure, with narrow hips and small breasts. Her hair was her best feature, thick golden blonde wavy locks that flowed down her back. Her big green eyes gave her a look of youthful interest in everything.

Karin worked in the most famous department store in the city, selling up-market, expensive clothing. One of her brothers had got her the position. She wasn't especially conscientious or good at her job, but she was so beautiful the store would use her as a model whenever they needed to. This was a nice distraction from the boredom of sales, so Karin didn't mind. She wasn't a stupid girl, but she was lazy. She was twenty-three years old, the youngest in her family, and had always been able to get away with sitting back while the others did all the work. Now that she was older and out on her own, she still continued with the same behavior. People let her get away with it, so she never changed. This job gave her a little pocket money to supplement the allowance from the trust fund left to her by her grandfather. He had founded a textile factory seventy years before, which was now a massive conglomerate, run by her father and uncle. The most important function of her job, to her anyway, was that she went to all the fashion shows in town and throughout most of Europe. She had to keep up to date with all the latest fashion trends. This was her passion and she had a reputation in town for being a trendsetter.

Karin picked up the phone and began punching in her travel agent's number again, this time to cancel the whole trip. Then the calming, rational voice of her therapist came into her head, reminding her not to put her happiness in the hands of others. "I am responsible for my own emotions, and just because things are not going my way, doesn't mean it is all bad." She chanted to herself, rolling her head on her shoulders and shaking her arms to relax. She had been seeing Dr. Gustaffson since she was fifteen and had been hospitalised with Anorexia. They had discovered together that her emotional problems had been triggered by her mother dying when Karin was thirteen and just reaching puberty. She was left in a household of men, her two brothers and father. They were good people and tried to help Karin through the mourning period as best they could, but they had not understood the mental fragility of a thirteen year old girl. She was an especially sensitive child. Her father had been busy maintaining the empire while her brothers, being older, had been better able to cope with the ordeal, throwing themselves into their studies.

She had been afraid of growing up and becoming a woman, of progressing into the future to a life without her mother. She had wanted time to stand still. Starving herself had made her feel powerful and in control of her situation. At school it became a power game with her girlfriends, to see who was the weakest and gave in first to eating. Karin was always the best at it. While the other girls tried hard to compete, they eventually had to concede defeat. Karin was able to go without food easily, although she did sometimes indulge in diet pills.

She would seldom look at her whole body in the mirror, just parts of it. The skin hanging under her arms had been an obsession for a while, making her do endless arm exercises while cloistered in her bedroom, supposedly doing homework. The gap between the tops of her thighs had been another obsession. She'd heard that men were very attracted to large gaps. No matter what slimming goal she aimed for, she was never satisfied with her look, although she did like the way her hip bones jutted out just like the skeletal models in the magazines. She kept many carefully cut out pictures stuck to her mirror and walls, as an incentive. All this hard work had kept her body in a pre-pubescent state, but it had almost killed her.

Her family only found out when she was sent home, for the third time, for fainting at school and her father had taken her to the family doctor, despite desperate resistance from Karin. She didn't want the old quack interfering in her well thought out plans to be a successful model. She was extremely malnourished, with anaemia and a calcium deficiency.

Initially her father had been angry, both at himself and Karin. Why would she starve herself? They were wealthy, they could afford all the food they wanted. She was a beautiful girl, why did she want to destroy herself?

After many phone calls to specialists and psychiatrists he managed a limited understanding of his daughter's problem. Karin received the best medical care available. There had been a couple of relapses, whenever she got stressed with school or boyfriends, but once she started to see her psychiatrist, she had improved dramatically. Her family were relieved, but always kept a close, protective eye on her now.

After sulking for five minutes or so, she rang Stefan back.

"I'm so sorry," she cooed. "Of course you can't leave right now."

Stefan's anger immediately disappeared on hearing Karin's soft, sweet voice. "I really think Ma will be fine by the middle of the month," he replied confidently, relieved that Karin was still talking to him. "I spoke with my travel agent and they are prepared to change my ticket, because of the circumstances, but you can't change yours."

"I know. I already asked them. I'll just buy another one and go with you in two weeks."

"That seems wasteful. Why don't you go and stay with those friends of your father's in Bangkok? They sound really cool, and I will meet up with you on the 15th. Then we can travel up to north Thailand and ride the elephants, like you wanted to. We would still have enough time."

"It won't be the same without you," Karin complained stubbornly, still trying to get her way.

"What about the beaches?", Stefan reminded her, trying to distract her as he would a naughty two year old. "Remember the brochures we looked at? There were some fantastic beaches. Go and lie on a beach and relax. I'll be there before you even realise."

"Well, maybe," Karin reluctantly started to agree. "I have been working really hard to get the winter season out, I could do with some sun."

Stefan beamed. He was always careful not to upset Karin too much.

LAURIE

As Laurie sat in the departure lounge of the Atlanta International airport she tried to ignore the admiring glances from passing travellers. She was still getting used to civilian life. After spending the last three years in the American Military, Special Forces Division, she had not expected to be out on her own so soon. She had dedicated so many years to dreaming about joining the specialised team. Now after the disgrace and forced resignation, Laurie was still very upset. She knew that it was her own fault, but being gay shouldn't be reason enough to destroy someone's career.

The whole affair had started innocently enough. The rules about fraternising within the group were very strict and Laurie could appreciate that, but she had met a woman who did consulting work for the Military and Laurie had reasoned that a consultant was far enough removed from her division to make it OK. The affair had been brief and passionate. It had started over a pool game, in the recreation room on base. Laurie had gone there at 9.00 p.m. that night, after three days of rigorous training in the desert. She was exhausted and dying for a beer or ten.

The woman had flirted openly. She was taller than Laurie with short, dark curly hair, a plain face but with beautiful, clear olive skin and sparkling, brown eyes. Her name was Meg. At first, Laurie thought the woman was just being funny, deliberately bending over the pool table to take a shot, right in front of her, revealing the back of her silky brown thighs in the tight, denim skirt she was wearing. Laurie tried not to look at her arse, but she was very attracted to the woman. She hadn't had any sexual contact for a year, since she had finished her long distance relationship in Atlanta.

It became very obvious that the woman was interested in Laurie when she came up close and whispered, her breath warm and inviting, "Are you dating anyone at the moment?"

Laurie stammered, flushed with desire and emotion, desperately wanting to get naked with this woman, but nervous about the other people around.

"No, uh no, um, I am not seeing anyone at the moment."

"I think you are very beautiful and sexy. I would love to be alone with you and share a bottle of wine and chat." The woman breathed teasingly into Laurie's ear while her hand caressed the small of Laurie's back.

Laurie had had a few beers by this stage, so with Dutch courage replied, "Umm, me too." Nervously she looked around to see if anyone had noticed this erotic exchange. No one was looking their way. The woman's hair smelt sweet and freshly washed and her hand was warm, caressing and sensual. Laurie's heart was racing.

"I was thinking about going into the mountains for a picnic tomorrow. Do you want to come, just you, me and Sam?", the woman asked, looking deeply into Laurie's eyes.

Laurie was alarmed. "Sam? Who's Sam?"

The woman laughed. "My Cocker Spaniel."

Laurie relaxed again, and laughed. "Yeah, that sounds nice."

They arranged to meet for a picnic the next day. For 'privacy' they would drive somewhere off base.

Meg arrived in a flashy red convertible, with a spotted black and white scarf over her dark hair and 'Jackie O' sunglasses. Laurie's heart skipped a beat as Meg flashed a dazzling smile and said, "Going my way, Baby?"

Laurie jumped in, flinging her backpack in the back seat with Sam. Meg rubbed her hand seductively on Laurie's thigh in a quick greeting and they were off in a roar of the engine. Meg chatted as she drove the car confidently up into the nearby hills to find the perfect picnic spot, and soon Laurie was at ease, laughing happily at Meg's stories about her dog. Meg seemed to know her way around the hills and had no problem finding a secluded place to lay the blanket. No sooner was the blanket down, than she grabbed Laurie hungrily, pushing her down and kissing her passionately. It had been one of the most exciting moments of Laurie's life.

They had met five more times in the ensuing weeks, before the affair had been discovered by passing hikers. The startled walkers had seemed more embarrassed than the reckless lovers. Meg tried to hide her face with her shirt, but was laughing raucously the whole time, while Laurie was like a deer caught in headlights and just stared at the intruders, mouth opening and closing stupidly.

The incident was reported to the base and that was when Laurie found out that her new lover was actually married to one of the Generals. There was a huge scandal; the General and his wife were transferred and Laurie was asked to resign, or be dismissed.

At first, Laurie had no idea what she was going to do. One moment her career was going to plan and the next it was all over. All the tumultuous feelings she had experienced when she was younger resurfaced.

She couldn't remember exactly how or when her childhood depression and anxiety had started, but her parents had noticed eventually and the family doctor had put her on anti-depressant medication. Once she had admitted she was gay, initially to herself, and then to her family and friends, a mountain of pressure had been released; she felt more comfortable with herself and her place in the world. Sometimes it was very hard and Laurie didn't know how she had got through those dark days, but one day in College she had a meeting with the guidance counsellor, who suggested a career in the Military. At a time when they were trying to encourage more females into specialised fields, Laurie had exactly the right personality for fast advancement through the ranks. Since she had made the decision to join, she had never felt depressed again. The first six months had been very rigorous and demanding, both physically and mentally, but Laurie had loved every minute of it. The training was demanding, but it gave her focus. Finally she had a direction and belonged to a group who accepted her as she was. For the first time in her life she felt together and valuable, as if she were really making a difference. She had made solid friendships with others just like her, her new family.

But now that was all over. She was ostracised and thrown out on her own. She went through the whole cycle of emotions; anger, fear, hate, self-pity. She didn't want to become a slave to depression again, so she moved back to her parents' farm, in a small community just north of Atlanta, to figure out what she was going to do with her life.

She had slept a lot at first but her mother had not allowed that for very long. Soon she was out in the fields helping with the labouring, which started to make her feel better; being surrounded by her loving, supportive family was vital. At the end of one rigorous day, Laurie slumped in front of the TV to eat her dinner. A travel show was on. A small group of backpackers were making their way around the world; tonight they were in Thailand.

"Wow, that looks like fun," Laurie commented absently.

Her father looked over at her, pleased that she was starting to return to her normal self and the strained expression was easing.

"You should do something like that, you have the time and some money saved." Her father took a quick sidelong look at Laurie's mother, checking her reaction.

"I dunno, I was thinking about maybe going back to school," Laurie shrugged, still watching the show.

"That's a good idea too, but there's plenty of time for school. Why not take off a couple of months and go on a holiday?", her father suggested casually. "It would be a good rest."

Her father had been her biggest supporter when the trouble in her Unit had started. He called in all favours owed to him to get Laurie's indiscretion overlooked, but they were using her as an example to discourage others.

"I'm going into town tomorrow, you should come with me and go see Auntie Jess at the travel agency. She could give you some options to think about," Laurie's mother offered.

Laurie considered this for a moment. School could definitely wait. Maybe a holiday away from everything, another country, would be a refreshing change. Maybe she needed a new perspective on life. "Yeah, OK, I'll come with you tomorrow."

Her parents beamed, happy to see the spark return to Laurie's face.

❖   ❖   ❖

Auntie Jess pulled out a vast array of brochures.

"I want an adventure holiday, with beautiful beaches, mountains to climb, old city ruins, jungles and strange animals."

"You would have to go to a few different places to get all of that, my girl," her aunt laughed.

In an afternoon of deliberation and intense brochure reading Laurie decided on a ticket to Asia. She felt it was time to move on from the protective circle of her family. She needed to build her confidence again. She would fly into Bangkok, Thailand, then travel up and down Asia for three months. It was a very full trip, it would use all of her savings, but she wanted to get away and broaden herself. She was unsure how her family would take the decision, but to her surprise they encouraged her one hundred per cent.

Now that she was finally starting her trip, she felt slightly better. At first she had been nervous about travelling alone, but she was highly trained in survival and combat, so back-packing around Asia shouldn't be too much of a problem. Laurie's figure belied how physically strong she was. At 5'5" with slim hips she looked almost delicate. No one would have guessed that she had a black belt in karate and was now very advanced in kick-boxing, having used the local gym as therapy since her "resignation".

From Atlanta she would fly through Los Angeles then on to Bangkok. It was a long flight, but after all these years on special operations she was used to long, uncomfortable travel. What she wasn't used to was how intimidating men's casual glances of desire could be. She quickly pulled back her curly blonde hair into a rough ponytail and cast her bright blue eyes down at her Lonely Planet Guide to Asia. She had gone over it a million times, but it was still exciting to think she was almost there. No-one was seeing her off. Her family lived too far away, and they were still busy on the farm. Spending the last two months working on the farm with her parents had been valuable, quality time and she was feeling very happy and carefree and ready for an adventure.

chapter four

KELLY

Finally the long awaited day had arrived and the whole family was at the Sydney International Airport to see Kelly off. At twenty-one Kelly was a very confident, friendly young woman. She was of average height, with long, straight strawberry blonde hair, sparkling green/blue eyes that changed colour depending on what she wore, or the mood she was in. Her small nose turned up slightly at the end. She always thought that it was ugly and looked like a ski-jump, and decided that when she was older and had the money she would get it straightened, but it was a feature that others found cute. Her full lips were always open in a dazzling smile, showing her perfectly straight, white teeth. She was used to being complimented on her smile, the result of being a tooth model for an orthodontist introducing a new technique into Australia. Her figure was very athletic and strong. Working out on the fitness equipment made by her design engineer father had kept her body lean and trim. Now she was wearing comfortable travelling clothes for the ten hour flight to Thailand; a T-shirt with shorts and sneakers. Around her tiny waist was the bum bag her mother had bought for the trip, securely holding her ticket, passport and money.

The closer the time came for Kelly to board the plane the more excited her three brothers became. Being the oldest Kelly was always the first to do everything. Her brothers had always complained that she was bossy and pushy, but they secretly admired her confidence and daring. All her life she had been instructed to look out for them and she was constantly fighting battles for them at school. Now they towered over her and she had given up fist fighting with them many years ago.

All three boys were boisterously pushing each other, laughing and joking, not knowing any other way to pass the time before Kelly left. Her mother was starting to look a bit teary, so her father had a comforting arm around her shoulders. Kelly started to do the rounds of goodbyes, hugging and promising to call regularly. She was not feeling upset or sad at all; she had been living away from home since she was seventeen, and had been looking forward to this trip for the last five months.

Kelly had quit her successful real estate sales job, after buying her first house at twenty, and decided she wanted a break from the humdrum of working everyday. A friend had suggested a season of working at a ski resort in the South Island of New Zealand, so they had flown over together. Kelly had worked in the ski apparel shop on one of the mountains above Queenstown, a hugely popular ski town. She had befriended a diverse range of international friends, from America, Europe and New Zealand, who had also been attracted to the area for the skiing and work. After getting a taste of the intoxicating spirit of travel, Kelly was easily convinced by her new friends to meet up with some of them in Thailand, after the ski season ended.

One of the American girls had stayed at a fabulous guesthouse in Bangkok, so it was decided that they would all meet there in five months. This suited Kelly as she really needed to save a bit more money before she could afford to go.

Their plan was to have a holiday on one of the islands in Thailand, to get thin and brown, before buying a cheap ticket in Bangkok and heading off to Tokyo to model and work in a bar. Japan was the place to be as a young Western blonde girl. The American girl had been over there already, and relayed thrilling stories about the money she had made modelling and serving drinks in one of the many hostess clubs. Kelly found it hard to believe that a bar would pay fifty dollars an hour to a pretty, blonde girl to just sit and drink and chat, but she had heard this same story from many other girls who had been to Japan. She was looking forward to seeing for herself.

Not wanting to delay and upset her mother further, Kelly walked towards the departure gate, and with one quick look and cheery wave goodbye, she was gone.

On the plane, Kelly was seated next to a lovely Maori boy, Jason. He was very effeminate, so she presumed he was gay. On hearing that Kelly had no accommodation booked in Bangkok he became very alarmed.

"You have nothing organised?", he queried in disbelief, one hand over his mouth and eyes wide.

"No. I have the name of a place and I thought I would phone them once I got there," she replied confidently.

"Do you know that we arrive at 1.00 a.m. Thai time? Nothing will be open."

Kelly had not even thought of asking the travel agent what time the flight arrived. She felt a little stupid now.

"No, I didn't realise we arrived so late," Kelly said, trying not to look nervous.

"Don't worry. I have a nice hotel booked in the heart of the city. You can stay with me if you like and phone your place in the morning."

"That's very generous of you, are you sure?"

"There is no way I can leave you at the airport with no-where to go. I am safe, and I have no ulterior motive," he reassured her quickly, looking very sincere.

Kelly had not even entertained the idea that he had sinister plans for her. "That would be great, thanks so much."

❖   ❖   ❖

Outside the Bangkok International terminal, the air was sticky and humid, even at one in the morning. Immediately Thai men were rushing up. "Taxi, taxi, you want taxi?"

"How much to the Novotel?", Jason asked.

"500 Baht!", one scrawny man shouted over the rest.

"That's $100," Kelly whispered, after doing a quick calculation in her head. "It seems a bit expensive. I thought Thailand was cheap." So much for being able to survive on five dollars a day, like some of the stories she had heard.

"OK, OK. I do special price for you," another driver piped up animatedly. "Just 400 Baht. No less!"

The group of taxi drivers now surrounded the pair, all shouting out different prices. Suddenly a uniformed Thai strode over and said in an authoritative voice, "Where do you want to go?" The taxi drivers all took a couple of steps back.

"We want to go to the Novotel," said Jason.

"You have to go to the taxi stand over there," the uniformed man said, pointing several hundred metres down. "Do not go with any of these drivers. They are not licensed, and the price should be no more than 250 Baht."

The crowd of drivers started to disperse sulkily as Kelly and Jason headed for the legitimate taxi stand. The taxi ride to the hotel was a rollercoaster. They both scrambled to put on their seatbelts, but discovered that there were none. The roads were huge, with four lanes in both directions. There seemed to be little observance of normal road rules. The driver swerved in and out of lanes, going right up behind the next vehicle, before quickly veering over without indicating. The roads were very congested, which seemed unusual for that time of night. There were motorbikes loaded up with what seemed like whole families. Children perched on the handlebars or on the mother's knee, behind the father. Very dangerous. Huge trucks lumbered past, spilling bits of whatever their loads were. Tuk-tuks, the traditional mode of transport, looking like a bicycle or motorbike attached to a covered cart that could fit three or four people, rode precariously on the sides of the road, swaying dangerously every time a big truck raced by. Was there no speed limit here? There were Police cars every now and then, but they seemed to be doing just as many illegal maneuvers as everyone else.

Kelly was starting to feel a little car sick when finally they arrived at the hotel. After paying an extra fifty dollars for Kelly to stay too, they were shown to the room.

Even though they had been travelling for over twelve hours, Kelly said to Jason, "It's only 10.00 p.m. our time and I'm not tired at all. Do you want to go out somewhere?"

"Yeah, I'm not tired either." Jason's eyes lit up with excitement. "Where should we go?"

"Let's just jump in a taxi and ask them where down-town or the night-life is," Kelly suggested eagerly.

They went out to the front of the hotel, where there was a line of taxis waiting. Hopping into the first one, Kelly asked the driver, "Can you take us to where all the bars are?" It took several tries before he seemed to understand what they wanted. Kelly was annoyed by this and wondered why the driver was waiting outside a big international hotel, if he could not speak English. All this was soon forgotten, as they raced into the night

At first, they were on congested main roads. They whizzed past massive department stores, their fashionable window displays brightly lit up, and street markets, with a diverse range of people wandering among the stalls, making late night purchases. Bright lights beamed and neon signs flashed. There was so much life and activity, nothing like her quiet home town in country Australia. It was very exciting being part of it.

After about ten minutes, Kelly noticed that the streets were getting smaller and more run down, with big spaces between the streetlights.

She looked at Jason and said, "This doesn't look like a very popular area. Do you think he understood where we wanted to go?"

The taxi turned into an alley. Starting to get a little nervous, Kelly looked out the window on her side. As the taxi was slowing to a stop, she saw a gang of youths coming out of the shadows, carrying chains and baseball bats. She screamed at Jason, "Lock your door!"

She banged her lock down and reached in front to lock the driver's door. By then the gang was all around the car, banging on the sides and trying to open the doors. When the driver started to unlock and open his door, Kelly realised he must be in on it. She leaned forward and kept her hand on the lock to prevent him opening it and yelled in his ear, "Drive!"

He turned around and was starting to say, "It's OK", when Kelly punched him in the head and screamed, "Go!"

He was shocked at her violence and seemed to hesitate for a second, but thought better of it as Kelly moved to punch him again. He hit the accelerator and sent both of them flying back into the seat. There was a scream of terror from one of the guys in the gang, as he rolled off the hood of the taxi and hit the ground.

The taxi driver was muttering abuse and rubbing his head, nervously looking through the rear vision mirror at the pair in the back seat. Jason was speechless and shaking, while Kelly leaned forward again and said to the driver, "Back to the hotel." There was no room for negotiation. After her initial bravado Kelly sat back shaking with adrenaline and shock. She couldn't believe her reflex reaction. It was then that their vulnerability hit her; they had everything of value on them in their bum bags. It could have been a disaster, two hours into her big adventure. Maybe she should have stayed home. Once back at the hotel, they quickly jumped out of the taxi, relieved at being back in a safe place. As they walked quickly into the hotel the taxi driver screamed at them for his fare. Kelly looked back.

"You've got to be joking!", she said incredulously. He started to pursue them, but when he saw Kelly go to the front desk, he quickly jumped back into the taxi and sped off. They reported the incident to the hotel staff, who suggested that they go to the Tourist Police. The Tourist Police unit had been set up specifically to punish any locals who ripped-off or harmed tourists, as the tourist income into the country was becoming vital. Locals who were caught were severely punished and often jailed. This process seemed a bit complicated since they didn't have the taxi number, so they decided not to report it.

The next day the whole experience seemed quite exciting and they talked at great length about it over breakfast, forgetting how dangerously close they had come to their holiday being over before it even started.

❖   ❖   ❖

On arrival at the guesthouse, Kelly was given some messages that had been waiting for her. Both the American girls had decided to return to their jobs and would not be coming. The English girl would be another two weeks, but was definitely coming, and excited about going on to Japan. The New Zealand girl had decided to go directly to Japan, and left contact details for herself there.

Kelly had two weeks to kill while waiting for Diane. Initially she was annoyed, but over the next few days she wandered around the typical tourist spots and found one area where all the young backpacking travellers went. Khao San road was a Mecca for young foreigners. It was a busy, congested road; a single lane each way, about two hundred metres long, full of restaurants serving a mixture of Western and Thai food, with televisions showing the latest pirated videos. Tailors' shops displayed a vast array of local cotton, silks and wool fabrics and made clothes to measure. There were hundreds of travel agencies, selling local and international travel, and cheap guesthouses. The key to this road being so popular with foreigners was that everyone in the shops, restaurants and guesthouses all spoke English, to varying degrees. The Indians were the best; they had the best shops, spoke fluent English, and were very polite.

Most people looked shabby and unwashed, in cut off shorts and ragged T-shirts, obviously seasoned travellers. Kelly stood out slightly with her styled hair, manicured nails and short summer dresses. She tried to dress down and be more casual, but could never pull it off. Where she came from, it was important to be well groomed and looking your best at all times. Being young and naive and new to travelling she was oblivious to the fact that in another country and culture her smart dress sense may be interpreted in a completely different way, especially by the modest Thai people. She never would have imagined what lay in store for her, just because she was trying to make herself look attractive.

On the Khao San Road everyone was under the age of thirty and very friendly. All were willing to exchange information and advice on places they had visited. Most people were travelling in pairs, but there were a few travelling alone and some were girls. Sitting in one of the many cafés, talking with them, Kelly became inspired, and the more she thought about it the more she became excited at the idea of travelling alone, not having to compromise, or ask another's opinion. The general consensus was that Bangkok was a dump and just a place you stayed for a day or two, while flying in or out. Kelly enjoyed Bangkok, but it was dirty and noisy, and the three days she had been in the city were enough. She called into one of the many travel agents and discovered there were overnight bus rides to other places in Thailand. One was to an island in the South East, called Kho Samui. It was starting to become popular and others had told her how beautiful the beaches were.

After the filth and chaos of Bangkok, a nice, quiet beach sounded wonderful. She went to one of the agencies that offered an international phone service to call home and tell her parents about her exciting new plans. When she arrived there was a wait of about an hour, so she decided to phone once she got to the island. She bought a ticket for the overnight bus ride down to the ferry that went across to the island. Others had also warned her not to eat the cookies and sodas that were offered on the bus, as they were sometimes drugged. The bus driver would wait until everyone ate their cookies and fell asleep, then stop at a pre-arranged spot and let bandits on the bus to rob the passengers. This was most alarming and as Kelly boarded the bus, she thought there would be no way she could relax and sleep. As the bus moved into the night she soon grew sleepy and was relieved when everyone was awoken in the early morning to catch the ferry, passports and money intact.

CAUGHT

The Boss drove Fiona to Heathrow airport on Thursday, still briefing her on everything she had to do. He was nervous about sending a dizzy junkie, but she was expendable if anything went wrong. This was his third attempt at sending someone, always the same type. No one could tie her to him, but most importantly, she had a clean passport, a steady job and no criminal record. The chances of success were high.

"Now, make sure you look out for the Thai driver picking you up. He will be standing at the gate you come out of, holding a sign with your name on it." He was looking at Fiona earnestly.

"You've already told me this a million times. I'm not stupid," Fiona retorted, feeling brave in this new relationship with the Boss. All she could think of was that she would be sunbathing on a tropical beach in less than twenty four hours, sipping a cocktail with cherries and an umbrella in it; something she had only read about in romantic novels and travel magazines. She would have the first six days to herself, on an island just outside Bangkok. Then on the return journey to the airport she would be driven by the Boss's contact. This man would give her a box with souvenirs and statues. Fiona was told that these had been stolen and would sell in England for a lot of money, therefore paying for her holiday and debt. She had not even considered the fact that they might be stuffed full of heroin.

On arrival at Bangkok it was not difficult to find her driver. It made Fiona feel very special to have someone greeting her and holding up a sign with her name. He was very friendly and tried to maintain a conversation with Fiona, but she was too busy looking at the sea of traffic and people to concentrate on what he was saying, and his accent was too difficult to understand. She had never seen so many Asians in one place. The buildings and neon signs were all very intimidating and overwhelming, but she was fascinated at the same time and couldn't tear her eyes away. The driver jabbered away on his mobile phone for a while and then said to her, "You hungry? We stop for dinner?"

"Yeah, let's go to a nice restaurant, I'm starving. The food on the plane was foul." Fiona wanted to get as much for nothing as possible.

The driver said, "My friend has very good restaurant, we go there, OK?"

"Yeah, whatever." Fiona was looking at some prostitutes on a street corner. "They're very beautiful, and so tall," she commented. "I thought Asians were small."

"They Lady-boys, Miss," the driver responded, looking at the group of scantily clad hookers, laughing and waving at passers-by.

"Lady-boys? What's that?"

"Boys raised as girls in their family from when they were little children."

"Why would their family do that?", Fiona asked, puzzled.

"If a poor family has no girls they can raise a boy like a girl and then sell him into prostitution and make a lot of money from him," the driver explained unemotionally.

"How bizarre. They look like beautiful, perfect women."

"Many have operation to be girl, make more money."

"Who are the customers?" Fiona was dumbfounded. What man would want to sleep with such a freak, even though they were very beautiful?

"Usually customer very drunk and don't know it not woman. Sometimes drugged. Very popular with big, rich white men from Europe." The driver was a mine of information.

"Yuk. My family doesn't seem so bad, now," Fiona joked, craning her head back to look at the prostitutes. "How can parents sell a child into prostitution, that's terrible!"

"Thai people are Buddhist religion. Some people think female is a low incarnation, and they have to make up for it in this life, so they can be born higher in next life. They are already low, so work as prostitute OK for them. They give money to family and help pay education for brothers and they will have better next life."

Fiona looked at him in complete disbelief. "You're not serious?", she asked, open mouthed.

"My older sister was prostitute, she paid for me and my brother to go to school, that was how we were raised. It is normal here."

"What is she doing now?" Fiona was fascinated.

"She dead. AIDS." A shadow of sadness seemed to flash across his face, but it could have just been a trick of the light. Fiona looked back out of the window, feeling grateful to have been born a female in a civilised country.

"This is my friend's restaurant." The driver leaped out of the van, which he had parked right outside the front, on the footpath.

They went into the dive that was supposed to be a restaurant. It was really just a lean-to up against a wall in an alley. There was a huge Thai man sitting on a tiny stool. You couldn't actually see the stool, but Fiona presumed there was one under the massive bum. His face lit up when Fiona was introduced to him.

"So you are the English courier, eh?"

"What do ya mean?" Fiona had forgotten that her main reason for being there was to take the 'souvenirs' back to England.

"You are the one taking the statues back to England aren't you?" His first thought was that the driver had picked up the wrong girl at the airport.

"Oh yeah, that's right, I am." Fiona understood what he was talking about now. She was finding it hard to remember everything; maybe she should cut back on some of the pills.

The huge Thai man was looking her up and down, appraisingly. Fiona was used to men looking longingly at her, so she politely turned her head away, pretending to look at the menu on the wall.

Finally, he said, "You are very beautiful. Are you hungry?"

"Yes, a little," Fiona responded appreciatively.

"Do you like fish? Very good fish here."

"That would be great. I like fried rice too."

He shouted towards the back to a very young Thai girl, who scurried to fetch the food. There was an awkward silence as they waited for the food and the huge man looked hard at her.

"You like drug, Lady?" She was startled at the question. She thought Asians were polite and quiet. She was unsure how to answer .

"You tried Opium?", he persisted. "I think you would love Opium, make you feel on top of the world."

"I've tried many things. I'm not sure about Opium. How do you take it?", Fiona asked, starting to get interested.

"Smoking is best. You want to try? I have some." He reached into his pocket and pulled out a small, stained, tin container. Putting it on the table, he opened it to reveal a small silver pipe and some black resin like lumps.

Fiona nervously looked around. "Can you bring it out in public like this?"

"Sure, no problem, no Police here. Police don't care anyway, I pay them."

He carefully spooned some of the black lumps into the pipe and pushed it down until it was packed tight, then handed the pipe to Fiona. "This will make you feel so good."

Fiona was a bit nervous, but it had been a long flight and she needed something to relax her. She sucked on the pipe as he held a light to it.

"Don't suck too hard," he advised.

She puffed and inhaled a taste of something she had never experienced before. It was bitter, but not completely unbearable.

"Strange taste," she said, after holding the smoke in her lungs for a while and breathing it slowly out, like she would with a joint.

"Try some more, it gets better the more you have."

The calm, euphoric feeling came over her in a wave, almost immediately.

"Wow, that's great," she murmured, feeling an overwhelming desire to lie down.

The Thai got easily off his stool and lifted Fiona like a doll.

"Do you want to lie down, Lady?"

"Mmmm, yes please." Fiona's eyes were already closed, as she drifted off into a blissful fairyland of careless, lazy days on the beach, drinking creamy cocktails, and having gorgeous men rub oil into her naked body.

chapter 6

S N A R E D

It was a tearful goodbye at Stockholm airport when Stefan saw Karin off. "Call me as soon as you get there," he insisted. She could hardly talk through her sobbing and she continued to cry on the plane, much to the distress of the businessman next to her. She had travelled alone before around Europe, but going to Asia alone was a little daunting, even though she was being met by her father's friends.

The driver met her at Bangkok airport. He had no trouble finding her, with her height and looks. The temperature had to be in the thirties. Karin groaned with exhaustion as she wiped a tired hand over her drenched forehead. It was a relief to get into the air-conditioned limousine, after waiting on the pavement outside the airport for the little driver to scurry off to get the car. She was irritable after the long flight. Even though she had flown first class, she had been unable to sleep.

Karin had never met her father's friends, with whom she was to stay for the next two weeks. Tim and Annika had lived all over Asia for the last fifteen years, running their own furniture export business. Their apartment was the typical ex-patriot mansion, unnecessarily huge with four bedrooms and maid's quarters. It was in a fashionable high-rise in the middle of the city, decorated in a myriad of different styles, from all the places they had lived in the region. Annika was very friendly and happy to have a distraction from the boredom of being the 'wife of a businessman', and took Karin to all the places she thought a young tourist would like to see.

At first Karin was fascinated. The temples were huge and elaborate, completely different from anything in Europe. The ceilings soared high above, making her dizzy as she craned her neck back to take it all in. The marble and stone walls were intricately carved with animals and people, so minute and detailed that she had to lean in very close to appreciate the years of work that must have gone into such creations. Sombre, shaven headed monks, draped elegantly in orange robes strode purposefully across the silent courtyards, heads bowed respectfully. They never stopped to talk, almost as if they had some pressing, Godly business to attend to, their minds calm and focussed, their hearts filled with peace.

In contrast the river markets were noisy, chaotic, and vibrant. Thousands of tourists and locals alike swarmed to the masses of rickety canoes and decrepit boats strapped flimsily together on the filthy water. Out of town villagers travelled for days to bring flowers, fruit and vegetables to sell in the city at an inflated price. The stink of the river was a little disconcerting but the assortment of colours and smells of ripe fruit and flowers were a real feast for the senses.

Karin particularly loved the department stores, the clothes were so cheap. She spent many hours wandering the vast malls, with Annika happily tagging along. On the fourth day Karin was feeling a little claustrophobic. Annika was generous and attentive, but Karin was used to doing what she wanted and being chaperoned everywhere was getting annoying. It reminded her of her family at home, constantly monitoring and organising everything she did. This was her holiday, she wanted to get away from all that.

Annika and Tim guessed Karin was getting a little bored with their mature company, so they had invited some young people from their office for a dinner party. That morning Karin had asked the older woman if she could accompany the maid to the local markets, to buy food for that night.

The markets were a semi-permanent set-up of rough stalls and benches, spilling over with brightly coloured fruits, vegetables and other kitchen necessities. Karin soon learnt to breathe through her mouth, as the unexpected stench of rotting vegetables and meat would assault the nose without warning.

Stall owners called out to Karin, "Lady, Lady, you want banana, peaches? Lady, come here Lady."

"You stay close to me, and don't talk to anyone," the maid instructed Karin carefully. Karin was in no mood to be bossed around and strode ahead by herself, ignoring the furtive looks from the maid. A straggly line of filthy children followed her, laughing and pushing each other. The maid was busy bargaining and bartering for different produce as Karin meandered along looking at live chickens in cages, turtles, snakes and live fish in big, dirty tanks.

As she passed a young Thai man leaning against a stall, he asked in a loud whisper, "Hey Lady, you wanna go beautiful beach?" This caught her attention. She was tired of the stink and heat of the city and going to a beach sounded like heaven. It was, after all, one of the main reasons for coming to Thailand.

"What beach?" She stopped to question him. He gave her a well handled but beautiful glossy brochure, featuring pictures of perfect little bays with white sands and palm trees. Western people were sitting in bamboo beach bars, laughing and drinking fancy cocktails. "Where is this?", she asked.

"Near here. Four hour drive. We have luxury van," he replied in halting English.

On closer inspection, he wasn't that young. He squinted against the sun, which accentuated the lines around his eyes. A few thick black hairs sprouted from a large dark mole on his chin and he had a smattering of whiskers above his top lip. His mouth twitched in a nervous smile, showing the few remaining dirty teeth. His eyes were very clear and sharp, following Karin's every move and gesture.

At that moment the maid came and grabbed her arm roughly, pulling her away and speaking quickly in Thai to the man in a harsh voice, a scowl on her face.

"You no talk to him," she said to Karin crossly, "Bad man!"

Karin snatched her arm back, irritated at being bossed around by the 'help'. She looked back at the man, who was still nonchalantly leaning against the stall with a big smile on his face, completely unaffected by the whole outburst.

That night, at the dinner party, Karin asked some of the younger guests about the beaches in the brochure.

"Are they really only a four hour drive away?"

"Oh yeah," one of the guests replied. "It's Koh Sammet, the closest island to here. Really convenient to get to and cheap. They have bungalows right on the beach and excellent food. You should go and check it out."

The next day, while the older woman was out, Karin rang the number on the brochure and got all the details. The woman on the phone was very helpful and friendly, her English was faultless. They would pick Karin up in a luxury van and take her to the ferry that went across to the island. They would arrange all the accommodation and her return as well. The only problem was that she could not pay for it with her credit card or travellers cheques, only cash. They had volunteered to drive her to an ATM after they picked her up. Karin was very pleased with her enterprising spirit. She was bored with the city and wanted to go off by herself to this exotic location, and hang out on a beautiful beach with people her own age. It was a much better way to spend time until Stefan arrived. The only dilemma was what to say to her hosts. She didn't want them volunteering to take her themselves. She would have to make up a bit of a story. First, she would book herself on the ferry for tomorrow. The sooner she was on her way the better, Karin thought smugly. The older woman returned and Karin was prepared with her lie.

"I spoke with a friend of mine in Sweden," she gushed quickly, thinking how clever her story was. "She has a friend who has a house on Koh Sammet. I just got off the phone with them and they have invited me to join them this weekend. They are picking me up tomorrow at 5.00 p.m."

The older woman looked slightly surprised, but pleased. "That would be lovely. Koh Sammet is beautiful. Where on the island is their house?"

Karin had not expected any specific questions. "I'm not sure, but I'll get their phone number there, so we can keep in touch", she replied non-committally. The woman seemed satisfied with this answer. She was starting to get annoyed with the spoilt brat anyway. It would be nice to have the house back to themselves.

Karin called Stefan and told him her plans to go to the island. "The beaches look so beautiful. I'll be staying in a bamboo hut right by the water," she explained excitedly, also filling him in on the lie she had told the Swedish couple. "I wish you were here. It would be so romantic."

"Just another ten sleeps baby, then I'll be there," Stefan breathed huskily into the phone. He was imagining Karin in her bikini and desperately wished he was there too.

"So where will I meet you then?", Stefan asked.

"I'll be back in Bangkok on the 15th to meet you. We'll pick you up at the airport."

"OK then, see you on the 15th. I love you."

"I love you too, babe, can't wait to see you." Karin was already thinking about her trip.

❖   ❖   ❖

Packed and waiting impatiently Karin jumped when the door buzzer rang. "Yes?"

"Hello Lady, pick-up Karin please," the man's voice chimed.

"I'll be right down."

Karin called out to the older woman. "They're here, I'm off now."

Annika had some ex-pat friends over for an afternoon bridge game. Putting her cards down she started to get up from the table. "I'll help you with your things," she volunteered.

"I'm only taking a small bag, it's just for ten days." Karin was eager to go and was starting out the door. "I don't want to interrupt your game."

"What about your friends' number on the island?", the older woman inquired.

Karin had hoped she would have forgotten. "I forgot to get it. I'll phone you in a couple of days or so, OK?"

Annika started to object but raised voices and friendly arguing over the next card distracted her.

"See you in ten days," Karin quickly shouted back, closing the door behind her and running to the elevator.

The driver was the man at the markets who had given her the brochure. His face lit up with a gap toothed grin on seeing her appear from the building.

"Hello Lady, you like go beach, eh?" He reached out for her bag and opened the back passenger door for her. She smiled at his child-like English and jumped in.

"Are we picking any others up?"

"Only you today, Lady." He was still smiling like the village idiot.

"Why is that?", Karin asked, not really interested.

"Off season, Lady." He was reaching into his top pocket as he swung dangerously into the steady flow of traffic, not bothering to indicate as he went. Pulling out a packet of cigarettes her passed them back to her. "Smoke, Lady?"

Karin was dying for a cigarette. She hadn't been able to indulge while staying at the old farts' place, unless she went out onto the balcony, but it was so uncomfortable in the searing Bangkok smog and heat.

"Love one." She leaned forward and grabbed one from the packet.

"Take the packet," he offered generously.

"They smell funny." Karin screwed up her nose on the first drag.

"Thai clove, very expensive," he answered and swerved into the next lane, honking loudly and shouting out in Thai to no-one in particular.

Karin settled back and smoked the strange cigarette, which made her feel quite heady. It was a nice feeling.

Stuck in the rush hour, Karin soon became bored and reached for another cigarette to pass the time. She wasn't sure whether she liked the taste and smell or not. It wasn't bad, just different. Half way through the cigarette, she felt very sleepy.

"Wake me when we arrive," she slurred to the driver.

Looking back in the mirror he was smiling. "Sure," he replied. "Sure will."

She lay down on the seat to be more comfortable and was soon fast asleep. The drug had taken effect.

TRAPPED

Laurie loved Bangkok. So different from Atlanta. She loved the hustle and bustle of millions of people, who all looked the same, racing around engaged in their daily activities. The smells of the spicy food, cooked in the streets on small carts; the flashy neon lights at night, indicating all the different eating, drinking and stripping places. Laurie had gone into some of the strip clubs, expecting them to be the same as at home, and had been shocked.

The nudity didn't shock her, she was comfortable with looking at a naked female body. But the way the girls performed shocked her. Legs spread wide, they would pull all sorts of objects out of their hairless pussies. A string of razorblades, small bottles of alcohol which the girl would open while the bottle was still half inside her, and then stand over a willing customer and pour the alcohol into his mouth, still clasping the bottle inside her vagina. This produced great back-slapping and applause from the customer's friends. Some girls spat ping-pong balls or darts from their vaginas across the room to customers who caught the balls or held balloons to be burst by the darts. Nude waitresses would open a bottle of beer at the table by placing one leg high on the table, thrusting the bottle inside the vagina and with a quick flick of the wrist popping the cap off. This is how they could justify twenty dollars a bottle. Most of the girls looked way below legal age, but Laurie found it difficult to tell with Asians. None of the male customers seemed to mind, but the other female customers appeared to be just as disgusted as Laurie and usually the girl would quickly drag her boyfriend or husband outside.

After being in the city for three days, she was over her initial cautious approach of just going to the main tourist spots, the markets on the riverboats, the Buddhist temples, the massive and diverse department stores. She was an adventurer and preferred to go off the beaten path, to experience life as the locals did. Her hotel was small and fairly clean. The reception staff were friendly and eager to help in any way. Her room had a double bed with a mosquito net and a large floor fan in the corner. There was a small bathroom. The walls of the room were bare, with paint coming off in places, but it all seemed to add to the charm of the place. She could have got a cheaper room with a shared bathroom at the end of the hall, but she had put up with that long enough in the Military.

Laurie hadn't really spoken to any other Western travellers. The other people staying at her hotel were all older couples. They were nice and chatty, but conservative in what they wanted to experience in Thailand. She had befriended a local boy, about sixteen years old, who hung out at her small hotel. He was very friendly and wanted to talk, although his English was difficult to understand. He had been a great help in showing her places that the average tourist never saw. He had been the one to tell her about the shuttle bus that went to the coast near Bangkok. It was a four hour ride and there were fabulous beaches and traditional Thai villages there. This sounded very appealing, so she had checked in her guide book. The place was called Kho Sammet and it really did sound beautiful. It was the closest of the islands to Bangkok and there were two major resorts there, but also many smaller bungalows and hostels, right on the beach, at amazingly cheap prices. These attracted many young backpackers and it was easy to meet fellow travellers and get feedback on where to go and where not to go. Laurie had booked her spot on the shuttle and was waiting to be picked up outside her hotel. It was coming at 1.00 p.m. and she would be sitting on the beach sipping a cocktail and watching the sunset by this evening. When the shuttle arrived, the driver explained, "You are first pick up, Lady. Let me help you with your bag." He threw her backpack in the rear of the van and she settled into her seat. Once on their way the driver shouted back to Laurie, "You smoke, Lady?" He reached into his pocket for a packet of cigarettes.

"No, thanks," Laurie replied with a friendly smile. "I'm too healthy for that."

"You hungry? There is cooler on seat, with drinks and sandwich, help yourself, please."

A sandwich sounded really good. Laurie hadn't had time to get any lunch and now realised how hungry she was. She opened the cooler and saw a great selection of juices, sodas and sandwiches in clear plastic wrap. Laurie chose a salad sandwich and a juice, and settled back in her seat. The sandwich was delicious and it was soon gone. Laurie leaned forward. "Can I have another sandwich please? I'm starving."

The driver gave a huge smile. "Sure Lady, many as you want!", he encouraged in his baby English. Laurie was most impressed with his generosity. The shuttle ticket had been really cheap, and now they included lunch! You didn't get this sort of service in the States.

While on military exercises that involved lengthy travel, Laurie had learnt how to lightly doze, so when she started to feel sleepy she was not surprised. She thought that she would wake up when they stopped to pick up the other passengers.

TAKEN

Once on the island, everyone seemed to walk in the direction of some waiting trucks. They were open backed trucks, with tarpaulin over the roof and the sides rolled up, acting as taxis that took everyone around the island to all the different hotels and resorts. Kelly was not sure where she was going, but everyone else seemed to know what they were doing, so she decided to pile in with them and get out when something caught her fancy. As the trucks drove around the island they stopped at different hotels and people disembarked, noisily chatting and laughing with one another. Nothing really appealed to her and she was afraid she would be back to the beginning of the island, without finding a place she liked. Eventually they came around a corner and there was the most spectacular little bay she had ever seen. It was picture perfect. Sparkling white sand and aqua water, with small waves. Coconut trees shaded the little bamboo bungalows at the water's edge. Kelly banged on the side of the truck to indicate she wanted to stop. No one else got off, and this surprised her a little. Was there a better place further on?

She approached what looked like a restaurant. The bamboo structure had no sides, because of the heat, and was filled with wooden picnic tables and chairs. There was a group of Thai people sitting around chatting and eating. One woman jumped up with a big, white smile as Kelly entered and said, "Hello Lady, you want food, drink?" Kelly was pleased with the friendly reception and asked, "How much is it to stay in one of the bungalows?"

"You stay with us, Lady, very nice here. Are you alone Lady?"

"Yes, I am. I'm from Australia," replied Kelly.

The woman looked Kelly up and down appraisingly and said, "Only 30 Baht." Kelly did the calculation in her head. "Really? Only 30 Baht?", she queried. That was very cheap.

"Special price for you, Lady," was the woman's quick response. "OK, I'll pay for two nights please."

The woman went to a desk and got out her ledger. "We have very good bungalow for you, Lady." Kelly was very pleased with herself, and thought what a good traveller she was, finding such a cheap, beautiful place. She paid for the two nights and was shown to one of the cute bungalows. It was made of bamboo with a thatched roof. The inside was just one room, with a raised bed that took up most of the space. Hanging above the bed was a mosquito net. She threw her bag on the bed and looked through the doorway to the bathroom. It was very small with a hole in the floor for the toilet, and a shower rose hanging flimsily from the wall. It was very primitive, but she thought it was perfect, and very romantic. Finally, she was travelling at the grass roots, living like a local. Kelly spent the rest of the day swimming and walking along the beach, talking with a few other people and sun bathing. She found out about a place called Flamingo's, a twenty minute walk further along the main road. It was a bigger beach and bungalow complex, which had great restaurants and a nightclub. After the relaxing day, Kelly was ready to meet other people and go dancing. She dressed up in a nice floral summer dress, with flowers pinned in her hair.

It was dark by the time she arrived. Even though there were no streetlights along the way she had been able to make her way on the road very easily. Kelly went straight into one of the restaurants and ordered dinner and drinks. There was a group of Australians and Americans nearby and it was not long before they spotted Kelly by herself and invited her into their party. They danced and drank into the early hours of the morning and Kelly decided to sleep over with one of the Aussie guys, rather than walk home. He was handsome and charming, so it was not a hard decision to make. In the morning, she hung out with the group again, before heading back to her quiet paradise to get some sleep. She had promised to meet them again that night, so just before dark she walked to Flamingo's to join them at the bar. When she arrived, the Aussie bloke told her that they were all planning to take some magic mushrooms and asked if she wanted to participate. Kelly had never been one to follow the crowd, or indulge in drugs, they scared her. "I'd rather drink and supervise," she said casually. "That's great", he replied. "We need someone who is straight to help anyone who has a bad trip." It seemed ridiculous to Kelly that people would take something like this with all the mental and physical risks involved, but that was their business. They all gathered in one of the bungalows. One of the boys carefully unwrapped the bundle he had just bought from one of the locals who hung out at the restaurant. The mushrooms looked harmless enough, but on closer inspection, they had small white lice on them. "Gross," Kelly squealed, screwing up her face in disgust. The others all laughed and debated how they were going to take them, in a tea or omelette or just as they were. One crazy American guy grabbed one and quickly ate it. "If I talk any more about it I won't do it," he said, draining his water bottle to help the hallucinogenic down. The others laughed again and all followed suit, then sat around looking at each other, expectantly.

"How long until it kicks in?", Kelly asked.

"Thirty minutes or so, depending on the strength of them," the American replied. After a while they all decided to go out to dinner. It ended up being one of the funniest nights of her life. Kelly was so glad she had not participated in taking the mushrooms, as watching their behavior was hilarious. One of the girls started to have a bad trip, but Kelly sat with her and talked her through. At about 3.00 a.m. Kelly walked back to her bungalow. She didn't feel like sleeping with the Aussie guy tonight.

The next day she decided that she would stay one more night before leaving for a popular beach on the other side of the island. They had a phone there and she wanted to call her family and tell them her new plans for travelling by herself. She went to the restaurant to pay for another night. There was the same group of Thai people sitting around. Kelly wondered if they ever got bored with their lazy lifestyles. There was one young boy aged about fifteen who was always hanging around. Didn't he have to go to school? Kelly spent the rest of the day lounging on the beach and swimming. By dinnertime she was bored with her own company, and decided to go to Flamingo's again. She put on a tight, white top and miniskirt to show off her nicely tanning slim legs. She loved dressing up and looking her best. Just before dark, she set off on the twenty minute walk. About halfway there she heard the buzz of a small motorbike coming up behind her. That was the main form of transport on the island and most of the tourists hired them too. The bike pulled up next to her. It was the young boy she saw all the time at her bungalows. He had a big smile on his friendly face.

"Hello Lady, you want ride to Flamingo's?", he asked helpfully.

"That's nice of you. Sure." Kelly jumped on behind him, and they started off. They putted along at a ridiculously slow pace with the weight of both of them on the small moped, but Kelly was in no hurry and it made the boy seem like a hero, she presumed. Then, suddenly, he turned right, into the jungle, onto a path Kelly hadn't even noticed before. She wasn't alarmed at all; this was a beautiful tropical island, there was no danger.

She leaned forward and asked, "Where are we going?"

"To get a bigger motorbike, from my brother's place." This didn't really seem necessary, as Flamingo's was only ten minutes further along the road. Kelly kept quiet, assuming he just wanted to impress her. A short time later, they came off the overgrown path to a clearing where there were several concrete block buildings with iron roofs. These were the first solid buildings Kelly had seen on the island; everything else was built from bamboo and thatch. On the porch of the first building was a huge, muscular Thai. He was standing with his legs apart and arms crossed over his massive belly, waiting, as if he was expecting them. He was wearing the typical attire that the Thais wore because of the heat — a T-shirt hanging over a sarong-like skirt. The boy stopped the bike outside this hut and Kelly jumped off.

"This is my brother," the boy said, and started moving off, shouting back, "I'll get the other bike."

"This must be the biggest Thai person I've ever seen," Kelly thought. He looked very unusual, probably because of his size. Kelly was not alarmed; she was busy thinking about catching up with her new friends and partying. The big brother smiled warmly and waved his arm at Kelly, indicating for her to come into the bungalow.

"Come in, come in. Wait in here," he invited casually, speaking perfect English.

Presuming the boy wouldn't take long, and not wanting to offend the brother by rejecting his hospitality, she climbed the three stairs onto the front porch and following his gesture she stepped past his bulk, into the subdued light of the bungalow. It looked similar to the bungalow she was staying in, a huge bed taking up most of the room, side tables and a chair, only this bungalow was a lot more solid than hers.

He came in behind her and closed the door. Kelly thought immediately that that was strange. Why was he closing the door? Then, she heard him locking the door! Panic flooded over her as she heard this sound and realised for the first time how foolish she had been. Here she was in a block bungalow in the middle of the jungle with a huge, strange man she didn't know and he had just locked her in. Her first thought was for her family. They would be so upset when she went 'missing without a trace'. No one knew she was on this island. She resisted the urge to swing around in wild panic and scream like crazy. Who would hear her anyway? The young boy? Was he in on this too? Instead she calmed her breathing and turned slowly around, to see the big man's face in the gloom of the room, wondering if maybe she was jumping to conclusions. His face had lost the friendly smile, and was now twisted in an excited grimace. Kelly's heart was racing in fear and panic. She felt hot and cold at the same time, but she seemed to know instinctively not to show it. She didn't want to excite him into doing anything rash.

"Sit," he said, and roughly pushed her onto the bed. Fighting the panic rising in the back of her throat, threatening to make her vomit, Kelly thought rationally, "I have to act calm and not let him see how scared I am. If I don't use my head I will never get out of here."

She sat on the bed hunched over, trying to look small and non-threatening, forcing her facial expression to look neutral. He stepped over to the corner of the room and stooped to pick up something from under the chair there. When he came up he was holding a large flay, a hooked knife they used to get coconuts out of the trees. Kelly's eyes widened, but she managed to stifle the gasp of fright. He could easily put it around her neck and pull, and it would chop her head off. Obviously the young boy was not about to come back, and this was all a set-up. She had been targeted, because she was young and blonde, and travelling alone. Information she had given them herself.

"I am so naïve", she admonished herself. Now the panic was threatening to overtake her, but she fought it back and tried to think of a way to get out of the situation, without alarming her captor too much.

"My friends are waiting for me." Kelly smiled and pointed to her watch, trying to look convincing. He didn't seem to hear her and just put a plate of food in her lap and said, "Eat!" It looked like cake and Kelly was sure it was drugged. Not wanting to alarm or antagonise him, she decided to pretend to eat it while distracting him with conversation. Kelly started a monologue of chatter, while putting the cake to and from her mouth without really eating any.

He seemed pleased with the progress and sat very close to her on the bed. In the middle of Kelly saying, "The beaches are so beautiful here, I have been swimming every day," he started to stroke her hair and say, "I love you, I love you." Kelly was glad that he didn't seem to notice that she was not consuming any of the cake. But she was not sure about encouraging him to touch her. He suddenly reached to the side of the bed and picked up a glass with a whitish liquid in it, and passed it to her, smiling and saying, "Drink!"

Kelly didn't take the glass, instead she lay back on the bed and said, "I love you too." She was desperate now. There was no way she wanted to drink the mysterious liquid. She knew once she was incapacitated there would be no way to escape. He looked a little surprised but lay down next to her, smiling. She took his hand and put it on her breast. He started to stroke her breast and squeeze her nipple roughly. Kelly groaned and closed her eyes in faked sexual excitement, blocking out his hideous image. He quickly lowered his hand and tried to pull up her tight miniskirt, probing roughly with his huge fingers. She fought the panic to stay calm and propped herself up on one elbow. "Can you wash your hands, please?", she asked in a hushed, throaty voice. His brow furrowed in confusion, his cheeks flushed with excitement.

"Fingers are dirty things." Kelly smiled nervously, wondering if she was pushing it too much.

He seemed to accept that explanation, and heaved his bulk up off the bed and lumbered through a darkened doorway, into what Kelly presumed was the bathroom. As soon as she heard the water running, she rushed for the door, quickly turned the key with trembling fingers, and raced out onto the porch and jumped down the three steps. It was now completely black. Kelly was very good with directions, and all her schoolgirl camping survival skills rushed back to her. She knew that they had come down a slight slope and gone into the bungalow on her left, so now she had to go right out of the hut, up the slope. She started blindly running, there was no light at all here in the jungle. She soon tripped on something and was scrambling to get up, when the big brother came tearing out of the bungalow, and started pursuit. He shouted after her, "No Tourist Police, no Tourist Police!"

"I have to get away!", Kelly thought, panic hitting her hard in the chest and making her gasp. "If he catches me and he thinks I am going to the Police, there will be no way he will let me go."

Fear made her run faster. Banging into trees and scraping past thick bushes, she scrambled and clawed her way up the slope, towards where she thought the road would be. She could not hear him running after her, but a few minutes later, she heard a motorbike start and head in her direction. Just then, she came bursting from the bushes out onto the main road. Which way to run? Right, to Flamingo's, where her friends were, or left, back to her bungalow? She decided the safety of people was better than her isolated bungalow. She started running along the road towards Flamingo's.

Suddenly the motorbike burst from the jungle onto the road. She hastily looked back over her shoulder as she ran.

"How stupid! I'm in plain sight on the road." She quickly dived into the bushes, hoping he hadn't seen her, and started to make her way along the side of the road. The motorbike roared in her direction.

"He must have seen me!" Kelly quickly crouched and froze, hoping desperately to blend with the darkened jungle.

The bike was moving at great speed, the engine roaring over the banging of her heart. It looked as if he would zoom straight past, but, at the last second he pulled savagely on the brakes, the bike swung around and skidded to a stop almost on top of Kelly. She squealed and tried to jump aside, but the wheel hit her leg and she collapsed in a heap right at his feet.

Quick as a flash he grabbed a fist-full of her long hair and yanked her up to her knees. Kelly screamed. It felt like a chunk of her head was being pulled off. She grabbed at his hand to lessen the pain as tears streamed down her face.

"Please, don't hurt me, let me go. I won't go to the Police." He yanked on her hair again, unmercifully, and Kelly staggered to her feet, squealing anew. He maneuvered her to the back of the bike. "Get on!", he barked.

Kelly swung her leg over and sat heavily behind him. He released her hair and held her around the waist, his arm twisted back awkwardly. He started the motorbike back in the direction of his bungalow, his grip loosening as they gathered speed. As he slowed to turn the bike off the road and onto the invisible path Kelly took the opportunity to make another run for it. She couldn't give up this easily. She wrenched his arm from her waist and jumped off the moving bike, hitting the ground roughly, rolling a couple of times before hitting a thick bush, where she stopped abruptly. Without missing a beat she crawled under the bush, out of sight. She heard him shout angry obscenities into the night as he slammed the bike around to come back to look for her. She crouched, shivering uncontrollably under the dark foliage. Her head ached where he had pulled her hair, but the pain felt very far away as she wiped her dribbling nose with the back of her grimy, scratched hand. He passed by her many times as he zoomed up and down. Eventually, her breath calmed a little and while he was out of sight, she crawled from her haven and in a crouching scurry, made her way to Flamingo's, keeping to the shadows.

It took her a lot longer moving in the undergrowth by the road, but it was worth it as he drove past her a couple of times. Eventually she got to Flamingo's and went straight to the Aussie guy's bungalow. There was no light on in the window, so Kelly went to the restaurant. It was surprisingly quiet and her group of friends were nowhere to be seen. Starting to panic she went to the reception desk and asked if they were still staying there. The young Thai girl explained that there was a big party on the other side of the island and everyone had gone there. "Oh no", Kelly thought in dismay, tears starting to prick her eyes. "I totally forgot about that. What am I going to do now?"

The Thai girl looked at her slightly confused and concerned, but before she could offer assistance Kelly had dashed off. She decided to head back to her bungalow, pack her bag and make sure she got up in time for the truck that went past at 7.00 a.m. to pick up people for the ferry that left the island at 9.00 a.m. each day.

She ran back along on the road, but stuck close to the bushes. Kelly was petrified that the big brother was lying in wait for her somewhere along the way, but she had no other choice than to make her way back to the safety of her bungalow. It felt as if she held her breath the whole way back. Once inside her bungalow she sighed with relief, slamming the door shut. She had made it! All she had to do now was stay in the hut until morning and get off this God forsaken island. She reached for the lock. Her stomach lurched into the back of her throat. There was no lock. She hadn't even noticed that before.

"This whole thing was a conspiracy," she thought, fear and panic rising in her again.

"I have been so stupid. How did I not notice that?" She started to throw her toiletries and clothes back into her pack, in readiness to leave immediately the sun rose. As she was stuffing her wet bikini into her bag, the door suddenly swung open. Taking up the whole doorway was the big brother. With a menacing smile on his face he approached her in two steps and forced her face down on the bed before she could even scream. There was no-one around to hear it if she had.

Twisting and struggling to get out of his vice like grip Kelly desperately tried to turn her face to get a breath. He held her head tightly. "I'm going to die like this", she thought desperately. Her lungs were on fire with lack of oxygen, but then he let her head turn to get a lifesaving deep breath. There was a strange smell, and everything went black.

HELD

When Laurie woke, she was on a big hard bed, with no covers. Opening her eyes she blinked repeatedly, trying to lubricate her dry, itchy eyes. All she could see was blurry white all around her. She closed her eyes and rubbed them gently with her fingers. Reopening her eyes she thought for a second that maybe she was blind, but gaining focus she realised that the white all around her was a mosquito net. Draped from the centre of the ceiling above the bed, it cascaded to surround the bed completely. It felt like she was in a cocoon, safe and protected.

She rolled onto her side and felt another body. She tensed in surprise. The other person didn't move, obviously still sleeping. "Who was this? Where am I?" Her mind was racing wildly. "Did I go out and get drunk and pick someone up? Where was I going last?" She bent her face closer to see what the person looked like. All she could see from behind was long, straight blonde hair. "Well, the back is OK", she thought. As she leaned forward over the girl, she started to stir. Laurie moved back to let her wake up. The girl rolled onto her back and put her hands to her head, then sat bolt upright, looking around wildly with eyes wide in alarm. Noticing Laurie, she went to jump off the bed, but got tangled in the mosquito netting and fell heavily onto the floor. Arms flailed desperately as she scooted backwards and banged into the wall, looking very confused, taking in Laurie and the room.

"Hey, calm down, it's alright," Laurie smiled and held her hands up in reassurance, trying to pacify the frightened girl.

"Who are you?", the girl demanded from her squatting position.

"I'm Laurie, who are you?" She noticed the girl's accent. Sounded like an Australian. Laurie tried desperately to remember how they had got here.

"I'm Kelly. Where's that big Thai guy?" Kelly's brain was hazy and her mouth was very dry, but she remembered the big brother coming to her bungalow and putting something to her mouth.

"What big Thai guy?" Laurie looked genuinely perplexed. "Where are we? Are we on Koh Sammet yet?"

"I was on Koh Samui, which is much further South." Kelly suddenly realised that she must have been unconscious for quite a while. They could be anywhere now. "Were you on Koh Sammet?"

Kelly slowly pushed herself up from the floor and sat back on the edge of the bed.

"I'm not sure. I have a splitting headache. I was on my way to Koh Sammet from Bangkok, and that's the last I remember. I think I fell asleep." Laurie rubbed her temples, trying to release the pressure.

"I think you were drugged as well." Kelly lifted the netting and paced quickly to the door of the room they were in. It was a similar size to the bungalow on the island; the bed took up most of the room and a small bathroom was off to the side, through a doorless opening. This bungalow was made of concrete block and the front door was very solid, dark wood and the floor was wood. There were no coverings on the walls or floor. The only other thing in the room was a small fan, high up on the wall, blowing a faint breeze around the stuffy room. Trying the handle, Kelly was not surprised to find it locked. She started to bang on the door, screaming loudly.

"Let us out, you fucking bastard! Let us out!"

Laurie was starting to look worried now. "What's going on, what do you mean, I was drugged as well?"

Kelly didn't seem to hear and continued to bang loudly on the door, screaming and kicking the solid door. Laurie leaped off the bed, flinging the net aside, and grabbed her around the shoulders. Spinning Kelly around to face her she yelled, "What are you talking about, what's going on?"

Kelly's face crumpled and she staggered back to the bed. Sitting down heavily, she started to cry. Alarmed by all this erratic behaviour, her head pounding even more, Laurie sat on the bed next to Kelly and put a comforting arm around her.

"What the hell is going on?", Laurie asked in a controlled, even voice, trying to keep calm.

Just then, there was a scraping sound at the door. Their heads jerked up in unison. Kelly instantly stopped crying. A small slot opened at the bottom of the door and a tray with rice and curry was pushed quickly through. They both jumped up and rushed to the door, but the slot was slammed shut with a resounding bang. They pounded on the door and shouted for a full ten minutes, until their hands were red and bruised, before they slumped back onto the bed again.

"Don't eat the food, whatever you do," Kelly instructed immediately, looking at the bowls with contempt and hatred. "It's sure to be drugged." Then she explained to Laurie what had happened to her. Laurie told Kelly all she could remember.

"Did you eat or drink anything they gave you?", Kelly asked.

"Yes, the driver gave me sandwiches and a juice. What an idiot I am." Laurie put her pounding head in her hands. She was more embarrassed than anything else. So much for all her specialised training. She hadn't even been away from the States for a week. They were both quiet for a long time, sitting side by side on the bed, lost in their own thoughts.

Kelly eventually crawled onto the other side of the bed, needing to be alone and have some space. She faced the wall and soon fell asleep. They both awoke to the sound of the slot in the door banging closed again. Sitting up quickly and rushing to the door they found the rice and curry still there along with a bottle of water.

"Don't drink it," Kelly said instantly.

"I'm so thirsty, I need water," Laurie said. She stepped into the bathroom and turned the shower handle. Nothing happened. The toilet was the typical hole in the ground, with no running water. Returning to the room, she found Kelly sitting on the bed staring at the bottle of water.

"How long can a person go without water I wonder?"

"About five days, sometimes longer," Laurie answered.

"I don't think I can last another five minutes," Kelly moaned. "I could practically braid the hair on my tongue."

"What kind of drug do you think they used?", Laurie questioned. Kelly seemed to know more about all of this than she did.

"I have no idea," Kelly replied glumly.

"One of us should try the water and the other can monitor the reaction," Laurie suggested logically.

"Who's going to be the Guinea Pig?" Kelly looked morosely at Laurie, then got up and went to the toilet herself. She tried the shower handle as well, hoping desperately that it would magically work. No such luck. They sat for another while; time was hard to judge in the room. There was a small window high up in the block wall, with steel mesh on the inside over the glass which let in a token amount of light.

"I'll boost you up, so we can see what's outside," Laurie suggested, desperately trying to think of a way to escape. Laurie cupped her hands on the support of her slightly bent knee and Kelly put her bare foot into it. Holding the wall for balance Kelly jumped up and grasped the bars over the window. Trying to support as much weight as possible Kelly peered out. The glass in the window was quite dirty, so it took a moment for Kelly's eyes to adjust to the grime and the pale light from outside.

"What can you see?", Laurie asked, not even straining while holding Kelly. She was used to supporting a person's weight and heaving them over an obstacle. Kelly was a feather compared to some of the men she had been required to lift in training.

"There are some other concrete block bungalows like this one. I can see three, and there is a bigger building, concrete block too." Kelly pushed two fingers between the mesh to rub a cleaner space on the glass.

"Can you see anyone?"

"No, no-one is about. There are some chickens over by the edge of the clearing, then the jungle starts. It looks very dense. I can hear a dog barking. Wait, here comes a truck!"

Laurie gasped, "Don't let them see you."

Kelly ducked her head down as the headlights of the truck flashed past the window. She slowly raised her head to take another peek.

"They're not looking this way. They've stopped outside one of the other bungalows." When the driver got out of the truck Kelly could see it was the big brother. Startled by his presence she almost lost her grip on the mesh and Laurie had to do a quick leg shuffle to maintain balance.

"That's him, that's the guy who tried to drug me on the island and then came to my bungalow later."

"Is there anyone else?", Laurie asked, squinting up at Kelly, starting to feel the strain of holding her weight.

"Yes, a young guy, he looks like a boy, I don't recognise him though." Kelly watched as the two went to the back of the truck. They had backed the rear of the truck up close to the door of the bungalow. The back of the truck was out of Kelly's view, but the door to the bungalow was visible. The two disappeared into the back of the truck and soon emerged carrying something between them.

"What are they doing?", Laurie asked anxiously. Her leg was on fire with the continued strain and her arms were starting to shake slightly.

"They are carrying something into the bungalow, I can't see what it is — oh no!" Kelly gasped in horror at the sight.

"What? What is it?" Laurie was alarmed by Kelly's tone and expression.

"It's another girl. I can see her long blonde hair. She looks unconscious."

"I can't hold you any longer, Kelly, can you boost me up?"

Kelly jumped down and Laurie stood upright, slowly, holding her back and stretching.

"Quick, hurry up." Kelly crouched, cupping her hands over her knee. Laurie quickly jumped up and grasped the wire mesh. Just then, the huge Thai man emerged from the bungalow.

"Wow he's massive."

"I know, I couldn't keep him out of my bungalow when he came for me," Kelly replied, shuddering at the memory. The boy followed behind and they both went into the back of the truck again.

"They've gone into the back of the truck again," Laurie whispered loudly, giving a running commentary, pressing her face to the mesh. "Now they're carrying out another person, I guess. They're covered with a blanket, so I can't see anything."

Just then, a small figure came out from the bigger building.

"A young Thai girl has just gone over to them," Laurie continued. "She's going into the bungalow as well."

Kelly and Laurie waited anxiously for the trio to come out of the bungalow again. The big brother said a few words to the girl as she stood quietly on the front balcony, looking at her feet. She nodded and then headed off back towards the bigger building.

"The men are getting into the truck again and the girl has gone back into one of the buildings. Am I getting too heavy?", Laurie asked considerately.

"Yes, you are a bit, but I want to know what happens," Kelly replied with a grimace on her face, sweat glistening on her brow.

"The truck is driving away." Laurie jumped down, feeling that Kelly was at her limit, and that there was really nothing more to look at.

"What are they doing?", Laurie asked, sitting back down on the bed wearily. "Why are they bringing us all here? If they wanted to rape and murder us they would have already done it. What do they want from us?"

"I have no idea. Other travellers warned me about being drugged and getting robbed, but no-one told me about girls being taken." Kelly sat back on the bed too, but couldn't relax, so got up and went over to the water bottle by the door.

"I can't take it anymore, I am so thirsty. I don't care if it's drugged or not. I would rather die of a drug overdose than of thirst." Tearing the top off the bottle Kelly drank most of the water down. Laurie looked on hungrily, but she decided to wait and see what it did to Kelly before she indulged. Once her thirst was satisfied Kelly started to look a bit worried and regretted her haste. She lay back on the bed and waited to see if she was going to die or not.

After about two minutes Laurie asked, "So how do you feel?"

Kelly went to turn her head towards Laurie, to say that she couldn't feel any change, when she discovered that she couldn't turn her head. Panic gripped her and she tried to sit up, also to no avail. Her body was not responding to her brain's commands. Laurie came closer in the dim room to see if Kelly had fallen asleep.

"Are you awake, Kelly?"

Kelly tried to say, "Yes, yes I am, but I can't move. Help me!" But her mouth didn't move. Her body didn't feel numb and she felt no pain. She couldn't move or talk, but she could hear and see.

Laurie saw Kelly's eyes open, but they were a bit glazed and she wasn't responding to her questions. Laurie grabbed Kelly on either side of her arms and shook her, gently at first, but then a bit more roughly. She was like a rag doll, moving in whatever direction she was pushed with no resistance.

"Are you alright, Kelly?", Laurie questioned, looking closely into Kelly's eyes and shaking her again.

A few moans escaped Kelly's lips, but that was all. Laurie didn't want to panic and upset Kelly. If Kelly was dying of a drug overdose or poison in the water, then there was no reason to make her feel worse.

"Should I get her up and walk her around?", Laurie asked herself. Maybe that would make the drug or poison work quicker. Would that be better for Kelly, make her death quicker, more painless? Laurie was starting to panic herself now. She had limited knowledge of drugs or poison and didn't know what she should do. Kelly looked relatively normal and peaceful, she was just lying there with her eyes open and moaning slightly. After a short while Kelly's toes and hands wiggled. Laurie grabbed one of Kelly's hands and squeezed it. Kelly squeezed back, but was still unable to move.

"Can you hear me, Kelly?"

Laurie could feel Kelly squeeze her hand lightly, a deliberate three squeezes.

"Are you in pain? Squeeze once for 'no' and twice for 'yes'," Laurie commanded. Kelly squeezed once.

Laurie couldn't think of anymore yes/no questions to ask. So she just sat there holding Kelly's hand, giving silent support. Then suddenly Kelly's leg raised up, bent at the knee, then the other one. Her arms started to move and she sat up, mumbling.

"You're OK! You're not going to die!" Laurie was ecstatic and hugged Kelly tightly.

Kelly started to get up off the bed and collapsed on the floor in a heap. Laurie jumped to help her up, and by this time she was starting to understand the garbled mumbles that Kelly was making.

"That was terrible, I was paralysed," Kelly blubbered.

"It lasted for about thirty minutes," Laurie responded. She didn't have a watch, but she was able to judge the passing of time quite well. "Was it painful or anything? What did you feel?"

"I didn't feel anything! I just couldn't move, but I could see and hear you. It was so weird." Kelly stood by the bed, shaking her arms and legs, just to make sure everything was still working and no permanent damage had been done.

"Are you OK now, everything back to normal?" Laurie looked most concerned.

"I, I think so," Kelly stammered, still unnerved by being paralysed, even though it was only for a short time.

"Well at least we know what happens when we drink the water. We're not going to die. I'm going to have a drink now, before I pass out." Laurie stooped and picked up the bottle of water and drained all that was left. It seemed to be soaked up by her throat before it even made it to her aching stomach.

"Man, that tastes so good." Laurie wiped the back of her hand across her mouth and decided she had better lie down before the paralysis kicked in. After about fifteen minutes she could move again, albeit slowly. Within a few more minutes, she was back to normal, with no noticeable side effects.

"That was so weird. I could hear and see, but couldn't move at all." Laurie was up and pacing around the bed, with a new appreciation of movement.

"I wonder why they have put that in the water. What do they want?"

"What about the food, do you think we should try that as well? I'm so hungry my stomach is sore."

"Well it looks like they don't want to kill us, so I think it would be OK. You try it and I'll take care of you," Laurie offered, not wanting to be the Guinea Pig.

Kelly picked up the tray with the curry and rice on it, long cold by now, and sniffed it cautiously. "It smells OK," she offered hopefully.

"Well, go on then," Laurie pushed, wanting to know what would happen.

"OK, here goes. I'd better sit on the bed." Kelly sat and gingerly put a spoonful into her mouth and chewed slowly. "Mmm, it's very spicy but tasty."

Kelly ate half of the bowl and lay down to wait for the results, hoping that it would be no worse than the water paralysis. She kept moving to see if she could or not, with Laurie watching closely. Nothing happened. It was only the water that was drugged. At least now they knew what would happen to them.

"I'm going to finish the curry off then." Laurie reached for the bowl and started stuffing the food in her mouth. Immediately she started hiccuping because of the spice, but this didn't slow her down at all.

They both lay back on the bed. The faint light from outside was growing dim so they presumed it was nearing nightfall.

"What do you think we are doing here? Why do they want to temporarily paralyse us?" Laurie was propped up on one elbow, looking at Kelly, unable to see her face in the shadows, but grateful for the company. It would be horrible to be alone in a situation like this.

"I really don't know. Other travellers told me about watching the locals for ripping you off or stealing your valuables, but no one told me about kidnappings."

"Do you come from a wealthy family or something?", Laurie asked, trying to come up with a solution for why they had been taken. "No, do you?", Kelly asked.

"No, just a farming family near Atlanta. They could probably trade some cows for me." Neither of them bothered to laugh at Laurie's attempt at humour.

"I wonder what they have done with all our stuff — passports and money and things?"

"They probably sold them. An American passport must be worth a lot. What passport do you have, Australian?"

"Yes. I wish I could have some of my clothes. It's getting cold." Kelly crossed her arms over her chest to warm herself. "And those mosquitoes buzzing around are driving me mad."

"We'd better close the mosquito net." Laurie stood on the bed and arranged the netting to protect them from the nasty bugs.

"Here, come closer and I'll spoon you," Laurie volunteered, moving closer to Kelly.

"What does 'spoon me' mean?" Kelly looked uncertain.

"You turn around and I hold you from behind to keep your back warm. It looks like two spoons together," Laurie explained.

"Oh, right. That is so much better." Kelly snuggled back into Laurie's embrace. "Are you warm enough?"

"Like this is much better." Holding another human gave great comfort in the stressful situation. Laurie put her face close to Kelly's hair to smell the sweet female scent.

"You smell and feel so good." Laurie's voice was husky.

"Yes, this is nice, much warmer," Kelly mumbled softly, and was soon fast asleep, all the stress of the last few days finally catching up with her. Laurie lay awake a while longer enjoying the soft feel of Kelly's body, her warmth and smell. Then soon she was asleep as well.

CAPTIVE

Waking up slowly, Karin was very confused about where she was. Mouth dry and furry, she raised herself up on her elbow and looked around at the dim surroundings. She was lying on a cot in the back of a covered truck. It was moving. She could feel the bouncing over the pot-holed road and taste the dust in the back of her throat. A dark shape came towards her.

"Are we on the island yet?", she asked sleepily.

"Almost," replied the young boy. "Thirsty?" He held out a small water bottle with the top off.

"Yes please." Karin drank gratefully, then fell back to sleep again, but not before noticing, in the gloom, another cot opposite hers holding a sleeping girl with long wavy hair.

❖   ❖   ❖

"Uhhh, my head." Fiona groaned and rolled over putting her hands to her head and slowly opening her eyes.

"What the hell?" She looked around the dim room and tried to remember where she was. She reached out to touch the mosquito net, not knowing what it was at first.

"This isn't my flat! Did I get wasted and leave the pub with a stranger again?", she wondered, squinting painfully at her surroundings.

She was on a double bed and, finally, could make out the shape of someone next to her. The desire to go to the toilet was stronger than her curiosity, so she swung her legs shakily over the edge of the bed, parted the netting clumsily and stood slowly. Holding the wall, she stumbled her way around the bed to look for the bathroom. She found an opening into a darkened room that she presumed was the bathroom. She felt the wall for a light switch, but there was none. Her eyes were starting to get accustomed to the dim glow from a high window, but Fiona was too absorbed in her throbbing head and full bladder to notice. Moving slowly into the bathroom she tried to make out a toilet in the shadows.

"What the fuck kinda place is this? What a dump." Fiona cursed under her breath, sliding her foot out in front of her and keeping hold of the wall, so she didn't trip on anything. The whole room looked empty. Suddenly, her bare toe nudged against something cold and hard. She looked down at the floor to what seemed to be just a hole in the ground, and that's exactly what it was. The foul smell of the open toilet finally reached through the fog in her brain and tapped on the olfactory sensors.

"Fuckin' hell! What a stink!" Fiona screwed up her nose in disgust and started backing up, but the need to urinate was more overpowering than the smell, so she took a deep breath, quickly pulled her pants down and relieved herself, careful to stay upright and not fall into the hole. She staggered back to the bedroom, taking deep breaths. She looked down at the sleeping person, but couldn't see the face through all the blonde hair.

"Looks like a girl," Fiona thought. "No one I know though."

Fiona brushed the hair from the girl's face to get a better look. The girl's eyes opened, startled, and she sat up, speaking quickly in Swedish.

It took Fiona a few moments to realise she didn't understand what the girl was saying. "Do you speak English?"

"Who are you, where am I?" Karin asked in English, confused, looking at the redhead.

"I have no idea where we are. Isn't this your flat?", Fiona asked unconcerned.

"My what?" Karin had trouble understanding Fiona's rough accent.

"Your apartment. Isn't this where you live." Fiona still wasn't putting anything together.

"No! Where are we?" Karin was repeating herself, but her head hurt so much. "Who are you?"

"I'm Fiona. Are you friends with those guys from the restaurant?" She was starting to recall bits and pieces from last night.

"What restaurant? What are you talking about? Who are you?" Karin was starting to get hysterical.

Fiona didn't like Karin's hostile tone. "Who the fuck are you?" They both glared at one another for a moment.

"I'm Karin."

They were both silent, trying to understand the situation. "Are you English?" Karin asked eventually.

"Yes. What about you?" Fiona had never met any foreigners, so couldn't pick the accent at all.

"I'm Swedish, from Stockholm. I have no idea what has happened. Where are we?"

"I really don't know, I just woke up too." Fiona sat cross-legged on the bed, massaging her temples slowly.

"I'm so thirsty," Karin said, trying to swallow and licking her dry lips. "Is there any water?"

"I'm not sure. It's too dark in here to see properly," Fiona said.

"I have to go to the toilet." Karin got up off the bed shakily, pushed the netting aside and took some wobbly steps to the bathroom, holding on to the wall as she went.

"Be careful, it's not very nice in there."

Karin was hoping to drink some water from the bathroom tap, even though it wasn't very clean. She was disappointed to find only a hole in the ground for the toilet, and no water came from the shower rose. Returning from the bathroom she saw Fiona looking quite nonplussed, lying back on the bed, hands behind her head as she stared blankly ahead.

"The shower doesn't work," Karin said bleakly.

"Really?" Fiona yawned.

"Aren't you worried about where we are?" Karin was surprised at Fiona's relaxed manner.

"No. This is probably the apartment of the guys I was with last night. I was quite jet lagged, so they more than likely just put me to bed. Don't you know how you got here?"

"No. I was going to an island near Bangkok, and that is the last I remember. I was riding in a van, with a young Thai boy," Karin explained, as she slumped back onto the bed, her pretty face twisted with fear and confusion.

"That's strange," Fiona acknowledged, still lying back, gazing dreamily at the ceiling.

After a few moments Karin went to the door and tried the handle. It was locked. "Why would your friends lock us in?"

"Well, they aren't really my friends. I just met them last night," Fiona tried to explain, but the other girl didn't seem to be listening.

Karin went over to the wall under the window, but it was far too high for even her to look out of. She tried standing on the bed and leaning over to see out the window, but with bars over the glass and the pane so dirty, it was hard to get a decent view.

"Can you give me a leg up, so I can see outside?", Karin asked Fiona, who was still just lying lazily on the bed.

"You're too big," Fiona said tactfully.

"Well, I'll lift you then, come on," Karin encouraged, grabbing Fiona's arm and pulling her off the bed.

Fiona groaned at having to move and stood next to Karin, an annoyed look on her pale face, the smattering of freckles on her nose standing out clearly.

"Why do you want to look out anyway? They will probably be along shortly, once they know we are awake. Let's just bang on the door and shout."

"Something is not right. I want to see where we are and if anyone's about first. Come on. Put your foot here and I will lift you." Karin prodded Fiona.

Fiona sighed heavily and put her foot where instructed. She grasped the wall for support as Karin heaved her up. Fiona pushed her slim fingers through the mesh and rubbed the glass to get a clearer view.

"There is nothing, we are in a clearing. There is another building like this one, but bigger. I see the edge of the jungle and some chickens. That's it."

"You can't see anyone? Look to the sides more."

"You're very pushy. There's no-one there." Fiona was annoyed and got down from Karin's supporting hold, and quickly lay back on the bed.

Karin stood with hands on hips, looking at Fiona. "So, you are not worried at all? Why don't you shout out to your friends then, to let us out?"

"OK, I will." Fiona got up again and went to the locked solid door, and tried the handle herself. There was no way it was moving. She started to bang on it with her fists, and shouted. "Hey, I'm awake. Open the door please."

"You'll have to do it louder than that." Karin looked unimpressed.

"It hurts my hand banging too hard," Fiona whined.

"Shout out their names then," Karin suggested.

"I don't remember their names."

Karin rolled her eyes in disgust and went to the door to start banging hard and noisily herself. "Help, let us out! Hey, come here, let us out!"

Fiona kept on banging as well, but not as loudly as Karin. She gave up very quickly and sat back on the bed. Shortly after, Karin sat back on the bed as well and started to cry softly. Fiona looked at her not knowing what to do, thinking Karin was a bit soft.

"It's not that bad. They will let us out soon, they can't have gone far away." Fiona tried to be reassuring, but doubt was starting to creep into her mind as well.

Just then, a small trap door at the bottom of the door slid open and a tray of curry and rice, and two bottles of water were hurriedly slid through, into the room.

Karin jumped up and ran to the door. "Let us out. Why are you keeping us here?"

There was no response from the other side, and just as Karin was going down on hands and knees to look through the slot, it was quickly slammed closed. She kept banging for a moment, but knew it was useless.

The water had distracted her anyway. She snatched up a bottle and drank half of it down thirstily. Then, she sat on the bed heavily, not knowing what they should do next. She started to feel a little strange and tried to rub her face, but couldn't lift her hand. Falling back with her legs over the side of the bed, she just lay and couldn't move.

Fiona ignored Karin taking up the foot of the bed. She pushed herself up and said, "I'm starving, do you want some curry too?

There was no response from Karin, even though her eyes were open, so Fiona just shrugged and said, "OK, I'll leave you some, in case you want it later."

She went over to the curry and returned to the bed to tuck into the food. She thought that Karin must be a very moody person, just lying there and not responding to her comments.

"She'll get over it," Fiona thought, so sat in silence eating the curry. It was too spicy and her nose and eyes were running, but she just wiped them on her sleeve and kept eating, hiccuping loudly. It wasn't as good as the Indian curry in London. She wanted to eat the lot, but thought she'd better save some for Karin. She put the curry on the floor and started to drink some water. She drank almost all of it, her mouth on fire from the spicy food. Moments later she found that she couldn't move. She was still in the sitting position, leaning back against the wall. At first she thought she was asleep and dreaming it, but she could see Karin at the foot of the bed, still not moving.

"What the fuck is going on?", Fiona thought angrily trying desperately to move, and just managing to mumble.

Karin tried to go into a meditative state, wondering if she was dying or would ever be able to move again. She thought about her family, Stefan, her job. She had a wonderful life and she had never really appreciated it. "When was the last time I told my father and brothers I loved them?", she wondered as she drifted along on her meditation. Finally, she found that the feeling was coming back. She was ecstatic. "At least I am not paralysed for life. If I'm going to die, this is not how I want to go. I have so many things I need to say to people, and places I want to see."

She could manage to sit up now and she turned to see where Fiona was. She was sitting back, awkwardly, on the bed. Karin thought she was asleep, but leaned forward closely to Fiona's face and saw her eyes open.

"Are you OK?", Karin asked.

There was no response. She must be paralysed as well. Karin saw the open bottle of water, almost finished, next to Fiona's body.

"The water must be drugged," Karin said to Fiona. "Don't worry, you will be alright. The same happened to me and I feel fine now."

There was no response from Fiona; her eyes were glazed over, but Karin knew she could hear what she was saying.

Karin sat on the bed to wait for Fiona to recover. She looked longingly at the curry and rice. She was starving, but was afraid to touch it in case it was drugged as well. She could go without for a while longer. A few days without food wasn't too hard.

Finally, Fiona started to stir. Groaning she pushed herself on to one elbow to look at Karin. At first she could only slur, until finally her mouth formed the words correctly.

"What the fuck was that?", she spat angrily. "I couldn't move at all."

"I guess there was something in the water, a drug. It happened to me as well." Karin stood up and stretched her long, lean body, stiff from lying in one spot for too long. She rubbed her neck and rotated her head a few times.

"I thought you were in a mood and ignoring me," Fiona stated simply. "Were you paralysed as well?"

"Yes, it was horrible. I think I'm alright now though. There doesn't seem to be any side effects. How do you feel?"

Fiona was gingerly getting to her feet. "I think I'm OK. I don't understand why they would drug us though. What do they want?" She stood with hands on hips, expecting Karin to have all the answers.

"Who were the people at the restaurant you said you knew?"

"I don't really know them. A friend of someone I know in England picked me up from the airport and took me to his friend's restaurant. A huge Thai guy. He seemed very nice and friendly." Fiona remembered him offering her the Opium pipe. "Oh that's right." She smiled at the memory and sat back down on the bed. She wasn't interested in stretching.

"What? You remember something?", asked Karin eagerly, hoping for an explanation for this whole misunderstanding.

"Yeah. The big Thai guy offered me some smoke and that's the last I remember." Fiona shrugged.

Karin sighed, disappointed. "I think they got me with a cigarette too. The young boy who picked me up in the van gave me some cigarettes."

Fiona didn't want to admit that she hadn't meant a cigarette, so she just said, "Must have been laced with something."

"Laced?" Karin didn't understand the word.

"Yeah, had a drug in it or something."

"Oh, right," Karin agreed.

Karin started pacing around the room, nervously, while Fiona lay on the bed, eyes closed, trying to ignore her. After a while Fiona asked, "Don't you want to eat the curry? I don't know why they don't eat proper food."

Karin kept pacing, pretending not to hear her. She didn't want to enter into a conversation with this strangely accented girl. "My English is better than hers," Karin thought snobbishly.

Fiona ignored the fact that Karin hadn't acknowledged her and asked, "Do you have any cigarettes?"

Karin gave a heavy sigh of annoyance and turned to face Fiona. "I have as much on me as you do." She patted the side pockets of her shorts. "Which is nothing."

Fiona didn't pick up on the sarcastic tone and replied, "I need a cigarette. If I don't have one soon I am going to freak out."

"What do you want me to do about it?" Karin rolled her eyes and looked at the ceiling, wondering how long she could put up with this dreadful person.

"I want you to pull a carton of cigarettes out of your pocket," Fiona shot back angrily. The lack of nicotine and pills was starting to make her feel very irritable and nauseous. She went into the bathroom and threw up all the curry she had eaten, eventually falling asleep propped up against the wall, holding her aching stomach.

Karin went into the bathroom and poured some water into Fiona's dry mouth, her lips were already cracked and sore looking.

"Come on, let's get you to bed." Karin groaned under the weight of lifting Fiona's lifeless body. Fiona felt Karin trying to help her to her feet, but she had no energy to help herself. Karin half dragged Fiona back into the main room, amazed at how heavy she was. They both staggered to the bed and fell onto it awkwardly. Fiona just moaned faintly, remaining in the same position, looking as if she were still asleep. Karin pushed Fiona into a more comfortable position, then sat back on the bed and looked at the left over curry hungrily. She was trying to remember the last time she ate.

"Has it been two days or three?", she wondered, having lost all concept of time, being in the dim bungalow and sleeping constantly. In reality, it had only been a day and a half. She sat back on the bed holding the curry cautiously. She looked at Fiona still sleeping and thought, "Maybe this is drugged as well. Maybe that's why she threw up."

Putting the spoon to her lips she took a tiny taste. It was sweet and spicy and totally revolting. She was too afraid to try any more, so lay back on the bed. Fiona was moaning and shaking. Karin looked closer and felt Fiona's forehead. She was dripping with sweat and burning up. Karin wished they had saved some of the water.

The room was hot and stuffy. The small fan on the wall buzzed back and forth, just blowing the hot air around, rather than cooling. She considered fanning Fiona, but decided that it would be too much of an effort and it probably wouldn't be appreciated. Eventually Karin fell asleep as well. It was more peaceful than Fiona's tortured nightmares and painful withdrawals, but neither girl felt refreshed when they were awoken by the trap door opening. Fiona hurt all over. She felt as if she had been hit by a truck. It took all her energy to remember where she was. She looked through bleary eyes at Karin. "Who are you?"

"We've already been through this. Can't you remember anything?" Karin looked annoyed.

"Oh yeah, you're that stuck-up Swedish bitch," Fiona retorted nastily and turned her back on Karin.

"Nice talking with you too." Karin wasn't affected by this ignorant girl's insults. She went over to the two water bottles which had been pushed through the trap door, picked them up and returned to the bed, throwing one next to Fiona's back.

"There you go princess, that might help your mood," Karin said sarcastically. She really did want Fiona's mood to improve if they were going to be stuck in this tiny room together. "Remember it could be drugged like the last lot."

Fiona rolled over slowly, grimacing with the pain of movement. She was hoping that it was drugged; she needed something to help ease the pain. She unscrewed the top and drank deeply, only just managing to put the top back on, before collapsing onto her back. Karin was watching closely. She didn't want to have to go through the paralysis again, but she was so thirsty after that mouthful of spicy curry.

"Maybe if I only have a mouthful, every so often, it might not have the same effect," she thought. She daintily took a mouthful, swilling it around in her mouth for a minute, just to savour the water a bit longer, before swallowing. It made her mouth go a little numb, but that wasn't so bad. What seemed like two hours later, but was really only ten minutes, Karin had another mouthful. Before she realised it, most of the bottle was gone. She lay back down and was soon asleep again. At least she didn't feel the paralysis.

PASSING TIME

They awoke in the same position in the morning, with the sound of the small trap door slamming closed. Laurie jolted upright, ready for flight, while Kelly stretched and yawned. Her eyes opened slowly and reality flooded in.

"They've given us some more water." Laurie got off the bed to retrieve the two water bottles.

"What about food? I'm starving." Kelly looked expectantly towards the door.

"No, just water." Laurie handed Kelly one of the bottles. "We should ration it, don't drink it all straight away. Maybe if we drink only a little at a time the paralysis won't be so bad."

"I can't drink only a little, I'm too hungry." Kelly's lip started to quiver and she lay back on the bed and turned her back on Laurie. Squeezing her eyes shut she started to sob. Not many tears came because of the dehydration, which made her feel even worse. Laurie returned to the bed and arranged the netting around them, blocking out the rest of the room, so they felt a little more protected. Laurie lay behind her and rubbed her back in sympathy.

"You just have to distract yourself from the feeling of hunger. Don't think about it."

"How do you not think about hunger when your stomach is hurting so much?", Kelly sniffled, feeling very sorry for herself.

Still rubbing Kelly's back Laurie said, "I remember this one time when I was on a mission in South America."

"What do you mean 'mission'?" Kelly stopped crying and rubbed her eyes.

"I was in the Military, in a special division. We did survival training all the time," Laurie explained.

Kelly looked over her shoulder at Laurie, to see if she was joking. "Really?"

"Yeah, this one time in the northern part of Chile, we were supposed to be in the jungle for four days without any food and water and try to hike to a pre-arranged pick-up spot. But we stumbled on this Cocaine plantation that none of the satellite pictures had revealed. There were some guards around the plantation who started firing at us, with these really old fashioned rifles, but they hit three of our people and killed one of them. We fired back and killed them all. But then we had to carry our two wounded men and one dead body to the pick up site. So instead of taking four days and being a simple hike, it took eight days and was really hard, carrying the bodies and looking for food."

Kelly rolled onto her back to get a better look at Laurie telling the story.

"Are you serious?" She wasn't sure if she could believe Laurie or not, but it certainly was distracting.

"Yeah. I was so hungry and tired, but we couldn't stop, because of the wounded guys and having to watch out for more Cocaine plantations and the guards protecting them. We chewed on some of the coca leaves to perk us up and give us energy." Laurie smiled at the memory.

"You did not!" Kelly chuckled at the thought of highly trained military personnel, traipsing through the jungle chewing on illegal contraband.

Laurie smiled also, glad that she had distracted Kelly from her hunger, and stopped her crying. Even though Kelly's eyes were all red, she was very pretty. Laurie had to look away from Kelly's face to concentrate on the story.

Laurie talked for a couple of hours about things she had done in the Military and places she had been.

"Wow, you have done so many things, and been to so many places. How exciting." Kelly was fascinated and hung on every word. "How come you are in Thailand at the moment? Are you on holiday?"

"Not really." Laurie's tone changed and her face became hard with the memory.

"What's the matter? Did you leave the Military?"

"I had an affair with a General's wife and had to resign." It was the first time Laurie had mentioned the event, since it had happened. It seemed such a long time ago.

"What do you mean 'had an affair with a General's wife'?", Kelly asked innocently.

Laurie looked at Kelly to see if she was kidding, and saw that she wasn't.

"I'm gay, I had sex with the General's wife, on a picnic blanket, in the hills near the base," Laurie stated blankly.

"I thought only men were gay. I didn't realise women could be gay too."

"Are you joking?" Laurie bristled, not sure if Kelly was making fun of her. "Haven't you heard of lesbians?"

"Yes, I suppose. I guess whenever an outspoken, politically active woman was on TV, or something, Dad would call her a lesbian, so I never really thought it was sexual."

Laurie laughed loudly, slapping her thighs. Kelly laughed with her.

"What about school, didn't you have girls that got together to experiment?" Laurie was still giggling, remembering her school years and many steamy study sessions.

"Not that I ever saw. I went to a co-ed school, so we always talked about the boys. But I remember this one time when I went on a holiday to a resort island," Kelly was casting her mind back, smiling. "I must have been about seventeen. I got really drunk and this girl started kissing me in the toilets. I didn't realise it could go further than that. Wow, I'd totally forgotten about that, it was really fun."

"So why did you stop?" Laurie asked, leaning in, interested.

"I'm not sure. I was really drunk and didn't know what to do, I suppose. We just laughed and went back to the party."

Laurie and Kelly talked the day away, getting to know each other and trying to distract one another from the pain of hunger and fear of not knowing what was going to happen to them.

Finally, when the light was starting to fade, Kelly said, "I can't stand it any longer, I have to have a drink of water. I don't care about the paralysis, it doesn't last long anyway."

Laurie agreed. "I know. I'm going to have a drink as well, but only a little to see if that shortens the paralysis time at all."

They both took a tiny sip of their bottles of water. Kelly took a couple more and then they both lay down again, awaiting the effects.

After a moment Laurie sat up. "I can still move, what about you?"

"Yeah, I can too." Kelly sat up and looked at Laurie, happily surprised.

"Do you think this water isn't drugged?"

"Maybe we should try some more." Laurie opened her bottle and drank half of it. Kelly followed suit. They waited another five minutes and both sat up again. "Nothing has happened. That's weird, why would they drug the first bottles of water and not these ones?"

Just then, the trap door in the main door opened and a tray of curry and rice and another two bottles of water were hastily pushed through. The hand was small and feminine, and Laurie said, "It looks like that Thai girl's hand." She jumped up and lunged for the door. Getting down on all fours pushing her face close to the opening she said, "Why are we here, what do you want?" But the door was quickly slammed shut, without a response, before she could finish her sentence.

"At least we have some food, yeah!" Kelly rushed over to the tray and picked up the curry, and started eating. "Here, you'd better have some."

Laurie slowly stood up and ate some of the offered curry. "I would kill for a roast beef sandwich with mustard and a beer right now. I am sick of this spicy crap."

"I'm happy that they are feeding us, but I could go for a chicken Caesar salad, from the café down at the shopping mall at home."

They both stood there, polishing off the curry and fantasising about the food they would love to have. With full tummies and most of the light gone, they lay back on the bed, cuddling up for warmth. It was the third night.

❖　　　❖　　　❖

In the morning they both woke early, feeling very stiff from so much lying down, but quite refreshed. Laurie returned from the bathroom. "I am so sick of lying around, I need to exercise."

"I know what you mean. Let's stretch. Do you know yoga?" Kelly got off the bed and stretched her hands up high and stood on tip toe.

"No, I mean real exercise, I need to run." Laurie started running on the spot, knees up high.

"You'd be surprised how strenuous yoga can be." Kelly was bending sideways at the waist with arms overhead, looking like an expert.

"OK, I'll try it." Laurie started imitating the movements.

After about an hour of exercise the girls collapsed back on the bed.

"I could really do with a shower now, I am so stinky." Kelly had her arm raised and she smelled her armpit.

"Tell me about it, I wish the shower worked." Laurie went into the bathroom to the shower and turned the handle hopefully. "Still nothing," she complained returning to the sanctuary that was their bed.

She adjusted the netting carefully so the mosquitoes that always hovered at the ready had to remain in the corners of the room, avoiding the breeze of the fan.

"My hair is so greasy, I'm glad there is no mirror in here. I must look revolting." Kelly groaned, pulling her sticky wet hair back from her face, red with the exertion of the last hour.

"You look fabulous dahling." Laurie sat cross-legged on the bed, looking at Kelly and mimicking a posh accent. They both laughed. They passed the day again talking about their lives. In the afternoon they did more yoga and stretching, and drank more of the water. Unsure of whether this lot was drugged or not, they lay down after drinking it. Again, to their relief, nothing happened.

GETTING ON

By the third day, both Karin and Fiona were spending most of the time just lying on the bed staring or sleeping. The mosquito net gaped open as neither of them had the energy to adjust it properly. Karin swiped angrily at any mosquito coming near her, but Fiona didn't appear to even notice them. They talked very little, mainly because Fiona was in such pain from the withdrawals that whenever Karin tried to talk to her, Fiona's responses were vicious and unintelligible. Karin herself was weak from lack of eating, so not talking saved energy.

Suddenly the door opened, the light blinding them. They covered their faces with their hands and tried to see who was at the door from between their fingers. It was the big Thai guy. He stepped into the room and the girls could see another figure behind him. They sat up and both started talking at once.

"Who are you? Why are you keeping us here?", Karin demanded, mustering all her strength to sound confident.

"What the fuck are you thinking? Why are you keeping me here? I'm supposed to be on a tropical island. I need my pills, I am very sick." Fiona used her most annoying grizzly voice.

"Shut up! Both of you." The huge Thai man bellowed, like a crazed monster, surprising them both with his fluent English and aggressive tone.

"Lie down, with your legs together," he instructed, stepping closer to the bed, his eyes flashing back and forth between them, lips pulled back in a snarl.

They both lay back as instructed, shaking with fear, wondering what he had in store for them. Were they going to die now? Maybe he wanted to cut them up and take their organs, to sell on the Black Market. Karin had read something about that, years ago, and forgotten it until right now.

"I wonder if it hurts being killed," Karin pondered, feeling quite separate from her body, lack of food making her very disoriented. Her body was the enemy, anyway.

Their captor came around to Karin's side of the bed and pulled some rope from his pants pocket. At the same time the other man, much younger, almost a boy, with red blotchy pimples all over his face, went around to Fiona's side, flung the netting aside and started to tie her ankles together as well.

"Why are you doing this? I'm the courier," Fiona stammered, looking pleadingly at the big man.

He ignored her and continued to tie Karin's ankles together, then the two girls were pulled to their feet.

"Follow me. Do as I say, and you won't be hurt."

With bound feet, they could only take small steps, so progress out of the hut was slow. The men walked slowly alongside, prodding every now and then, and they made their way across the dirt path and into another, bigger hut. Fiona kept her eyes down, stumbling more than necessary. Karin tried to look around and take in the surroundings. She squinted and made out a few other bungalows in varying sizes. There was a small clearing before the thick jungle started, with chickens pecking at the barren, dusty path and a mangey dog lying in the shade of one of the huts.

They were led across the dirt path and into the biggest bungalow.

At first they had trouble seeing anything after the bright sunlight outside. When their eyes adjusted they could see it was a kitchen and dining room. The dining table was a long, wooden picnic bench. Already at the table were two other girls, one with long, blonde, straight hair and one with shoulder length, curly blonde hair. Another man was guarding them and a young Thai girl was standing in the kitchen watching everything with alert, beady eyes. The two girls already at the table looked dirty, but their eyes were sharp and aware. They didn't seem surprised to see Karin and Fiona. They all stared intently at each other. Fiona was the first to speak. "Who are you?"

The big man grabbed her roughly around the arm, dragged her to the table and pushed her onto the seat. "I will do the talking."

Karin quickly shuffled to the table and sat, before he grabbed her as well. She looked at the other girls and gave a half-hearted smile. They both gave a weak smile back, then quickly diverted their attention back to the man in charge.

"You are all here for a reason. I have a business and I need your help for a short time. If you do as I say, I will look after you and you can go home. If you don't I will punish you and you will never go home. You have probably noticed that the first bottles of water I gave you had a drug that paralysed you temporarily. I will not drug your water or food if you do what I say. Also in the water is a contraception pill, so you do not get a period."

"What do you mean, not get a period?" Laurie asked, looking angrily at him. He lunged forward, thrusting his face millimetres from hers and screamed, "Do not interrupt me when I'm talking!" Spittle shot out of his mouth onto her face as he shouted.

Laurie pulled back as far as she could without falling off the bench seat, but kept her eyes fastened steadily on him.

"I have some very important customers that like to be entertained by blonde Western girls, and you are going to help me. We are very far out in the jungle here, so escape is impossible. You will only be here for a couple of weeks, then I will take you back to Bangkok and give you some money." He looked at each of them individually to make sure it was all sinking in. He made a mental note to keep an eye on the curly haired one; she looked like a trouble maker, typical opinionated, bossy girl. The type he hated the most. "Now follow me and I will show you where you will entertain the customers."

He headed for the door, while the girls scrambled to their feet, with pushes and shoves from the two guards. They filed out into the heat and searing sun. Sweat was soon running down their faces and bodies, making them even more uncomfortable, as they were marched, very slowly because of their bound ankles, across the dirt clearing to another bungalow. The big man pulled a massive bunch of keys from his pocket and started to unlock the door. The girls all huddled together, heads down, squinting at the bright sunlight, feeling hot and dirty. He flung the door open and they all entered a beautifully decorated room. The bungalow was a little larger than the huts they were staying in, but the bed still took up most of the room. The colour scheme was rich red and gold, with matching curtains over the high window. Mosquito netting hung from the ceiling over the bed. It looked very romantic, like a honeymoon suite. Bedside tables had lamps with tassels and large embroidered wall hangings hid the solid concrete block behind. A fan attached to the wall was buzzing away, spreading cool air around the room. It looked liked a picture from a Home and Garden magazine. Everything looked very expensive and beautiful and elegantly arranged. Kelly was the closest to the bathroom, and she craned her neck to see in. Laurie crowded closer to look in also. It was very extravagantly outfitted as well. There was a clean, free-standing bath, with claw feet, and a modern toilet. Luxurious thick red towels hung on a rail. Kelly looked longingly at the bath. "I'd love a bath," she ventured bravely, avoiding looking at the menacing captor.

"You can have one soon," he offered generously. "I have a customer arriving in one hour, you can take care of him."

"What do you mean 'take care of him'?"

He ignored her, and strode over to a bedside table and opened the drawer. "Condoms are in here, and other things." He lifted up a purple vibrator and a tube of lubricant.

Laurie had gone completely white. "I can't do that," she stammered, eyes wide with alarm, shaking her head defiantly.

"You can and you will!", he shouted, pulling a machete from behind the door. "Or I will slit your throat right now!" He started to move closer, holding the weapon threateningly.

Kelly stepped in front of Laurie to distract him and asked, "When can I have my bath?" She didn't do it out of bravery. It was just an automatic reaction, which she regretted immediately. She gritted her teeth to keep her expression neutral and hoped Laurie would stay quiet and the man would calm down. He stopped moving forward, but held the machete in place, looking at Kelly, then back to Laurie. After a nerve wracking few seconds he replied evenly, "The girl will come and get you just before the customer arrives." He jerked his head indicating the young Thai girl standing unobtrusively to one side, then lowered the weapon.

"Now get out of my sight. I am sick of looking at your ugly faces."

The other guards grabbed their arms and started to lead them away, out of the bungalow. Laurie panicked. She lurched sideways and punched the pimply young guard full in the face, sending him flying backwards into the concrete block wall. He screamed as bright, red blood spurted from his nose.

Trying to run, but hampered by her bound ankles, Laurie managed a few wobbly steps out onto the balcony, before she tripped and went sprawling onto the dirt. Dust flew around her as she came to her knees quickly and started to crawl. She was soon stopped in her tracks by the huge Thai man kicking her viciously in the stomach. She gasped loudly, and rolled onto her side, winded. The Thai girl stepped forward with a syringe. Sweaty and puffing slightly the big man bent and injected the liquid quickly and expertly into Laurie's rear. Her gasping for breath eased and her body immediately went limp. Kelly hobbled to her side and knelt by her head to look into Laurie's eyes. They were completely glazed over.

"What have you done to her?"

"What I will do to you all, if you disobey." He grabbed the stupefied Fiona and Karin and strode off in the direction of their hut. They stumbled along pathetically, arms flailing, trying to keep up.

The third guard grabbed Kelly roughly at the wrist and forced it up her back. She winced with pain as a small squeal escaped her dry lips, but he didn't push any further. The injured guard stooped to pick Laurie up, blood wet on his face and shirt. He twisted Laurie's arm awkwardly up her back as he half carried, half dragged her back to their bungalow.

Kelly had no idea what Laurie had been injected with, but she seemed to be half conscious. "Maybe it is the same stuff they put into the water to paralyse us," Kelly thought as she lay next to Laurie, stroking her hair. Trying to comfort Laurie, as much as herself, she tried not to think about what lay in store for them. One thing she knew now, was that trying to physically fight was not an option; to get out of here alive, she was going to have to be clever.

It reminded her of some advice her mother had given her years ago when she lived at home. Kelly had always clashed with her father. He was very strict and only interested in results, not excuses. Kelly would enter into heated debates with him on many things, arguing that he was unfair and didn't listen. It would usually end with her in tears of frustration and TV or car privileges taken away. She would suffer the punishment, knowing that he was wrong and she was right. Her mother's advice was that it was not necessary to always bang up against him and argue the point. The result was the most important thing. She used the example of Kelly's younger brother, who also disagreed with their father most of the time. He would just nod and agree with the father when being lectured, then do it the way he wanted anyway. Usually by the time the father found out it was too late, or it didn't really matter. The point was, that the younger brother was agreeable at the pertinent moment and not argumentative, like Kelly, and he always got what he wanted without a fight.

In this situation, Kelly decided she would go along with what they wanted, biding her time until she could get away.

THE JOB

About an hour later, the door to their bungalow was flung open. One of the younger guards strode in, holding some noisily jangling shackles in his hands. He motioned for Kelly to sit up on the bed, his eyes hard and his mouth a thin line of concentration. The other guard hung back in the doorway, holding a machete in front of him, keeping a menacing gaze on Kelly.

The guard knelt at her feet and hurriedly locked the cuffs around her dirty ankles. She sat calmly, although her insides were churning and her heart raced. He stood and grabbed her roughly around the top of her arm, hauling her to her feet. With her ankles bound, she slowly stumbled alongside of him, back across the dusty yard, to the beautiful bungalow.

The young Thai girl was waiting inside the bathroom. The guard released his hold and backed quickly out of the room, locking the door carefully.

The room smelt of incense, which always reminded Kelly of the hippy shop in her home-town that sold cheap jewelry and large flowing dresses. She suddenly felt very homesick and alone.

"Come." The young Thai girl motioned for Kelly to come into the bathroom. The bath was filled with steaming perfumed water. It looked so inviting after days without washing.

Kelly put her hand into the water. "Oh, wow. That feels lovely." She smiled at the girl.

"In water," the young Thai girl demanded in hesitant English, indicating with her hands for Kelly to get into the bath.

Normally Kelly would have been shy about undressing in front of a stranger, but the girl was already starting to help her undress, and she was desperate for a bath, so all modesty was forgotten. Once in the water the young girl helped Kelly shampoo her greasy matted hair, then heaped on conditioner. The warm bath water was comforting and Kelly lay back enjoying the moment.

It didn't last long, as the young Thai girl prodded her and said strictly, "Wash."

Kelly took the soap and started washing herself as the girl watched. When finished she handed the soap back.

"Wash pussy," the girl instructed bluntly, handing the soap back again to Kelly.

"What?" Kelly was shocked at this order.

"Wash pussy," the girl repeated, pointing to her own privates.

Kelly took the soap back and washed herself more thoroughly, turning red with embarrassment under the girl's supervision. The young girl passed Kelly a razor. "Shave."

Kelly dutifully shaved her legs and underarms. "Pussy too."

"What?" Kelly wasn't quite sure she had understood the instruction.

"Shave pussy, quick!" The girl was getting annoyed with the delay.

Kelly was mortified. She wasn't going to shave her pubic hair. She had done it once, years ago, for a boyfriend; it had given her the worst rash and she had been itchy for days.

"No, I'm not going to shave my pussy, thank you!", Kelly responded indignantly, throwing the razor onto the floor.

"I will get boss man to do it!" The Thai girl started for the door.

Kelly balked in horror. "No, wait. OK, OK, I'll do it." Kelly scowled at the Thai girl, as she retrieved the razor and handed it back to Kelly, with a slight smirk on her face.

Once Kelly was dried, the girl got another towel and briskly rubbed Kelly's hair to try and dry it as much as possible, then passed Kelly a long red silky dress.

"This is nice," Kelly smiled, her voice heavy with sarcasm.

"Put on," the Thai girl snapped.

She slipped it over her head and sashayed around the room, like a catwalk model. She was so nervous about her impending plight that she tried to distract herself with humour.

"Dry hair," the girl instructed, pointing to the fan and handing her a comb. She turned it on full and Kelly tipped her head upside down to dry her hair in front of it.

"The customer come soon. Be nice and give good sex and you get good food and money," the young girl explained in faltering English. "If customer no happy you big trouble." She mimed an injection in the arm.

"So, I have to have sex with the customer?", Kelly asked nervously. "What if he's fat and ugly and I don't like him?"

"He is ugly," the girl stated simply and turned to go. "Wait here." The young girl knocked on the door and it was unlocked and opened by the guard waiting outside.

"Yeah, sure I'll wait," Kelly thought miserably. She continued to dry and comb her hair, nervously awaiting the inevitable.

It wasn't long before she heard the key in the lock again and the heavy door swung open. The young girl came in carrying a tray with two plastic glasses and a carafe of what looked like wine. Behind her was the big man ushering in an old man, presumably 'The Customer'. He was fat and ugly, but had on a very beautiful suit and sparkling gold glasses. Kelly was very nervous as she sat on the bed and the old man came up very close to inspect her. He looked at her face, then slowly down her body. Kelly couldn't tell if he was pleased with what he saw or not.

"What happens if he doesn't like me?", Kelly wondered, suddenly panicked at the thought. "Will they give me another chance? I should have put some make-up on!"

The customer spoke very quickly in Thai and the big man responded, gave a small bow and backed out of the door. The young girl made motions for Kelly to pour the drinks and she also left the room. The old man sat on the bed next to Kelly and started stroking her hair slowly, gazing at her with a silly smile on his face.

Kelly felt, simultaneously, both relieved and revolted that he had accepted her. Now, unsure what to do, she sat there, frozen, waiting for her cue. There was no way she wanted this man to be unhappy and complain about her; she was terrified of being injected.

Suddenly, she had a brain wave. Maybe he would be happy with just talking and holding hands. With renewed vigour she tried to make conversation.

"My name is Kelly, what's yours?" She produced one of her winning smiles and turned to face him, holding his dry, thin hands in her hot, sweaty palms.

"I love you, I love you," was his immediate response, as he grinned happily and continued to stroke her hair, lovingly.

"I'm from Australia and I'm here in Thailand on holidays," Kelly continued courageously, now looking straight ahead while he played with her hair.

"I love you," he repeated, and started to slip one of the dress straps off her shoulder. Kelly grabbed his hand quickly and smiled. "Oh, um, well, you are friendly. Um, let's have some wine."

She stood quickly and wobbled over to the tray with the glasses and picked one up, pouring the dark coloured liquid from the carafe. Her hands were shaking and she spilt some of it on the brightly patterned rug. She offered the glass to the old man, who couldn't stop smiling and looking at her breasts. He took the wine and tried to make another grab at her with his free hand. It brushed her bum. Letting out a small squawk she straightened and continued to fill her own glass.

"Maybe, after a couple of shots of this stuff, it won't seem so bad", she thought. Going back to the old man, she held her glass up to make a toast. He seemed to be enjoying the whole charade and eagerly raised his glass also.

"Cheers," Kelly chimed, with false enthusiasm, standing in front of him.

"Cheers," he parroted. They clinked glasses and both drank the contents down in one gulp. It was like fire water, not like any wine Kelly had ever tasted! She coughed and spluttered, grabbing her throat with one hand and fanning her mouth with the other. The old man laughed. This girl was really funny! He would definitely have to see her again, after he had seen all the other girls.

The wine did give her a slight heady rush, but that might have been due to the lack of food over the last three days. She took his glass and went back to the tray for a refill. When she turned back he was already on his feet, taking off his jacket and shirt.

"Here you go, have another drink." Kelly tried to distract him from undressing. A very optimistic thought. He downed the second shot in one go, smacking his lips together with loud satisfaction. He continued to take his pants off and lay them neatly at the end of the bed. Kelly sat with a fixed expression on her paling face. The old man wobbled slightly on thin, hairless legs as he hurriedly ripped off his underwear. Not wanting to watch, but unable to turn her head away, Kelly caught sight of the impending monster; the tiny purple penis standing erect and demanding, pointing straight out from a tuft of straight black pubic hair.

Still holding her full glass, Kelly suddenly seemed to come to her senses. This is going to happen! The alarm was rising in her throat, she felt hot and unable to breathe. He took a quick sidelong glance at her, happy that her excitement was causing her to pant.

He pulled her gently up, off the bed, to stand in front of him, Kelly was slightly taller. He went to take the glass from her shaking hand, but she quickly put it to her trembling dry lips and sculled the lot again. Gagging a little she took several deep, calming breaths.

He started to roll the straps of her dress off her shoulders; the dress fell to the floor, revealing her total nakedness. He gasped with pleasure, transfixed by her body and reached his hand between her legs to spread apart the soft nude lips of her vagina. He was breathing hard, mouth gaping and pushed her gently back onto the bed. She fell back with her legs spread apart and dangling over the bed. He stood between her legs looking at her open vagina. His breath coming in gasps now, he quickly licked his fingers and started stroking his erection. Kelly lay frozen, not knowing what to do.

"Should I get a condom?", she wondered. "I hope they are small condoms, a normal one would just fall off that little cock."

She almost laughed out loud, at the image she had of the little dick draped in an enormous latex sheet. The alcohol was having an effect, thank God! Then suddenly, the old man made a few jerking movements, gave a deep groan, and spat his cum onto her thigh. He picked up her dress and wiped off a few sticky drops hanging on the end of his cock. He was still smiling as he scooped up his clothes and quickly got dressed.

Kelly just lay there. "Is that it?", she wondered hopefully.

He pulled a few notes from his pocket and placed them on the bed next to her, then walked to the door and knocked. It was opened by the guard and the old man left without looking back.

Kelly snatched up the money and put it into the pocket of her dirty pants, which had been stuffed under the bed. She grabbed the crumbled, discarded dress and wiped the cum off her leg, groaning with displeasure. She went into the bathroom to get into the comforting bath again. Shortly after, the young Thai girl came bustling in, retrieving the wet towel from the floor.

"Customer very happy," she said smiling cheerfully.

"Good. I'm hungry! Can I have some more food please?", Kelly asked tetchily, thinking she had a better bargaining position now.

"OK, I ask boss man," the girl replied, holding out the towel, indicating that the bath was over.

"Can I have a cover for my bed too? I get cold at night." Kelly thought she may as well try for as much as possible, if she was on a roll.

"I ask boss." The young girl was starting to look annoyed. So Kelly left it there and quickly got out of the bath. It was lovely to feel clean again. If that was all that was involved, then Kelly thought it would be no problem lasting for a couple of weeks, until they let her go. She was feeling quite elated.

The girl held out some fresh clothes for Kelly to wear, then, to Kelly's dismay, she scooped her dirty ones from under the bed and stuffed them into a plastic bag.

"Can I have my clothes, please?" Kelly wanted to get the tip money she had hidden in one of the pockets.

"No" the girl replied sharply, making it clear that there would be no more talk about it.

Disappointed, Kelly put on the fresh clothes, a long sleeved shirt and sarong, with no pockets.

"Oh well, I'll just have to wait until next time and be more careful with the tip," Kelly thought, as she was led back to her hut.

JUDGEMENT

Laurie was still in the same position on the bed. Kelly's elation with the bath was forgotten, as she raced to Laurie's side.

"Laurie, are you alright? Can you hear me?" Kelly bent close to Laurie's face to see if her eyes were open. They were closed and there was no response. Kelly suddenly felt sick with fear.

"Oh God, I hope she's not dead." Kelly started to shake Laurie. She was limp. Kelly felt her neck for a pulse, but all she could hear was her own racing heart. She tried to calm herself and concentrate. There was a faint pulse. Kelly hugged Laurie with relief.

Suddenly the trap door was opened and a bed cover was stuffed through. Kelly jumped up and grabbed it.

"Thank you," she shouted at the door, presumably to the young Thai girl.

Then a tray of food and water was pushed through as well. This time it was meat sandwiches, chocolate cake and Coca Cola. There was also a magazine. It was in Thai, but it looked like a fashion magazine.

"Yeah! Real food." Kelly was so excited. "And a magazine. Cool. Look Laurie, real food. Come on wake up." Kelly stood over Laurie, shaking her for a response. Still nothing. Kelly put the cover over Laurie and undid the rope around both of their ankles, then went back to the tray of food. She wolfed down the first sandwich, but saved the other for Laurie. She decided that she deserved all of the cake though. She hopped onto the bed and snuggled next to Laurie under the blanket, trying to look at the magazine in the fading light. She had never realised the luxury of a magazine and the pleasure it could give her, even though she couldn't understand the text and all the models were Asian. She sipped on the Coke, trying to make it last, and wanting to save some for Laurie. She would probably really love to have some Coke, being American and all. Soon she was starting to nod off. Putting the magazine and Coke aside, she fell asleep.

Kelly had no idea how long she had been asleep when she was awoken by Laurie throwing up over the side of the bed onto the floor. There wasn't much for her to bring up so it was mainly a lot of loud retching and sobbing. Kelly rubbed Laurie's back in sympathy, until the spasms had finished.

"How do you feel now? Better?", Kelly asked, concerned.

Laurie groaned then finally replied. "I feel like shit!" Her voice was raspy with exertion. She rolled onto her back wiping the back of her hand over her mouth.

"What happened to me?"

"Don't you remember?" Kelly handed her a bottle of water.

"The last thing I remember was being in that horrible room and that fat fuck said we have to have sex with men. What happened after that?" Laurie's voice was indignant at the memory.

"Well, you freaked and punched one of the guards in the face, then you tried to run, but tripped because of the rope around your ankles and the big guy kicked you in the stomach and then injected you with something."

"How long have I been out for?" Laurie looked towards the window to see how much light there was outside. It was dark except for the faint glow of the bare bulb outside one of the other bungalows.

"It's hard to tell. Maybe ten hours or so," Kelly tried to guess. "It must have been afternoon when we went to that bungalow and it's the middle of the night now."

"I wonder what he injected me with, I feel so sick and crappy." Laurie groaned, with her arm over her face. "I had to do so much specialised training in the Military, but nothing prepared me for this."

"Would you like some Coca Cola?", Kelly asked excitedly, remembering she had saved some for Laurie.

"What? How come we have Coke?" Laurie looked over at Kelly.

"Well, I'm in the good books now and they gave us some beef sandwiches, Coke and a blanket too. Do you want a sandwich?"

Kelly got up and went and brought the tray back to bed. Laurie looked at the blanket covering her, seeing it for the first time.

"What? What did you do?" Panic flashed across Laurie's face, fearing the answer.

"I had to see a customer," Kelly stated simply, trying to keep the guilty look off her face.

"Oh my God! You didn't!" Laurie sat up, and winced at the effort, rubbing her bruised stomach. "How could you?"

Kelly was annoyed with Laurie's horrified response. "It wasn't that bad. It only took five minutes and he didn't even put his cock in," she explained.

"No way! What happened? What did he do?" Laurie babbled, trying to come to grips with what Kelly had done, holding the cover up to her chin, as some kind of protection from what was in store for her.

"The guard took me to the nice bungalow and the Thai girl was there and I had a lovely hot bath, washed my hair and everything, in perfumed water." Kelly felt as if she was trying to sell the whole idea to Laurie, who was just looking at her in disbelief and horror.

"Then she gave me a beautiful red silky dress, and the customer came into the room, we had some drinks and he jerked off onto my leg and then left."

"Are you serious? He didn't kiss you or touch you or anything?" Laurie couldn't believe it would be so easy.

"He touched my hair, and took off his clothes, then my dress and then looked at my pussy and came on my leg. That's all." Kelly looked innocently at Laurie.

"Wow, how creepy." Laurie lay back under the cover, starting to feel quite chilled, not sure whether it was still the effects of the drug or the horror of what they were there to do. She drank some Coke, tentatively, then started to nibble on the sandwich. She was amazed at how delicious the sandwich tasted.

"How long have we been here?", she wondered. With all the drugging and sleeping, she had totally lost count. "Was it four or five days now? When will my family start wondering about me. They probably wouldn't even know where to start to look for me either." Laurie groaned, feeling very depressed and isolated. She was glad to have Kelly with her, but it looked as though Kelly was starting to enjoy captivity.

"Are you feeling OK?", Kelly asked, concerned about all the groaning Laurie was doing.

"Kelly, I don't know what I'm going to do. I can't be with a man. I never have and I never will." Laurie put her arm back over her face to escape Kelly's innocent and concerned look.

"But, it's not that bad, compared with the rewards you can get. His cock was so small you wouldn't even feel it anyway!", Kelly sniggered, trying to lighten the mood. Laurie flinched. "You just don't get it." She got up from the bed and went to the bathroom to gargle the hairy taste from her mouth. When she returned to the bed Kelly was lying there looking solemn and hurt. Laurie immediately regretted how she had spoken to her; Kelly didn't deserve it.

"I'm sorry, Kelly. I didn't mean to sound so harsh. It's just I have had experiences in my life and I thought I had come to terms with them, but this situation has brought it all back up for me, and I'm finding it very hard to deal with."

"You're not the only one who has had experiences, you know! Why are yours more traumatic than mine?" Kelly was offended and angry at Laurie's judgment.

"I was raped by a neighbour when I was ten years old." Laurie sat heavily on the bed and started to cry.

Kelly felt so guilty for thinking her experiences were as bad as Laurie's. Nothing like that had ever happened to her. Kelly had a fleeting thought about how glad she was to have the family she did. No bad experiences or abuse. Just a normal family. Was she ever going to see them again?

"God, when was the last time I cried?", Laurie thought to herself. Even through all the drama of being kicked out of the Military, she hadn't cried, just been angry. Maybe it was a delayed reaction.

Kelly sat next to her, with her arm around her. "It's only for a couple of weeks, then they'll let us go. It will pass very quickly." Kelly tried to reassure Laurie.

"Are you really that stupid?" Laurie looked at Kelly, who quickly withdrew her arm from Laurie's shoulders and looked hurt and confused.

"They aren't going to let us go, not after all of this. They know we would go straight to the Police."

"We could promise that we wouldn't," Kelly volunteered.

"Don't be so naive. They are never going to believe that. We are going to be prostituted until we die of disease or drug overdose or something just as horrible," Laurie explained morosely.

Kelly suddenly had a picture in her mind of her mother, when she found out that Kelly was missing. It was a physical pain to think how her mother would feel losing her only daughter; never finding out what really happened to her.

"I'm getting out of this. It doesn't matter what I have to do, how many men I have to have sex with, I am getting out of this alive!"

Laurie looked at Kelly, impressed with her conviction and bravado.

"We need to make a plan to get out of here." Laurie looked thoughtful.

"Well your way didn't work, did it?" Kelly leaned back against the wall, with the blanket over her legs. "You are going to have to do it my way, until we can get out."

"What is your way?" Laurie asked. "Fuck every guy that comes along?"

"If that's what it takes, then, yes!" Kelly looked indignant.

Laurie shuddered and said aggressively, "I will never do that!"

"Well you can bang up against them and be punished for it, but I'm not going to. Next time I get nice food and a blanket, I won't share with you." She yanked the blanket, wrapped it around herself and lay down with her back to Laurie.

Laurie wished she hadn't spoken so harshly, but she was damned if she was going to go along with the captor's plan. She lay back down, but it was cold without the blanket. She edged closer to Kelly to get some warmth on her back. Without turning around Kelly released some blanket from around her and flicked it towards Laurie, who grabbed it gratefully and snuggled closer, murmuring a quick thank you.

WORKING

Returning from the beautiful bungalow Karin and Fiona sat on the bed and removed the ropes from around their ankles, flinging them to the floor in disgust.

"So we are here as prostitutes, is that it?", Karin asked, looking dazed.

"Looks that way."

"Doesn't it bother you?" Karin was surprised at Fiona's lack of reaction or emotion.

"What am I going to do about it? Yell and scream and try and run away? That won't get me very far will it? We're in the middle of the jungle, God knows how far from civilisation, no money or anything. I'm not going anywhere. My friends in England will start to wonder where I am and send someone to look for me." Fiona lay back on the bed looking confident, thinking about how angry the boss in England would be when she didn't show up. He would definitely start looking for her.

"What about those other girls? I wonder if that American girl is OK?"

"What American girl?", Fiona asked stupidly.

"The one that the big guy kicked and then injected."

"How do you know she's American?" Fiona was quite serious.

"Her accent, dummy." Karin wondered if Fiona really was that stupid, or if she was just too busy thinking about herself.

"I hope they bring some food soon, I'm starving." Fiona completely changed the subject.

Karin sighed and rolled her eyes. She got up off the bed and started to pace nervously. Her long legs looked even longer with the weight she had lost over the last few days. Starving was getting easier as the days went by, just like in high school.

"What are we going to do?", she said more to herself than Fiona, her brow furrowed in thought and worry. Her long hair still looked beautiful, but very dull and greasy at the roots. She pulled it all back with her hands and twisted it into a rough bun.

"I could do with a happy pill, I know that much." Fiona's stomach was still cramping with the withdrawals.

"Do you think of nothing but yourself?" Karin was getting sick of being diplomatic.

"Shut up Princess. Don't tell me you're constantly thinking of others?", Fiona shot back, ready for a full confrontation.

Karin sat on the bed with her back to Fiona. She wasn't going to enter into a stupid argument with this nasty girl. Fiona smiled, thinking she had won.

They remained in silence for a few hours until, suddenly, the door opened and the big man and one of the guards came in, closing the door quickly behind them. The big man still had the machete in his hand and the guard held a very thick, menacing knife. Even though the girls were tall, the thought of physically taking them on never crossed their minds. Karin had never been in a physical fight, so would never have entertained the thought and Fiona had been punched by a couple of boyfriends in her time, so knew how much it hurt. Both girls stayed on the bed and didn't move, just watched the men's movements with eyes wide, trying desperately not to do anything to make the big man angry.

He moved the netting aside and stood over them, looking from one girl to the other, assessing. Finally, his eyes rested on Fiona.

"You want something nice?"

"Like what?", she asked warily.

"A little smoke. Make you feel very relaxed."

"Like the stuff you gave me at the restaurant? It wiped me out." Fiona wrinkled her nose.

"You took too much, just a little this time." He pulled the pipe from his pants pocket and passed it to her. She took it willingly, grateful for anything to take away the cramps and headaches.

"Do you have any valium or sleeping pills? I like those better."

"I'll get some for you, if you're a good girl." He smiled as he leaned forward with the lighter. His teeth were visible, all dirty and stained. His head was large, with a constant film of sweat on the brow. He was very strange looking, not like the other Thai men at all. Even though the girls hadn't washed in four days, he still smelt worse than them. Fiona inhaled deeply as he lit the pipe.

"That's good, good girl." He smiled again, nodding approval.

"The girl will come back soon and you can have a bath." He was starting back to the door, taking his pipe with him.

The other guard was still near the door, knife held up ready. His eyes darted back and forth with anticipation, waiting for the slightest threatening move from the girls.

"Can I have a bath too?", Karin asked timidly.

"If you're good, you can."

Karin smiled sweetly at him, hoping it would have some effect, but he had already turned and was going out the door. The other guard never turned his back on the girls. He backed out of the door and slammed it solidly shut. They could hear the key turning in the lock immediately.

Fiona was leaning back against the wall, her eyes glazed and a smile on her face.

"Are you OK?", Karin asked, looking closely at her.

"I feel marvellous, absolutely marvellous," Fiona smiled back, not moving at all.

Not long afterwards the door opened again and the young girl came in, accompanied by the same guard as before.

"Bath time," the young girl said, moving to the foot of the bed and tying Fiona's motionless ankles with the rope again.

"What about me?" Karin propped herself up on one elbow, and looked questioningly at the young girl.

"You wait," she said gruffly, then helped Fiona to her feet. Fiona moved very slowly and the tied ankles didn't help progress at all, but she was giggling and laughing and soon they were out of the hut and heading back towards the bungalow, leaving Karin to worry and fret by herself.

"Where are we going?" Fiona's eyes were still glazed over and squinting. She was smiling from ear to ear.

"You have a customer."

"A customer?" Fiona was confused, but continued to follow the young girl, assisted by the surly guard, who was proving to be more of a hindrance than a help. The young girl and Fiona entered the bungalow and went straight to the bathroom. The guard waited outside, ready for the slightest trouble from Fiona. Fiona looked at the bath filled with sweet smelling water.

"It's beautiful," she said smiling.

"Get in," the young girl ordered. Even though she was much smaller than Fiona, her manner suggested a hidden strength. She was already taking off Fiona's clothes and throwing them aside. Her hard, calloused fingers worked quickly and efficiently.

Fiona sank gratefully into the bath; it was warm and felt fantastic on her dirty body. The young girl handed her the soap and started to rinse and wash her hair. Fiona half-heartedly washed herself, her mind floating somewhere else, with the effects of the drug. She loved the pampering and wanted it to go on forever. She had heard some of the girls at her work talking about going for facials and massages, but she had never been able to afford it. Suddenly the girl pinched her arm and said, "Up."

"A wee bit longer, luv," Fiona whined.

"Get up!" This time she pinched much harder.

"Oww, don't do that." Fiona squirmed away from the mean fingers, and quickly stood, about to get out of the bath.

"Wait," the young girl instructed. She bent in front of Fiona with a tiny pair of scissors and started to trim Fiona's dark red pubic hair. Fiona stood patiently, slightly confused and uncomprehending, but too happy in her own dream world to question the girl's behaviour. The young girl passed her a silky red dress, wet in patches.

"It's wet," Fiona stated unnecessarily, sitting on the bed, holding the garment loosely in her lap.

"Hurry up. Get dressed," the young girl snapped impatiently. She went to the door and popped her head out, speaking quickly to the guard outside.

"Hurry, hurry, no time," the girl hissed to Fiona and then slipped out of the door, locking it after her.

Fiona was sunbathing on a tropical beach, wearing the red bikini that the boss had bought for her at the local department store. It went beautifully with her hair and had tassels on the sides of the briefs. She was sipping her cocktail and laughing with a handsome man next to her, when the clouds rolled over and blocked the sun. It became colder instantly and the cold pressed down on her. Pressed down hard on her breasts and stomach. She opened her eyes and saw the old man lying on her, his face coming close to kiss her. She didn't have the strength to move, just squirmed against the weight and moaned. The old man was very excited by this encouragement and pressed his lips hard against hers, breathing heavily, his fish breath unbearable on her face. She turned her face, eyes clenched shut in revulsion, moaning deeply. He interpreted this as ecstasy and pushed his hard cock further into her. It was only then that Fiona felt him inside her. She squirmed harder. His breath was coming in gasps; a few more thrusts and he groaned loudly in completion.

Collapsing onto her limp, warm body, he took a moment to catch his breath again. Fiona was trying to stay as still as possible now, to give him no further encouragement. He pushed himself up, quickly dressed and strode out of the bungalow, smiling from ear to ear.

Fiona slipped back to the beach again, laughing and sipping the frothy cocktail, the sun warm on her skin, as the handsome young man rubbed oil onto her body. "This is fantastic." She smiled dreamily to herself, the brief interruption soon forgotten. Then she felt the strong, determined hands of the young Thai girl.

"Get up, get up," she insisted, pulling Fiona to her feet. Fiona was disoriented and confused, staggering to the bathroom, with the assistance of the young girl, the slippery sperm sliding down the inside of her thigh. The girl noticed the sticky mess as Fiona raised her leg wearily, to flop into the bath. Fiona could hardly muster the strength to keep her head above the water. After being thoroughly scrubbed and rinsed by the young girl, Fiona was instructed to stand up in the bath. It took a lot of pulling, but she finally got to her feet. The young girl pushed the tops of Fiona's legs apart and inserted something into her vagina. Fiona's eyes opened wide.

"What the fuck are you doing?" She tried to push the young girl's hands away, but she was stronger and pushed the device deep into Fiona's vagina.

"Owch, that hurts, stop it." Fiona started to cry feebly.

"Stupid girl, you didn't use condom. You get bad infection. This help you. Must use condom."

The girl squirted a cool stinging liquid into Fiona's vagina, quickly followed by some clean water from a nearby bucket. Fiona didn't even struggle the second time; she just stood there, tears and snot wetting her face.

"Next time use condom, stupid girl."

Once scrubbed, Fiona was given a shabby but clean sarong and long sleeved shirt to wear. She would never see her own clothes again. The young girl and the guard escorted her back to her bunglow where Karin was sitting up in bed looking most concerned. Karin stayed on the bed until the guard closed and locked the door, then jumped up to help the freshly scrubbed, but forlorn looking Fiona onto the bed and untie her bound ankles.

"What happened? Are you OK?"

"Yeah, I'm alright, thanks." Fiona was grateful for Karin's concern and friendship. She lay on the bed and curled into the foetal position.

"Do you want some water?" Karin held out the bottle.

"Mmm, yes please," Fiona mumbled, but didn't move.

Karin held the water to Fiona's lips and poured a little in.

"Is that better?"

Fiona was too tired to answer. Her eyes closed and soon her breathing was slow and even. Karin watched her for a while. The trap door opened and a tray of food was pushed through, then a bedcover.

"Yeah, more curry," Karin thought and went over to the tray. She couldn't stand the smell of the food being in the same room with her. To her surprise, there was a huge beef and salad sandwich, chocolate cake, Coca Cola and a magazine. "Yuk, how disgusting!" Karin spoke aloud in Swedish. The thought of any food revolted her. The continued stress of not knowing what was going to happen was making her stomach cramp and knot. Just like when she was younger, she felt scared and helpless, with no control over what happened to her. How could she have an appetite under these conditions? But she was happy with the magazine and soft drink, they were a welcome distraction from the boredom of the room and the miserable company. She returned to the bed with the magazine, Coke and bed cover. Leaning over Fiona she shook her gently. "You have some food, wake up." Fiona didn't even stir.

Karen draped the new bed cover over their legs, trying to ward off the damned mosquitoes, then lay back to enjoy the magazine and coke, but the smell of the beef sandwich was too much for her. Even from across the room the stench irritated her delicate nose, making her feel nauseous. She took the tray into the bathroom and placed it in the far corner.

Fiona awoke after a few hours, feeling very groggy and disoriented, as if she were hung-over and had been partying for a week. She raised herself, tentatively, onto one elbow and looked around the dim room. Karin was sitting up in bed, trying to look at the magazine in the small amount of light.

"Hello Sleeping Beauty, how do you feel?" Karin smiled, lowering the magazine, relieved that Fiona seemed OK.

"I feel like shit, as usual," Fiona answered grumpily, scowling, annoyed at Karin's smile and enthusiasm. Fiona was so tired of feeling like crap. She rubbed her sticky eyes with her knuckles.

"Why can't I just fall asleep and never wake up?"

"Come on now, it's not that bad. Look, we have Coke and a magazine and there are sandwiches and cake in the bathroom. They're being nice to us now." Karin got up from the bed to retrieve the food and drink and passed it to Fiona, thinking that this would perk her up.

"You shouldn't be depressed, you're the one who has had a bath, I haven't." Karin tried to joke and make Fiona feel a little better. She wished Fiona was nicer and could comfort her when she felt low.

"What a moron you are. Don't you know why I've had a bath and we're getting better food now?" Fiona looked daggers at Karin.

Karin's smile instantly evaporated. "You are such a bitch! I have tried to be nice to you, but it is impossible." Karin started to sob. " Why are you taking your anger out on me? I'm a victim too you know." She stomped into the bathroom, not wanting to be in the same room as Fiona or the food any longer. She stood there confused and hurt, sniffing loudly.

"All this stuff is mine", Fiona continued to bellow from the bed. "You had no right to any of it. I'm the one who did the work. You're not the victim," Fiona screamed in Karin's direction. She snatched up the sandwich and started to eat, fury overtaking the pain in her head. Karin came back into the room, the tears wet on her cheeks.

"Why is it all yours? What work did you do?"

"I had to fuck an old, ugly Thai man, that's where I've been. Where did you think I went, to the spa for a massage? You're so naive!" Fiona was talking with a mouthful of sandwich, little pieces flying out onto the bed.

Karin gasped, hand to her mouth with her eyes wide.

"Did you really have to do that?" Karin sat back on the bed, her face much softer and forgiving of Fiona's bad attitude. "What happened?"

"Well, whatever the big guy gave me certainly helped. I had a nice bath and the girl washed my hair. Then I woke up with this old fart on top, fucking me."

Karin's eyes were still wide, but she lowered her hand from her mouth.

"My God. I'm going to be next. I can't do it." Karin jumped up off the bed, suddenly panicked and paced around the bed, shaking her head and mumbling, slipping into Swedish every few sentences, working herself into a frenzy.

"Take whatever the big guy gives you and it will be OK. We're only here for a couple of weeks anyway, then we can go home and just forget this whole nightmare." Fiona sipped on the Coke casually, her fury spent.

"How do you know they will let us go in a couple of weeks?" Karin's brow was wrinkled with worry; some greasy locks of hair were dangling around her pale, frightened face. Fiona thought about this for a moment, obviously she hadn't considered that their abductor had been lying.

"Why wouldn't they let us go? The longer we are here the more trouble our family and friends will cause," Fiona replied, the confidence in her voice belying how she felt. She knew her family would take a couple of months to even notice she was missing. She had told her mother that she was coming to Thailand, but she was pretty sure she hadn't believed her; she was used to Fiona's lies. Her younger siblings still hung on her every word every time she went around to visit them, but they wouldn't be any help to her. As for her friends, well they had shown their true colours when all of this started. No one wanted to be involved with her problems.

"But our families have no idea where we are, or even where to start. My family has friends in Bangkok, but I lied to them about where I was going." Karin sat heavily on the bed, head in her hands. "I'm so stupid." She started to cry softly again. Their situation seemed hopeless.

"Stop blubbering, you're getting on my nerves," Fiona snapped, turning her back on Karin, so she could hide the tears that were streaming down her own face.

DISILLUSIONED

Karin and Fiona were both shaken awake at the same time. The big man was standing over Karin and one of the guards over Fiona. Both held machetes.

"Busy day today, many customers coming." He grinned his dirty mouthed grin, running his eyes over Karin's long, thin body. Karin cringed and drew her legs up to her stomach and pulled the cover over her body, trying to make herself look smaller, or even invisible.

"I'm ah, I'm sorry, but I, I'm afraid I can't do it," Karin stammered.

"I can give you some smoke to relax you, or some water to paralyse you, or you can do it straight, it's your choice. Or if you give me trouble I can bury you in the jungle, where you will never be found, only by the maggots." He leaned his face closer to Karin.

She shuddered involuntarily. "I won't give trouble. What is the smoke? Hashish?"

"Something similar, but much better, makes you feel fantastic." His smile was more like a grimace.

"OK, maybe I'll have a little, so I am not so nervous," Karin whispered. She was feeling weak with fear, and just wanted this all to be over. The big man pulled the pipe from his pocket, all ready to go. Karin sat up slowly and took the pipe, with a shaking hand. He leaned over with the lighter, as Karin sucked cautiously. She drew away quickly, coughing and screwing up her face.

"It tastes very bitter, what is it?"

"Have a little more. You need to have a bath before first customer comes, hurry." He shoved the pipe, still in her hand, back up to her mouth. Already she had felt a slight change. She was starting to feel very relaxed. She took a bigger drag from the pipe and started to smile. Looking at Fiona, through the haze that was closing in, she could see concern, but Karin was beyond caring now.

The big man tied her feet loosely with the rope and led her slowly out of their hut, across the clearing to the bungalow. She felt as though she were floating, the euphoria was wonderful, as she tagged along, feet bound, behind the hulking back of the big Thai. The grass looked green and beautiful, the sky a brilliant blue with a few puffy white clouds dancing merrily. The cute dog came to sniff at her briefly, before being kicked away. Everything looked so lovely and peaceful to Karin as she trotted along; she had even forgotten where she was going.

Karin entered the bungalow where the Thai girl was bending over the bath, hand in the water, testing the temperature. The door was closed behind her by the big man and she heard him locking it.

"Quickly, girl. No time," the girl snapped. She pulled Karin roughly into the bathroom by her skinny arm.

"Quick, clothes off." The girl was pulling the T-shirt over Karin's head and unbuttoning her shorts before Karin realised. She didn't put up any resistance, there didn't seem any reason to. Karin stepped out of her shorts and underwear, not shy about her nudity at all.

"Mmm, the water looks great." She bent to put her hand in. "Lovely."

The girl didn't understand any of what Karin was saying, because without realising it, Karin was speaking Swedish.

"Quick, girl, get in." The Thai girl was pushing Karin and slapping her leg to indicate for Karin to lift it and step into the bath. Deftly she washed and conditioned Karin's beautiful hair. Karin laid back with eyes closed and a smile on her face. She thought she was back in Sweden at her local sauna, where she went for facials and massages regularly. She felt so happy and at home, the feelings, the smells, all so reassuring.

"Wash yourself, hurry," the girl instructed, handing Karin the soap.

Karin couldn't even lift her arm. She was too relaxed and the warm water was so nice. Clicking her tongue in annoyance the girl grabbed Karin's arm and started to scrub. She moved the soap quickly and efficiently over Karin's body, making sure to wash her genitals thoroughly; Karin just moaned, with enjoyment it seemed, and lifted her pelvis to help the process.

Karin was soon pulled to her shakey feet and towelled off roughly. The young girl pulled some small nail scissors from her baggy pants and trimmed Karin's thick, curly pubic hair.

"That's better." She smiled at the tidy results. "Put this on." She handed Karin a silky red dress. Karin just stood there, smiling with eyes glazed, not really seeing. She had difficulty putting the dress over Karin's head, due to the difference in height, so she stood on the bed to reach, while Karin obediently stood next to the bed. Karin's white nakedness stood out in the dimly lit room. Her small, perky breasts with delicate pink nipples and the trimmed, brown pubic hair between her long, graceful legs were just what the customers loved. Even the Thai girl stopped to appreciate the beauty of her body. "This one will make a lot of money for us," she thought. She knew she would not see any of the money, but at least the Boss would be in a better mood and not hurt her anymore. He was dreadful when the money was not coming in and always seemed to take it out on her.

The Thai girl laid Karin on the bed and put a bit of red lipstick on her dry white lips. The Boss unlocked the door and quickly stepped in, still holding the machete.

"Ready? Does she need another hit?" He went close to Karin and slapped her face lightly.

"You awake?"

"Mmm, yes," she answered dreamily.

"You feel good? Want more smoke?"

"Mmm, yes." She opened her eyes halfway and smiled.

"OK, quickly, customer here." He pulled the pipe out and placed it between her absurdly red lips. "Suck."

Karin sucked on the little black pipe with its bitter taste, which seemed to taste better this time. The ecstasy was instant. The Boss snapped something to the Thai girl and quickly left the bungalow, not locking the door.

"You must use condom, girl. Don't get sick." The young girl took some of the condoms from the bedside drawer and placed them under the lamp. Taking one, she put it in Karin's slack hand. "You hear me, girl?"

"Mmm, yes," Karin answered obediently, grasping the condom.

Then Karin felt Stefan's arms around her. He was smiling at her and telling her it would be all right. She felt weak with relief and hugged him tightly, moaning with happiness. She felt him take the condom out of her hand and put it on.

"That's strange," she thought. "We don't use condoms." Soon he was inside her, thrusting mightily. Whispering that he loved her, she was so beautiful, he wanted to see her again.

"Of course you can see me again." She smiled her enthusiasm and kissed him deeply. He came quickly, got up and left. The young Thai girl soon appeared, helped Karin to the bath, and douched her with warm liquid from a bucket. Karin's eye's were still glazed over, but the smile was gone.

"Where did Stefan go?", she asked in Swedish.

The girl didn't respond, leaving Karin to talk with herself. "Another customer here, get dressed again." She helped Karin with the dress again, lay her down and put another condom in her hand. She picked up the used condom from the floor and straightened the bed. A knock on the door and Stefan came in again.

"Oh, you're back, where did you go? I thought you left me." Karin chattered away in Swedish as the new Stefan got undressed and quickly mounted her.

"I'm so glad you came back, I missed you so much. How did you find me?" Karin looked at Stefan, but he was coming in and out of focus and she couldn't quite see him clearly. He was smiling and kissing her, going all red in the face with exertion. He was pushing with rapid little thrusts, getting close to orgasm.

"That's very quick, usually you last much longer," Karin murmured into Stefan's neck as he shuddered with the pleasure of orgasm. He got up, ripping the condom off and placing it on the bedside table. He got dressed and then pulled a few notes out of his pocket and placed them next to the dirty condom. Smiling he patted her on the head and left the room. Karin was starting to get a bit confused. Why did Stefan keep leaving?

The girl hurried back in, pulled Karin up from the bed and rushed her into the bathroom to douche again. Her rough, stubby hands handling the equipment expertly.

"Good girl, you use condom. Not get sick. Very good, very good. Boss man happy."

Karin looked at her, not really understanding what was happening.

"Did you see Stefan? Where did he go?" She was still speaking Swedish, so got no response, which confused her more.

"Very busy today, four customers waiting, hurry." She pushed Karin to the bed so she could stand on it and help Karin dress. Karin was in a blur. She wasn't sure why she was getting ready over and over for Stefan to come in for a short time, have sex then leave again. Even he was behaving strangely, sometimes smiling and friendly, other times rough and not affectionate. Even his face was distorted, sometimes she hardly recognised him.

"How many times has Stefan come in and left?" He had just walked out again, when the Boss came in with the young girl. They were both smiling heartily. He gave Karin's nakedness a cursory glance and said to the girl, "Wash her and send her back to her hut in clean clothes. Feed her well and make sure you put the right amount of contraception into her water. Give her massage too."

The young girl bowed her head and lowered her eyes in compliance. "Yes, Sir." Her obedient manner belied her inner anger and contempt for the four 'white witches'. She would be damned if she was going to massage one of the spoilt, pampered bitches. She did all the back-breaking work, all they did was lie on their backs, legs spread. There was no hardship in that. She should be getting a muscle relaxing massage herself; her back was killing her with all the lifting and hauling she had to do all day.

Quickly, she pulled Karin off the bed and into the bathroom for the final wash of the day. She had learnt through hard knocks not to backchat or disobey this cruel man. It didn't seem to matter how far she kept away from him, his arms always managed to reach her.

As she scrubbed the white girl briskly her thoughts drifted; it was pointless dwelling on how she had ended up belonging to this horrible man, but sometimes she needed to remind herself of where she had come from, that there were people out there somewhere who loved and missed her.

Li had been sold to him by her parents when she was seven years old. Her family was from a poor village in the country, which relied on the nearby crops of sugar cane, which the whole village cultivated and sold to one of the bigger villages. It had only taken a couple of years of drought and insect infestation to change Li's situation forever. When the gang of recruiters came through the village to buy young girls cheap, her parents had thought it was their only option to save the rest of the family. Li had been on her way home from school when her older brother had run up and said that she had to come home immediately. Grasping her only school book tightly she had struggled along behind him, complaining the whole way. Her brother was always bullying her, she was sick of it. When she stepped into their ramshackle old hut she saw her mother and father sitting at the table with two strange men. One was huge, very tall and fat, the other was typically small and skinny. Li couldn't take her eyes off the big man, she didn't know him, but instinctively she knew not to trust him, and to keep a safe distance away. Her parents were smiling encouragement and summoning her forward.

"Come here, girl, quickly." Her father was smiling, but his voice was very serious.

Li edged forward slowly, eyes fixed on the big stranger. He was forcing a smile and his teeth were very dirty and stained. Stubbing his cigarette out roughly he stood and took two steps towards Li's tiny, quivering side. He crouched next to her on bended knee and reached his smelly, nicotine stained hand out to hold her face and turn it this way and that in the light to get a proper look at her features. Li hated being that close to him and tried to pull her face free, but he held it tight.

"Now don't be silly, hold still," her mother admonished, as she leaned back in her chair and lit her pipe. She could be unpredictable when she smoked the pipe, so Li held still and did as she was told.

"She is very pretty and strong, she will make a very good maid to the working women. I am sure she will make a fortune, if she has the right temperament."

"She is very quiet and obedient, an excellent worker," her father hurriedly added.

The big man held her hands towards him, while he scrutinised her palms.

"Good, not too soft, she is used to hard work." He nodded approval. He stood upright, showing his impressive size and returned to the table, but, before he sat, he pulled a huge wad of notes from his pocket and placed it nonchalantly on the table, then lowered his bulk. Li's parents couldn't take their eyes off the money. That would save the whole family.

Despite all her begging and pleading she was given the privilege of joining the gang that would take care of her, feed and clothe her and help her into the specialised and potentially profitable art of prostitution. She was a very clever girl, but she was not sure whether this was a good or bad thing. She kept her intelligence a secret as much as she could, but was caught out every now and then, and put back into her place. Usually, with a very hard backhander. Nothing to leave too much damage, or reduce her value, but definitely painful.

Her virginity had been sold for a very good price, on her eighth birthday, to a very wealthy, fat, white man. Li had known what was going to happen, as she had seen the older girls before her go through the process. They had explained what the man did with his pee pee. At first, she had thought they were telling a perverted joke. Why would a man want to piss into her piss hole? But she had had to help look after some of the girls that had gone before her. One girl died from a bad infection a few days after her virginity fuck. A letter to her parents, instructing them to come and get their liability, was sent out. The girl had not repaid her debt yet.

Some of the older girls put their fingers into her piss hole to show her how the man would feel. It was horrible, very uncomfortable and weird.

"Why do they want to do that?", Li had asked the older girls.

"It feels good for them. You might even grow to like it." Li couldn't imagine that she would ever grow to like it.

On the day of her initiation, one of the older girls put a little slippery gel into her piss hole and said, "This will make it hurt less. You have to relax and it will not be as painful."

The girl had kissed her tenderly on the mouth and she was on her way to joining the status of the older girls. It wasn't as bad as she had thought. Sure it hurt, but the man had given her a bag of sweets and rice cakes. All the other girls made such a fuss over her, washing, stroking and comforting her that she had thought it was well worth it.

The fact that Li felt no sympathy for the four foreign girls was not because she had no compassion, it was just that they were adults who had had sex before, many times with different partners probably, so this wasn't such a trauma for them. They were just soft, pampered brats.

Li had learnt a lot about foreigners in the two years she had lived with Richard, an American. He had walked into the brothel one day looking for a live-in maid/girlfriend. She had been fourteen at the time, but with a very well developed figure for her age. Some men really preferred the under developed girls, but they always tended to be a bit strange, so Li was happy they never chose her. Her face was still young looking, but she had rounded breasts and curvy hips. The Asian men didn't really like this shape, but she was very popular with the Western men, and they paid more money. Almost as much as the Japanese, who were the most generous. Richard was very kind. He taught her English and how to cook the Western food he liked. It was a comfortable, enjoyable two years. His fantasy had been very easy to satisfy; he liked to have sex with two girls at the same time. As she had no shortage of brothel friends, catering to this desire was no problem at all. And sometimes he brought home Western women.

After two years in Thailand Richard's contract was finished and he returned to America. He had given the brothel the payout fee to free Li, but they said he was giving them a 'Thank you' present. Li could do nothing about it, so was still owned by the Boss. Her life wasn't so bad now that they ran Western prostitutes. Business was booming and all she had to do was look after the girls, and make sure they took the contraception that was in the drinking water so they didn't get a period.

This was the fourth 'white gang' the Boss had set up. He would run them for a couple of months then put in a manager while he went off to find more girls. Most of the girls only lasted three or four months. Usually they died of a drug overdose or infection. The Boss liked to get them addicted to heroin; it made them nice and passive and they would do anything to keep the supply going and their health would last a lot longer. When the girls died the guards would bury them in the jungle or dump their bodies in some back alley in the city. If the bodies were discovered by the police, their families were informed that their child was an addict and had died of an overdose. No further investigation would be needed.

The camps they had set up were all very close to each other and just on the outskirts of Bangkok. Most of the customers lived and worked in Bangkok, so the gang needed to be close to the city. Even though the camp looked as if it was in the middle of the jungle, it was actually in a very built-up suburban area.

Li really missed her friends from the brothel. She was very lonely by herself at this new compound. She had another year of working for the

Boss and her debt would be paid. She had been away from her family for such a long time, she was very much looking forward to being reunited with them.

Her father had died in a farming accident three years ago, so it had been a real burden to send more money home for her mother and younger siblings, but it was all worth it, judging by the letters she received from them every month.

It would be only another three months until Li found out that all those letters she had received, once a month since she was five, had been fake. The letters were written by another kept woman, who wrote an average of three hundred letters a day. The letters were what kept the working girls going, day after torturous day. It was a very clever idea.

ESCAPE

The moment that Laurie had feared finally arrived, as she heard the lock scraping open and the Boss came in with the guard. She wasn't sure which was worse, the waiting for the moment or the actual moment. Either way she was paralysed with fear. She knew that fear was her enemy and she couldn't operate at maximum strength or efficiency if clouded with fear, but all logic and her years of training were over-ridden by the chilling childhood memory of a forced sexual act. Whether this violent act on her when she was a child made her gay or whether she was born that way, Laurie hadn't thought much about. She just didn't like sex with a man, and she wasn't going to have sex with a man, ever!

"You need smoke?" The Boss held out the pipe to Laurie as the guard approached to tie her feet.

Laurie was backing up on the bed as far as she could go, pulling her shaking legs to her chest.

"Don't make trouble, you'll get hurt." You just had to look at his eyes to know that to fight him was to end up second best.

"Please, please don't. I can't, I'm sick." Laurie was stammering, speaking in the high pitch of a panicked child, her eyes wide with fear, her face white.

"Have some smoke, you'll feel real good." He tried to smile encouragement, but his face just looked more demented.

The guard had hold of one of Laurie's ankles and was grabbing for the other, when she lashed out and kicked him squarely in the chest, sending him flying back into the wall. He gasped, as the wind was knocked out of him, and he slid to a sitting position on the floor, his legs sprawled in front of him. Instantly the other guard was in the room, holding a machete at the ready, eyes quickly scanning the room, assessing the situation.

Kelly just lay as still as possible on the bed, the magazine still in her hand. She was not about to give any trouble, she had other plans on how to beat these circumstances.

"Your choice, girl. This or this." The big man held his pipe in one hand and a syringe in the other.

"Come on Laurie. You'll just get hurt if you fight." Kelly tried to reason with her. "It's not that bad, please do as they say."

Laurie's eyes were wide open, and darting from one man to the next, sizing them up for her next move. She had been in mock fighting scenes before, with multiple enemies, but the odds were certainly against her. Her logic was saying give up now and fight when the odds are better, but her emotions seemed to be over-riding at the moment.

"OK, chop off her leg." The huge guy said in English, then followed quickly with something in Thai.

The guard stepped forward, with the machete raised high over his head, eyes squinting with determined focus, his mouth a thin line.

Kelly screamed. "No, please stop! Laurie, do as they say!"

Laurie quickly raised her hands defensively in front of her. "OK, OK, I'll do what you want, please stop, I'll do anything you want. Please, stop!"

"That's better." The Boss spoke quickly to the guard on the floor, who staggered up and moved gingerly around the bed to grab at Laurie's ankles again. Her legs were pulled up tight to her pounding chest, but she relaxed them and allowed him to tie her ankles. The machete wielding guard stood menacingly close, still with the weapon raised, ready to bring it down on a soft body part.

"Turn over," the Boss said.

"Please don't chop my leg, I promise to do whatever you say."

"Roll over. Quick!"

Laurie rolled onto her stomach, eyes closed, sobbing quietly.

"Please don't hurt her. She'll do whatever you say," Kelly volunteered, but edged away from Laurie slightly, just in case they followed through with the threat.

The Boss grabbed one of Laurie's arms and twisted it up her back, until she gave a small squeak of pain. He leaned his weight onto her torso and stuck the syringe roughly into her bottom, right through her shorts.

"You still need a little, I think." He injected only a quarter of the dose, but Kelly saw Laurie slump immediately. He got off her back and pulled her up off the bed. Her eyes were glazed over and slightly closed and she was smiling.

"That stuff is effective, whatever it is," Kelly thought, but knew that she didn't want to try it. She wanted all her wits and faculties about her at all times. That was the only way she was going to get out of this mess.

The men marched Laurie out of the bungalow.

Li was waiting in another fancy bungalow. It had a navy blue decor, but was as beautifully decorated as the red one. She had the bath filled with steaming, scented water. Laurie was shoved roughly into the bathroom. She staggered slightly, but was still smiling carelessly as Li steadied her.

"Hurry up, clothes off," Li instructed, undoing Laurie's shorts and lifting off her shirt. Laurie raised her limp arms, obligingly. She almost fell into the bath, but Li grabbed her expertly, and helped her in. Water slopped over Li and wet most of her sarong and she slapped the back of Laurie's head in annoyance. Laurie didn't even register it, she was caught up with how amazing the warm water felt on her dirty skin.

"This is great." Laurie smiled warmly at Li, her eyes still unfocused. Li was busy getting the shampoo and washing Laurie's greasy hair. "Wash yourself," she snapped.

Laurie tried to pick up the soap, but it slipped from her wet hands. Skidding around in the bath trying to retrieve the slippery soap Laurie started laughing uncontrollably. Even the slaps to the back of her head couldn't stop her giggling mirth.

"Hurry, girl, customer waiting," Li reprimanded.

Laurie started to soap herself, still giggling like a school girl. Li pulled Laurie to her feet in the bath and told her, "Open legs. Your pussy too hairy."

Laurie stood with legs apart as Li started to shave her pubic hair. Big wads of dark brown pubic hair floating in the bath water made Laurie laugh all over again.

Li finished the job swiftly and pulled Laurie out of the bath, towelled her off and steered her over to the big, luxurious looking bed. Laurie's white skin was pink from the warm bath, her hairless pussy looking very dramatic now that it was bare and visible.

"Customers will like that." Li smiled her approval at Laurie's tidy pussy. It was nice and small with no hanging down labia, that was good. Her clitoris protruded slightly in the front. Very nice.

There was a sharp rap at the door, and the guard yelled something.

"Quick, onto the bed, customer coming."

Laurie was happy to lie on the beautiful bed. She was starting to feel sleepy after the lovely warm bath. She closed her eyes and started to dream about her ex-girlfriend, Amanda, in Atlanta. One time they had got drunk at home and decided to have a candle-lit bath together, with red wine, very romantic. In their drunken excitement they had shaved each other's pubic hair, just to see what they looked like. Laurie wasn't sure if she liked it. It kind of felt a bit creepy as it made them both look like little pre-pubescent girls. They had both let the hair grow back and never did it again. She felt the hard warm body lie on top of her.

"Amanda," Laurie thought absently.

Laurie felt the kisses all over her body, slight nibbling at her nipples.

"Mmm, that feels great," she moaned.

The kisses went lower and she automatically moved her legs apart. The tongue was warm and gentle, then started to get hard and fevered in its probing and sucking on her clitoris. Laurie moved her hips in rhythm with the licking and sucking, she had not had an orgasm in what seemed like a lifetime. She felt so warm and light, as if she were floating on a cloud. The kisses then moved up her body, lingering on her taut erect nipples. The hard, scratchy face started kissing her.

"That's strange, why is her face so scratchy?" She opened her eyes dreamily and saw a man. Flushed red with excitement and exertion, eyes wide and mouth hanging droopily open, he was breathing in gasps and groping for his penis to shove inside her.

She screamed and tried to push his weight off her. He had her pinned and she couldn't budge him at all. She pushed her head back into the bed and then thrust it forward with all her might, smashing her forehead into his nose. Blood spurted instantly in all directions. He reeled back holding his nose, screaming in pain. She lifted her legs and pushed him squarely in the chest back off the bed. He tumbled heavily to the floor. Immediately the door opened and the two guards came running in, machetes at the ready. The poor customer was sprawled naked on the floor, nose grasped in his bloodied hands. Laurie looked like a deer caught in the headlights, frozen with fear and confusion on the bed, blood spots all over her face and chest. One guard helped the wounded customer to his feet, speaking quickly in Thai and ushering him out of the door, while the other approached her on the bed, machete held high. Laurie thought that this was it. He was going to bring the blade down on some part of her body, with all his might. She had no choice but to go out fighting, she was not going to lie down and take it calmly. In one fluid movement she grabbed the two pillows and leaped towards him, pushing them against the massive knife with all her weight. The guard was completely caught by surprise; none of the girls had attacked a guard before. He stumbled back and banged his head on the concrete wall of the bungalow. In that dazed second Laurie was off and running out of the open door. The sunlight blinded her for a moment, but she didn't let it slow her down. She knew which direction they had come from her hut, so she started off in the opposite direction, running initially on the path, but then across the clearing and straight into the jungle. It was thicker than it looked. Her naked body was soon red and bleeding from all the scratches. She couldn't feel any pain, in fact she was feeling very exhilarated by the freedom of being out and running. It was like being on a training exercise, without the uniform. At first, she could hear the shouts and yelling from the guards at the camp; it seemed they were not prepared for a situation like this. But she was soon far enough into the jungle to hear only her own heavy breathing and the noise of the bushes and branches being pushed aside.

She wasn't sure how long she had been ploughing through the jungle, but she was very tired, so stopped for a rest. The adrenaline stopped pumping through her body as she sat and tried to steady herself. The tiredness and nausea hit at the same time; she wanted to throw up and sleep. Her head felt as if a locomotive was racing through it. She lay down in an exhausted heap. When she woke up, it was dark and she was cold. Now the scratches were starting to hurt. She looked up to see if there was any light from the moon or stars, but no light penetrated the vegetation. She knew it was too dangerous to set off walking in the dark, unable to see her hand in front of her face. She would probably end up walking in circles. She would stay put until morning. Laurie started to dig a hole in the jungle floor with her bare hands. The ground was quite soft, with a deep layer of rotting leaves. It didn't smell too good, but once she burrowed herself into the hole and covered herself with the leaves, she felt much warmer. She started to think about her friends and family so far away, totally unaware of her plight. She felt so alone and helpless. She had worked so hard over the years not to feel like this. Was it all going to be for nothing? She fell into a deep fitful sleep, dreaming about military exercises with people chasing her. She was running, trying to escape, but couldn't see where she was going, everything was very dark and blurry; she kept running endlessly into the unseen.

She woke to birds chirping loudly all around her. It took a moment for her to remember where she was and what had happened, but the frightening reality soon came flooding back. Her legs were stiff from sleeping with them cramped under her in the hole, but at least she was alive. For how long? Were they searching for her now? She listened intently for a moment. Were there any sounds of search dogs barking? Or people running through the jungle looking for her? There were only the sounds of the noisy birds going about their daily business.

"OK, now what?", Laurie mumbled to herself, trying to think logically. She rubbed her temples and stood slowly, shaking out her sore legs, filthy from her makeshift nest.

She set off to find the nearest village. She made sure her progress was straight by constantly looking up and checking the sun; she couldn't see it directly through the thick tree tops, but she could see generally where it was. Her scratches were aching and her tummy rumbling, but she reasoned that it was better than feeling nothing at all. As she trudged along, she thought about the girls she had left behind.

"I hope they are not being punished because of what I've done. I had no choice. I had to make a run for it. I'll get help and we will all be out of there by tomorrow." Every now and then, she would stop to listen for the sounds of people chasing her, but the jungle seemed very quiet, except for the birds and a distant droning, that she couldn't identify. She kept ploughing on. After an hour or so she thought she could smell something. Smoke, from a fire? She stopped, closed her eyes and put her nose in the air, sniffing deeply. Yes, definitely a fire, but from which direction? She turned this way and that, trying to determine which direction the smell was coming from. She started off in one direction, but then seemed to lose the smell, so went back until she found it again and then went off in another direction. Finally, on the third go, the smoke smell seemed to get stronger. The jungle was as thick as before, so progress was still slow. Now Laurie was being more careful of the scratchy branches, no need to hurt herself further. Help was nearby. Suddenly she heard a dog barking. She froze. Then a woman's voice, speaking sharply, maybe telling the noisy dog to shut up. The dog kept barking, so Laurie moved towards the sound. She almost fell out of the jungle, it ended so abruptly. She staggered a few steps, then regained her balance and squinted against the sunlight, now much stronger. There was a woman holding a fat baby on her hip and a scruffy dog yapping incessantly.

"Hello." Laurie smiled her relief at finding salvation. She walked towards the woman, who screamed and grasped the baby tighter and turned and ran back into the ramshackle house. The baby started crying loudly and the woman was talking quickly to someone, in her high-pitched, panicked voice. Laurie could hear another voice now, an old man. Laurie banged on the door.

"Please, help me, have you got a phone? Call the Police!" Laurie realised she was jabbering too quickly. They probably didn't understand a word, and they were afraid of her. She must have looked quite a sight, naked and covered in dirt.

"Hello, please help. Call Police." Laurie spoke slowly, pronouncing all the syllables clearly.

The baby was still crying heartily, most outraged at the sudden interruption in his quiet life.

"Please, help." Laurie banged on the door again. Then she tried the handle and the door swung open easily. The inside of the room was very dim, after the bright sunlight.

"Hello, do you have a telephone?" The woman was wide-eyed, sitting on a wooden chair near the baby's cot, rocking it, and shooshing the baby to be quiet.

Suddenly Laurie was grabbed from behind. She panicked and automatically dipped her shoulder, pushed out her hip and flung the attacker over her shoulder onto the hard, dirt floor. The old man screamed with pain as he was dumped roughly on to the ground. The woman had her hand over her mouth and tears were pouring down her face. Laurie bent over the man.

"I'm sorry, I'm sorry, I didn't know who you were. Are you OK?" The old man was shaking and trying to back away from Laurie, who was shuffling after him on her haunches, still apologising.

Then she was hit on the back of the head. When she woke up she was still on the floor in the same spot, her legs were bound with a man's business tie, her hands were tied behind her back and there was something over her mouth. Her head pounded, she probably had brain damage after that blow! The old man was sitting in the wooden chair holding the massive frying pan, looking at her with pure hatred. Laurie tried to talk, but it was just a mumble behind the gag. Her hands were starting to feel the pain of pins and needles, they were tied too tightly and the blood wasn't getting through. She twisted her wrists and hands to loosen the bonds, but they held fast. Her hands were going to turn black and fall off at this rate. There was noise behind her, someone, a few people were coming. Laurie started to writhe.

"Please, help me," she groaned into the gag. She turned onto her back and looked up into the face of the Boss.

Laurie started to cry. It was becoming difficult to breathe through her nose, as snot and tears ran down her face. The Boss got out a syringe and injected her in her dirty, naked buttock.

LIFE GOES ON

Karin lay back on the bed flicking through the magazine for the millionth time. The boredom was driving her crazy. She wasn't a person who did too much anyway, but all this lying around was starting to get tedious, even for her. Fiona was asleep, as usual, next to her. She was even more lazy, plus the pipe she smoked all day long didn't help at all. At least Karin only took a couple of tots a day, just when she needed it. The screaming jolted Karin from her blank staring at the page. First a girl's scream, then a man's. Karin tried to stand on the edge of the bed to look out of the small barred window. Where had the scream come from? Suddenly she saw the young Thai girl and one of the guards come tearing out of the kitchen and run in the direction of the bungalow.

"Wow, what's happening?", Karin said aloud. Fiona hadn't even stirred, so Karin got down and shook her awake.

"Fiona, wake up, something's happening, wake up!" Fiona screwed up her face and pulled the blanket over her head.

"Leave me alone," she grumbled. Karin pulled the blanket away.

"Get up, you lazy bitch! Something is happening." Karin slapped Fiona's bare leg, already red with mosquito bites.

"Aww, stop it. That fuckin' hurt." Fiona rubbed her leg.

"Whad-di-ya-wan?", Fiona mumbled incoherently trying to raise herself onto one elbow and rub her gluey eyes.

"I heard a female scream, then a man scream and when I looked out the window the Thai girl and the guard were running to one of the bungalows. Something is happening. I bet it is that American girl again. She's a fighter," Karin babbled quickly to catch Fiona up on all the excitement.

"Is that all? Probably got a customer that liked a bit of 'slap and tickle'." Fiona lay back down, exhausted. "I'm so tired all the time."

"You should stop smoking that pipe all day long then." Karin got back up on the bed, to look out the window for more developments.

"Mind your own business, you smoke it as well, you hypocrite." Fiona shuffled off to the bathroom. They had a few luxuries now, a blanket, magazines, water, better food, the water for the shower had even been turned on, and they had soap! Life was getting better.

Then all the shouting started. Karin couldn't see what was happening, but the big man had come lumbering out of the kitchen as well and was yelling furiously.

"Wow, he's not happy." Karin still peered out of the grubby window. Her arms and legs started to ache, with the stretch from the bed. Fiona slouched back into the room and looked up at Karin stretched out to the window sill, her shirt and sarong hanging loosely on her.

"I didn't realise how skinny you were," Fiona stated candidly. "Have you lost a bit of weight?"

Karin quickly jumped down, looking guilty. "No, not really. I've always been slim." The fact that she was only drinking a small amount of water and hardly eating anything was having a very dramatic effect on her.

Fiona had already lost interest and was back on the bed, flicking through a magazine.

Karin hadn't noticed the change in her body so much, but she was having more dizzy spells and seeing Stefan over and over during the day was really taking its toll on her emotional and mental state. Sometimes he was friendly and affectionate, then he would leave the room and come back acting like a totally different person. It was very confusing. She had asked him when they were going to the beach, but it was as if he didn't even speak her language. It was confusing moments like that, or when Stefan's features distorted, that she took a couple of puffs on the pipe, then everything was wonderful.

"Do you want some of this sandwich, before I polish it off?", Fiona asked, not even looking up.

"No, I've had some," Karin lied. Fiona didn't even notice.

"I'm sick of looking at these Asian models, they all look the same. Why don't they have any real models?", Fiona asked annoyed, flicking rapidly through the magazine.

"They are real models. It is for the Asian market after all." Karin was glad the conversation was off her. She flopped back down on the bed, weary, covering her skinny legs with the blanket. The shouting from outside had stopped, so the girls soon forgot about the incident.

The Boss and a guard came for Fiona a few hours later to service some night clients. Now that they had the two bungalows operating the girls were seeing about six to ten men a day each. They would see a man for an average of half an hour, but most of the clients were finished well within the time-frame. Sometimes they would spend the remainder of their time just lying next to the girl, even falling asleep briefly, and sometimes they would just leave.

The Boss seemed very pre-occupied tonight and was much rougher when tying the restraints on Fiona's ankles. The other guard stood back with a worried look on his face, his beady eyes darting from one girl to the next. He held his machete ready for the slightest move.

"I need more smoke," Fiona demanded bluntly. Her features were hard and mean in the dim light. Dark circles were appearing under her eyes and her normally fiery red hair was dull and lifeless.

"I gave you some pills yesterday," he shot back angrily.

"I've finished them, they were weak crap anyway." Fiona was rolling her eyes in annoyance.

"You'll become too expensive to keep at this rate," he said menacingly.

"I'm ready to go anytime." Fiona was really starting to push her luck with her insolence. She never did know when to shut up.

"Don't push me, girl." He pulled her off the bed, squeezing her soft arm unnecessarily hard. Fiona grimaced, but didn't let any sound out. Maybe she could learn to keep quiet.

She shuffled her way alongside the guards, getting an unnecessary push every now and then when she slowed down too much. Her thoughts were miles away, disjointed and blurry; she was starting to be unable to discern between dreams and reality. She was sleeping all the time, but not feeling rested at all. Her mind flicked between thoughts of her family, her job, the drug boss and her loser friends.

She had dreamt that the drug boss and her mother were having an affair and had come to Thailand to get married. They had found Fiona in the jungle and been very disappointed that she was working as a prostitute for very little money. Fiona had tried to explain that she didn't want to be here, that she was being forced, but they hadn't listened to her, they shook their heads with disappointment and said they were on their honeymoon, and couldn't be bothered with any more of Fiona's selfish lies and bullshit.

Other times she would wake up with her legs and arms itching unbearably. She would lie in the dark and scratch them raw, listening to Karin in the bathroom, making funny noises, as if she was talking to someone. She'd had a fleeting thought of saving all the powder the Boss gave her to take all at one time, just to end this nightmare, but she could never remember to save it.

Fiona entered the romantically lit bungalow and felt a little comforted by its familiarity. She would have a lovely, warm bath in perfumed water and lie around for a couple of hours; it wasn't so bad. Someone would come and rescue her soon, until then she could put up with it all. There must be worse jobs.

PLANNING

Kelly sat demurely on the bed as the next customer was shown in. She smiled radiantly as she saw it was one of her regulars. She would rather a regular than a new client; they were predictable and she could talk more.

This afternoon she was wearing a new, white, see-through gown. Her normally straight blonde hair was pinned up, with wisps hanging strategically down around her freshly made-up face. Li was getting more generous with providing dresses, hair accessories and make-up. Whenever Kelly asked for something, it usually appeared the next day. Maybe she should ask for her passport and some get-away money.

The customer hurriedly rushed in; red with excitement and smiling smugly, like a child. It was the one she called 'Baby', in her mind, anyway. He had asked her to call him Mr. James, although she could tell he was Thai and it was probably a fake name.

"Guess what?", he said childishly, giggling with glee.

She smiled seductively, pleased it was him. She couldn't be bothered with a hard sex session right now, she was sore from the last customer, who had had an unusually large penis and seemed very proud that he could pound away with it for the whole half hour. Baby was always happy just lying next to her and sucking her nipples for an hour. Sometimes he even extended to two hours. She had been surprised to learn from Li that he was very high up in the Police force. Li could be quite friendly and chatty when it suited her. The Boss had warned her never to upset Mr. James, as he was one of their most important customers.

The second time she saw Mr. James she had told him that she was being kept there against her will. He became angry with her talking about it and told her to shut up or he wouldn't come back and he would tell the Boss.

Luckily Baby had taken a shine to her and he would come and see her every second day. Kelly had asked him how he got all that time off work and Baby had laughed and said he worked thirty minutes away, so it was very convenient.

"You work in the jungle?", Kelly had asked, confused. He had laughed. "No, in Bangkok." But then suddenly he seemed to realise what he had said and became very quiet.

Kelly had not asked anything more; she didn't want to raise suspicion or make Mr. James angry again, but now she had a clue that they were not in the middle of nowhere, miles from civilisation. She couldn't wait for Laurie to be released from solitary, so they could plan their escape. After much coercion Li had told her that Laurie had been in solitary confinement for two days now.

"You know how you said you really loved jewelry?", Mr. James continued, lifting his briefcase onto the bed.

Kelly gave her standard, 'I can't believe you remembered, you are so wonderful' look. She had been planting that seed in a few of her regular, good customers, the ones she felt she could trust.

"You didn't show anyone, did you?", Kelly asked earnestly.

"No, of course not." He put his finger to his lips mockingly. "I know how to keep a secret." He pulled a tiny black velvet bag out of his case with a flourish.

"Wow, you shouldn't have," Kelly squealed excitedly, grabbing the delicate bag from his hand. It contained a pair of black pearl earrings.

"They're fantastic, you are so thoughtful. Thank you so much." Kelly flung her arms around him, making him feel very special. Her plan was to get as much jewelry as possible from the customers. It was small and easy to carry, for when she escaped. She would use it as bribes to get to the city and find the Australian Embassy. She hoped she could use the jewelry to bribe Li. With her help, it would be much easier. Li was starting to be friendlier, but Kelly wasn't sure she could be trusted yet.

Kelly was shaken from her thoughts of escape by Baby's grizzly voice. "Mummy, can I suck titty?" He had removed his thick glasses and jacket and sat on the bed looking childish and stupid.

Kelly groaned inwardly at this perverted little man. "Have you been a good little boy?" Kelly spoke her part in the little charade.

"Yes, Mummy." Mr. James sucked on his thumb solemnly, eyes wide and innocent, nodding his head up and down, like a big overgrown baby.

"OK, lie down next to me." Kelly lay on the bed, undid the top few buttons of her gown, and pulled one of her full breasts out for Baby to suck on. She leaned back with her arms behind her head and eyes closed, pretending to enjoy it, while Baby sucked furiously and played with himself. He would eventually ejaculate on her leg and then say, "Sorry Mummy, sorry Mummy. I'm a bad boy." Kelly would either put him over her knee for a spanking or reassure him that he wasn't such a bad boy, depending on her mood.

"Today I think I'll spank him," she thought absently as she planned her escape.

Soon Mr. James' time was up. He couldn't stay longer today. There was a big case he was working on. He pulled his boxer shorts up over his red bottom, smiling broadly.

"See you Thursday, Kelly."

"OK Mr. James, see you then, I can't wait. I'll be thinking about you." Kelly played with her red, chewed nipple, as she looked at him from the bed. He shivered with excitement and hurried out the door, saying a few words to the guard standing outside. Li scurried in soon after.

"You good girl, make lots money." Li beamed as she fussed with running the shower and tidying up the towels.

Kelly took a deep breath and put on her dazzling smile. It was time to start the second part of her plan for escape.

"Li, you look very nice today, have you done something?" Kelly looked at the shy girl, who started to grin and duck her head away. "You've got lipstick on, come and show me." Li shook her head and kept her face turned away, but Kelly knew her well enough by now to know that Li was dying to have some attention and friendly human contact. Kelly had been watching Li intently for some time now, looking for a chink in her armour. She thought there must be some way to get Li on her side, so she could help them to escape. Kelly had spent many sleepless nights planning. She had learnt to stop thinking of sex as being associated with love and relationships. She was beginning to see sex for what it was to these men; a commodity to be used, sold or exchanged for favour or finance. Once she began to think this way it became much easier to deal with her predicament and concentrate on surviving to see her loved ones again. She had decided that maybe this whole situation was normal to Li, that she must have her reasons for being here. She just had to find a way to befriend her and get her trust.

"Come on, show me. You look so pretty. Come here." Kelly held her hand out to the girl, who turned slowly, and started to move towards Kelly. Kelly sat on the edge of the bed, and when Li was close enough she parted her legs, so Li stood between them. Because Li was so small and petite their faces were almost at the same level in this position.

"Can I try some on?", Kelly whispered, pulling Li closer and puckering her lips. Li leaned forward and pushed her lips onto Kelly's. Kelly opened her mouth slightly and slipped her tongue into the girl's mouth. Li took it and held the position for a second, before pulling back.

"Did I get any?", Kelly asked smiling mischievously.

"A little," Li replied, smiling her very rare shy smile.

"Give me some more!" Kelly pulled Li close again. Li laughed and came forward, kissing Kelly with an open mouth this time. It was brief but Kelly could feel the girl's excitement.

"That's better." Kelly giggled and pulled Li onto the bed next to her. The buttons on her gown were still open and Li looked quickly at Kelly's full breasts.

"Do you want to touch them?" Kelly took one of Li's tiny calloused hands and brought it to her breasts. Li licked her lips nervously and flicked a hesitant look towards the door.

"Feel's good, doesn't it?", Kelly murmured huskily, making Li tweak her already sore red nipples. As Li was stroking her breast Kelly asked casually, "When is the Boss letting Laurie out?"

Li seemed very preoccupied and took a moment to answer, "Dunno."

"Why's that?" Kelly tried to keep her voice even, but fear was starting to creep in, and her voice wavered slightly. Li didn't seem to notice as she kept stroking Kelly's breasts tenderly.

"She a stupid, bad girl," Li commented absently.

"Why, what has she done now?" Kelly was afraid to hear. Laurie was well trained and capable, but she was still no match for three men with weapons, especially when she was weak from lack of food and the effects of the drugs.

A terrible image flashed across Kelly's mind. "They didn't chop off her leg, did they?" Surely they wouldn't do that. It would be hard to market a one legged girl, definitely wouldn't get as much money!

Li looked up at Kelly's worried face and was about to reply when suddenly they heard someone unlocking the door. They both jumped up off the bed in fright and raced for the bathroom together. The shower was still running, and in one motion, Kelly had her gown off and was under the tepid water.

The guard shouted something from the doorway in Thai to Li, who, in turn, shouted at Kelly to hurry up, another customer was coming.

"Why am I doing all the work? What about those other two girls? What's happened to them?", Kelly complained, while she washed quickly.

"They working, they working," Li hissed, afraid the guard would hear.

"Where?", Kelly asked, trying to look nonchalant.

"Too many questions," Li snapped, holding out the towel for Kelly. "Quickly!"

"Are they still here?", Kelly persisted, turning off the shower and grabbing the towel.

"Yes, they working too. No more questions. Please," Li pleaded.

Kelly slipped the white gown on again and rushed to the bed. She saw her sarong hanging out from under the bed. She had stashed the earrings into it, so carefully pushed it back under with her toe. She would tie the velvet bag into the sash of the sarong when she got dressed to go back to her bungalow.

Li banged on the door and shouted to the guard. He opened it and she slipped out. She would go and greet the customer in the lounge, where he would be waiting, having tea or wine and bring him back to the bungalow. She was glad things were running smoothly, because it meant the big Boss was always away, generating more customers. Her work load was getting bigger and bigger. Mountains of towels and bedding to wash, food to prepare and looking after the girls. It was hectic.

Kelly was fun to look after though, not as selfish and silly as the other girls. None of the girls before had ever been nice or paid any attention to her. The friendly female contact reminded her of the brothel she had worked in and all her friends. It was nice to have Kelly now. If any of the others found out, she would be in big trouble though.

At first the Boss had been concerned with how easily Kelly had accepted the situation, without taking any drugs, but he soon concentrated on other things when he saw how popular she was. Li hurried into the waiting lounge to greet the next customer.

"Hello Mr. Tang, Sir. How are you today?" Li followed her standard greeting script, bowing respectfully with her palms pressed together in front of her.

The customer just nodded and continued to sip his tea, not even looking in her direction.

"I know you usually see the fire haired girl, but we have another stunningly beautiful white girl that I think you would really love. She has a fantastic body, and long blonde hair. Very nice. Very friendly."

The old man continued sipping his tea as if he hadn't even been listening, then spoke from the corner of his mouth.

"Not the skinny, tall one, she's no good. I don't like her, she's very strange."

"No, no, Sir, different girl, very nice girl, the most popular girl," Li stammered hurriedly. She had to make sure the customer was happy. If their quota started to slip the Boss would spend more time here and no-one wanted that.

He raised an extremely bushy eyebrow and looked at Li. "Most popular, eh?" He turned his gaze upwards, appearing to be thinking hard.

Li prayed he would go for it. Kelly was ready in the red bungalow, but the fire-haired girl and the tall, skinny one were not in very good shape at the moment. Both had been working during the day and Li had given them pills to help them through, but, maybe a little too many and now they were too drugged to be any good. The Boss would not be happy if he found that out. The angry one who escaped was still in the lock-up cell, for punishment and cooling down. The boss was still not sure what he was going to do with her. One more step out of line and she was going to be killed. Li nervously awaited the customer's response.

"Is she young? Don't like those old, used women." He puffed out his chest and glared at Li.

Some of the white women they had first used had been bored wives of ex-patriots in Thailand, looking for extra money and free drugs. Not exactly spring chickens.

"Oh yes, Sir, she is only seventeen years old, very fresh and young," Li lied. Well, Kelly looked seventeen. She wasn't far away from it.

"OK, I'll see her, but she'd better be good." He adjusted his position in the chair and held out his cup for more tea. Li dutifully filled it.

"Yes Sir, she's very good, very beautiful girl."

He pulled out a fistful of cash and started peeling off the notes. Li looked on greedily, wishing the money were hers. She could buy her freedom with what he held in his hand. But, it didn't help to think like that. He handed over the agreed amount and Li hastily stashed it in her pants pocket, thanking him.

"Please come this way, Sir. The girl is ready for you." Li lead the way to the red bungalow. She poked her head in first, to make sure Kelly was ready to receive a client. Kelly was pacing around the room, scowling. Li asked the client to wait a moment and went in to deal with Kelly.

"I'm tired, what's going on? Take me back to my bungalow." Her tone was annoyed and tetchy.

"Customer here, get on bed," Li hissed, their earlier intimacy forgotten.

"I've done enough today, I'm too sore." Kelly whined like a two year old, standing in the middle of the room, eyes flashing defiantly.

"This is all I need," Li thought. She didn't want a fuss, especially with the customer waiting outside. Nor did she want the Boss to find out she was not managing the girls properly.

"Do this one now, no problems, and I will give you a slow day tomorrow, OK?"

Kelly smiled to herself, triumphant, but was careful not to change her expression. If Li owed her a favour, then she was in a better position to get what she wanted; one step closer to getting out of here.

"OK, but just this one," Kelly agreed slowly, watching Li's reaction carefully.

"Three more. I give you extra food and rest tomorrow," Li countered. Kelly wanted more than food.

"I'll do these three now, without complaining, and I will give you some jewelry and I will work extra tomorrow even, if you give me a key to my hut, so I can escape tomorrow night." Kelly had really laid her cards on the table now.

Li just looked at her, stunned. How had the conversation turned to her helping this girl escape? She looked fretfully towards the door, terrified that they might be overheard. This customer couldn't be kept waiting any longer, he was too important. Li started to panic, what could she do?

"OK, OK, I help you, but no more talk." Li hurried to the door to let the customer in, before Kelly could say anything more. She had no intention of helping this girl escape. The Boss would find out for sure and she would be killed, maybe even her family too, as an example to the others. Li shivered at the thought.

Kelly smiled inwardly. Not much longer and she would be out of here. She knew her way was better than Laurie's.

PRIVATE HELL

Laurie awoke to darkness. The pitch black enveloped her so completely that she reached up to touch her eyes to make sure she had them open. It was too dark for her to see anything, even her hand in front of her face. She lay for a moment taking in the blackness and fighting the feelings of needing to throw up and go to the toilet. She forced herself to take deep, calming breaths to squash the fear and panic creeping in on her.

Her whole body ached and her head pounded. She gingerly reached her hand to the back of her head and winced in pain as she touched the huge egg shaped lump caused by the frying pan. She moaned pitifully, raising herself up slowly to a sitting position. Initially she was too afraid to check the rest of her body for damage, but she knew it needed to be done. Although her hands and feet were no longer bound, her wrists were still very raw and painful. She was still naked, but it was very warm. She anxiously ran her hands over her legs and arms, no serious cuts, only the scratches from the bushes. Nothing broken. She was filthy from spending the night covered by the leaves in her makeshift bed and she stank, but aside from the pounding in her head, the nauseous feeling in her stomach, and the fullness of her bladder, she seemed OK.

The only way she could measure time was by how much her pubic hair had grown; she must have been here for only a day. Getting onto all fours, Laurie crawled her way around her cell, exploring nervously with her hands. It was a very small room, maybe a cupboard of some kind. There were shelves along one wall, but nothing on them. She knocked something, a plastic bottle. She lifted it close to her face trying to make out the shape of the container in the blackness, presuming it was water. Carefully she undid the lid; there was no smell so that seemed like a good sign. She took a tiny sip and decided that it must just be water. It might contain the paralysis drug, but she didn't care and took a big swig.

She lay back down to ease the pressure on her bladder, but trying not to think about needing to go to the toilet just made her need to go more. Moving over to the side as much as possible she relieved herself. Now she could drink some more of the water, saving some for later. God knows how long she would be here.

Laurie stood, stretching her arms high above her head and standing on her toes. She was stiff and sore, but stretching made her feel so much better and reminded her of Kelly and the yoga they had done to ease the boredom when they first arrived. She smiled at the memory.

"How life changes so quickly and without warning. What are they going to do with me now," she wondered miserably.

The heavy feeling of depression was starting to take hold of her again. For a second she contemplated just going along with what the captors wanted. Kelly had and she seemed OK with it all. She contemplated having sex with old ugly men for money, but the thought was just too revolting to her and she quickly dismissed it. She had to find a way out.

Sitting in the dark became increasingly difficult. The silence was deafening. She had trained for all kinds of terrible scenarios in the Military, but the reality was so much harder. She tried to meditate, to project herself to another place, but fear hovered at the edge of her thoughts, distracting her.

She would sleep and wake up to the darkness, stretch, have a sip of water, piss in the corner, then sleep again. She had no idea how much time was going by. The blackness seemed to be consuming her. There was no life anymore, just this cupboard. How long would it take for her to waste away?

The sounds of movement nearby brought her out of her thoughts. A door opened and light came pouring in to blind her temporarily. She turned her head and squinted against the brightness. She slowly made out the shape of the huge Boss and one of the guards, who stood back holding the machete ready.

"Lie on your front, hands behind your back." Laurie knew better than to talk or answer back, she just quickly lay on her front and put her hands behind her back. He stepped forward and put a heavy boot clad foot onto her lower back. She grunted with the weight. He bent over and injected half the dose into her naked, dirty buttock. At least now he knew that a quarter dose was not enough for this one.

"That should keep you nice and calm," he grunted into the back of her head as he stooped again to grasp her elbow and pull her roughly to her feet.

"Come on, work waiting. You've wasted enough of my time." He escorted her to the red bungalow, with Laurie staggering and swaying the whole way.

Li was waiting with the hot bath ready. She helped Laurie into the water slowly, feeling slightly sorry for her cut and bloody body, but she had been asking for trouble going up against the Boss.

"You lucky still alive," Li whispered to Laurie, scrubbing her back as softly as she could. "Don't make trouble, you get hurt."

"I'm afraid. I can't do it." Laurie's voice was emotionless, her eyes dull.

Li looked at her in confusion. "Why problem? Sex with man so easy."

"It hurts." Laurie winced, more because of the memory of her attack from the neighbour when she was young, than with the hot water and soap on her cuts.

"Have to relax, think about other thing you like. I always think about swimming in the river near my house when I was little. Sometimes the elephants would come too, they so funny in the water." Li smiled to herself with the memory.

"I can't do it," Laurie said morosely, slipping further into her familiar depression.

"Have some smoke, make you feel very good," Li suggested helpfully. Most of the girls ended up taking to the Opium pipe. Usually once they did, they were hooked for life though. Li had never tried it, she had seen what it did to good people and she was afraid of it.

"I hate smoking, I get asthma." Laurie's voice was small and childish as she slowly got to her feet and stepped out of the bath, standing still, with head bowed, while Li towelled her off. Li didn't understand that word, but she was busy thinking about the next client now and told Laurie, "Hurry, put on dress. I get customer. Remember, relax and no trouble, don't make boss mad. He very dangerous." She pulled the red dress over Laurie's head, adjusting it neatly over her small frame, and hurried out the door.

Laurie looked down at the dress, running her hands over the silky fabric. She never wore dresses. It reminded her of Prom night. She had gone with a boy in her class, and it had been a disaster. She had watched all the pretty girls, all completely unavailable, as her date had desperately tried to please her, running and getting drinks and food for her, lavishing compliments on her dress, her hair. All of this going straight over her head, as she fantasised about the Homecoming Queen.

"How am I going to get through this?" The drug was making her feel very neutral about everything, but she still knew she couldn't have sex with a man.

The door opened and the huge Boss came in. He saw her sitting hunched on the bed, deep in thought. Her hair was still wet and dripping. The fan was on in the corner, so it would soon dry, as it blew back and forth, rustling the netting around the bed. The clingy red dress hugged her taut figure, making her look extremely feminine for a change.

"OK, no trouble from you, or I will kill you. You want smoke or needle?" He stood back from her, just inside the door. He was much stronger than her, but he was not underestimating her strength and cunning this time.

She hadn't even noticed him coming in.

"Umm. I don't know. How about some anti-depressants?"

Finally, he knew her vice. Everyone had one, it was just a matter of finding out what it was.

"I'll get some, but for now I have strong wine. You want that?"

"OK." Laurie shrugged her shoulders, still looking down.

He knocked on the door and quickly departed.

Li returned carrying a tray with two plastic glasses and a plastic jug of tea coloured liquid. She placed the tray on the bedside table with a plonk and started to pour a generous glass for Laurie.

"Drink quickly, customer coming," she said, passing the glass to Laurie.

Laurie sculled the drink quickly and held the glass out for a refill. The wine burned her throat, but it felt good.

Li smiled and poured another drink. "Good girl." Then she went to the door and scurried out to bring in the customer.

Laurie quickly drank another three glasses before the customer arrived. By that time, she was feeling quite giddy. The door opened and a young, handsome Thai man came into the room. He looked more frightened than Laurie felt. She looked at him in surprise, through her haze.

"You're young," she blurted before she could stop herself, then blushed deeply. She didn't know how to behave around men who weren't her squadron buddies. He closed the door and stood there, looking around nervously. Laurie reached for the half-empty jug of wine.

"Want a drink?", she asked him, already pouring herself another.

"Yes, please," he responded in perfect American accented English.

Laurie looked up, again surprised. "You speak like an American."

"Yes, I went to college in L.A." He started to move towards her slowly, accepting the drink she held out. He was tall and athletic, with smooth milk chocolate coloured skin and perfect white teeth. Laurie couldn't stop staring at him. He was nervous under her gaze and tried to look everywhere but at her.

"What did you study? Laurie asked, trying to make conversation, all the while thinking about how this young man could help her get out of here. After all, he was educated in the States.

He sipped on his wine, his hand shaking slightly and replied, "Economics."

"At UCLA?" Laurie wondered why a handsome, educated young man would want to have sex with a Western girl being held against her will.

"Yes." He was starting to relax and calm down a little as well, but continued to stand awkwardly in the middle of the room. He swallowed all his wine in one go and held his glass out for more. Laurie poured two more glasses. She was starting to feel quite light-headed and drunk.

"Do you know that I am being held here against my will?" Laurie's words tumbled over each other in a confused jumble. Her tongue felt thick and awkward and her eyes drooped heavily. "I was travelling around Thailand when I was drugged and brought here to be a prostitute. They are still drugging me and won't let me go. They even threatened to kill me."

The young man shifted his weight from one foot to the other, avoiding her gaze.

"I don't think it is that bad." He smiled hesitantly. The big man had told him that this girl had a mental problem and thought she was somewhere else. She indulged in the Opium too much.

"Did you hear what I said?" Laurie looked at him in disbelief, mouth open. She stood up, but swayed and staggered a little, so sat back quickly on the bed.

"Can you help me?"

"I will try." He nodded reassuringly, edging closer to the door. He banged loudly and it was quickly opened by the guard. He was breathing quickly, relieved at being outside in the fresh air. This was very awkward. The girl was obviously wasted and quite delusional; he would ask to see another one instead. Laurie lay back on the bed with a sigh of relief. A local was going to help them. Soon this nightmare would be over. Within minutes the door opened and Li raced in looking very stressed and frowning with worry.

"You need water, girl?" She leaned over Laurie with a bottle of water, putting it to her lips before Laurie could even respond.

"Mmm, OK," Laurie murmured as she drank the water thirstily. She gasped for air as Li held the back of her head and pushed more water upon her. "Drink more."

"Enough!" Laurie gagged, dribbling water down her front.

Before long, the door opened again. Laurie went to push herself up to see if the young man had come back to save her, but discovered she couldn't move! Panic flooded over her. Li had given her the paralysis drug with the water! The young, handsome man, stood over her, looking her up and down, from her face all down her petite body, taking in her small, firm breasts and slim legs.

"She's very pretty," he thought. "The big man was right, she is much better after taking her medicine." Her face was relaxed and she appeared very calm.

She could see his face from the corner of her eyes, but the image was blurry. She was shocked and furious. "How could he do this? He was supposed to help me, supposed to be civilised. He studied in the States for Christ's sake!" Laurie felt so disappointed and betrayed.

He started to run his hands over her body. The sexy, red dress clung to her every dip and curve. Slowly slipping the straps off her shoulders to expose her lovely white breasts, he bent to gently suck on her nipples and kiss her navel. He thought he heard a faint moan. Her face looked peaceful and content. He could see the corners of her mouth turned up in a small smile and this encouragement made his heart beat rapidly.

He undressed quickly, not taking his eyes off this beautiful vision as she lay shy and quiet, waiting for him to take her, just like the sweet American girlfriend he had had in the States. He opened the bedside cabinet drawer and pulled out a condom, then hurriedly pulled it on, fumbling with anticipation and desire. He pulled the dress off in one quick movement. Her vagina, covered in a blond shadow of re-growth, looked fresh and inviting. He could wait no longer and shoved his penis into her. She was very dry, so he spit a little onto his fingers and rubbed it around the entrance of her vagina. He started thrusting slowly to enjoy the tight sensation, but could control himself no longer. Thrusting harder, he admired the way her breasts wobbled back and forth and her eyes were half closed with ecstasy. He came quickly and lay on top of her warm, soft body to recover, inhaling deeply her clean smell. He could see why his uncle came here so often and recommended it. What a fabulous birthday present. He would start saving so he could come here again and see one of the other girls. Pulling the condom off he was surprised to see blood. He was pleased with himself and his huge appendage. He dressed and kissed Laurie firmly on the lips before leaving, smiling and whistling to himself happily.

Laurie felt like dying. All the memories of her rape, which she had spent years trying to forget, were now back, darker than ever. She felt sick and dirty all over.

Li returned with the armed guard. They pulled Laurie to her feet and helped her to the bath. Feeling was returning to her limbs as she wobbled and leaned heavily on the guard for support. Plopping down into the bath with a splash, Laurie's feet hung out over the edge. Li had to quickly grab her by the arm as her head slipped down under the water, making her splutter and choke on the swallowed, soapy bath water. The guard stood nearby, emotionless, staring straight ahead, but not missing anything.

"This is the lowest I can go," Laurie thought darkly to herself. "I don't want to go on from here. Please God, just let me die". Li washed her swiftly but gently as Laurie just sat with a morose expression on her face, the freckles standing out against her pale skin.

Soon, Laurie was washed and dressed in a loose, long sleeved yellow shirt and a tatty navy sarong. She had to sit on the bed as Li cuffed her ankles together and the guard supervised.

They both escorted her back to the hut where Kelly was on the floor doing sit-ups. She jumped up to greet Laurie as she entered, ecstatic that her friend was all right. The guard pushed Laurie roughly into the room and Kelly had to grab her to stop her from falling. They fell on to the bed together and Laurie started to cry.

S I C K

It was morning again. The dim light filtered through the grubby window, casting the shadow of steel mesh across the bed. Outside birds chirped merrily, completely unaware of the sadness within. Karin had been awake all night, although it felt as if she had been awake for ten years, she was so desperately tired. Having Fiona passed out next to her, snoring loudly in a fitful sleep, sometimes crying out, was making Karin a nervous wreck.

The trap door opened and a tray of food was shoved through. Karin heaved herself up to retrieve the tray. The smell of the food was making her nauseous, but she carried it over to the bed. Fiona was sprawled out on her stomach, still sleeping. The cover had come off, exposing the nasty scabs and sores on her legs. She had not been careful about avoiding mosquito bites and now they were badly infected. Karin leaned closer to look at the festering wounds, but quickly withdrew, wrinkling her nose at the horrible smell.

"Wake up. Food's here." Karin prodded Fiona. It always took ten minutes or so of complaining and moaning before Fiona was completely awake.

"What? Leave me alone," Fiona grumbled moodily.

"They'll be here for you soon." Karin went into the bathroom.

"Already? I just got to sleep." Fiona rolled over and flopped a scabby arm over her eyes. Soon the smell of the food was too much for her, so she propped herself up on an elbow to pick at the food on the tray, scrambled eggs, sausages and thick, white toast.

"You've been asleep since yesterday afternoon, you lazy cow," Karin shouted. She readjusted the sarong which kept sliding off her narrowing hips. She washed her hands to rid them of the smell of food, not seeing how bony they had become, nails all soft and broken. Fiona had finished most of the breakfast by the time Karin returned to the room.

"You want some of this?", Fiona garbled, cheeks bulging with food. She licked her greasy fingers.

"Umm, no thanks." Karin looked at the leftovers, revolted. She never felt hunger pains anymore. She enjoyed the dull ache in her stomach. It reminded her of how powerful and in control she was.

"Hope we don't get those damn meat balls for dinner again," Fiona moaned. "I'm so sick of those."

"Mmm." Karin didn't want to talk about food. It made her feel sick. Instead she flopped back onto the bed and grabbed a magazine from the bedside table and turned her back on Fiona to read, or look at the pictures, anyway.

The guards opened the door to collect Fiona. She sat on the bed and held her feet out to be shackled. She had become very timid and co-operative lately, the drugs had really calmed her down. One of the guards looked at her scabby legs and made a comment to the other, which made him laugh and come closer for a look.

"What the fuck you lookin' at?" Fiona pulled her legs away. He grabbed them back, careful not to touch the weeping scabs and clicked the cuffs closed around her ankles. These cuffs were new, much more efficient than the rope. The guard muttered under his breath about the stink of her sores, while the other stood back and chuckled. Fiona continued to scowl, twisting her normally pretty features into the look of a haggard, old woman.

"Maybe you should ask for some cream for those sores," Karin suggested to Fiona, trying to be helpful.

"Mind your own fuckin' business," Fiona spat, quickly pushing herself up from the bed and hobbling out of the room with the guards.

"I hope your legs rot off!", Karin shouted after her in Swedish. She would normally never say such nasty things, but Fiona really knew how to make her angry.

"She is such a mean, self centred bitch," Karin fumed to herself, flicking the magazine pages so hard one of them ripped.

The cuffs rubbed painfully on Fiona's scabs as she shuffled across the clearing, so now they were sore and bleeding. Her body was in so much pain lately, she was even starting to hallucinate. Whenever she looked at Karin, all she could see was a skeleton with a mop of hair, dressed in ridiculous baggy clothes, like a scarecrow in a field.

Sometimes she caught Karin just staring at her, and heard her talking about her in the bathroom. When she was sleeping, she could feel Karin watching her. No wonder she woke up exhausted every morning.

"How much longer can I put up with this?", Fiona muttered to herself. She staggered into the room with a push from one of the guards.

"Arsehole," she muttered under her breath.

Li looked up, frowning disapproval, as Fiona struggled over to the bed and sat down with a weary groan.

"I need some pills or smoke before I can do anything," Fiona mumbled incoherently, eyes droopy and head wobbling unsteadily on her hunched shoulders. She was finding it increasingly hard to focus or even string a sentence together.

"Bath first," Li insisted, going over to Fiona to undo the shackles. She bent down with the key, then gasped, looking at Fiona's legs in horror.

"This very bad, stupid girl," Li admonished, scowling at the weeping, smelly sores all over Fiona's legs and arms.

"You need medicine. Cannot bath."

Fiona looked down at her legs, they were coming in and out of focus, but now that she thought about it, her legs were hurting quite a bit. They had been itchy for a while now, she couldn't remember exactly how long.

"What's wrong? Just a few bug bites."

"Very bad, infection." Li screwed her nose up at the smell and the sight of the ugly spots. "Wait, I get medicine." She went to the door, knocked and ducked out, leaving Fiona to sink back into the bed gratefully. She was feeling very hot and achey now. All she wanted to do was sleep.

Li returned with the Boss. She scurried into the room and over to Fiona, holding a medicine bottle. All her mannerisms were cowed and submissive in the presence of the vicious man. He was going to be very angry that she hadn't noticed these sores before they got so bad. She was supposed to make the girls understand the importance of the mosquito net. Li almost stepped in a pile of smelly vomit next to the bed. Fiona had lost her breakfast.

They both bent over Fiona's shivering body. At first they thought she had fallen asleep, but looking closely, they saw she was covered with sweat, her teeth were chattering and her eyes were glazed over.

"What have you given her?", the Boss raged, pushing Li roughly out of the way. "This is worse than infected mosquito bites. How did this happen? You are supposed to take care of them!"

"I didn't give her anything. She was OK just a moment ago," Li stammered fearfully. "These white girls are weak, they always get sick."

"You can't do your job properly, stupid incompetent girl." He was furious. There were two clients waiting to see Fiona. This was very bad timing.

"Go and get the tall, skinny girl. Quickly!", the Boss shouted at Li. "And clean this stink up!"

He picked Fiona up and marched to the door, bellowing for one of the other guards as he strode off to another hut, a storage shed, carrying the limp, shivering body as if it were a rag doll. He dumped Fiona down on some hastily arranged blankets on the floor. Her hair was drenched in sweat and the dark circles under eyes were black smudges against her yellow, waxy complexion. She was mumbling incoherently, shaking her head back and forth, delirious. He stood over her for a moment longer, then instructed the guard to get some iced water and cloth and hold it to her brow. The guard looked on in fear, not wanting to touch the sick, white witch.

"Go!", the Boss screamed, startling the guard out of his frozen panic. He turned on his heel and raced off.

The Boss was annoyed. He had seen Malaria many times before and the girls never recovered from it. This could be Malaria or just bad blood poisoning from the infected bites. He hoped it was just blood poisoning, otherwise he would have to go out and find another girl just when everything had been running so perfectly. That stupid Li should have been more careful, she would have to be punished for this.

Watching Fiona toss and turn reminded him of his past. He squeezed his eyes closed with the pain of the memory. When he was born, his mother had been only thirteen years old. Giving birth to such a big baby had almost killed her. An emergency Caesarean had been performed, which saved her life.

His earliest memories were of helping the other girls in the big house. He fetched this and that for them as they laughed and praised him. He was happy to get attention from them, both positive and negative, just as long as he was being acknowledged. His mother could barely even look at him. She would snap and curse at him without warning or reason. Sometimes grabbing his chubby toddler's arm as he passed, she would give him a mean pinch or vicious shake. He learnt early on to avoid her.

The girls called him a nickname, which he liked until he found out what it meant, 'Half Devil'.

It was years later that he found out from the older girls that his mother had been raped by a huge white man, while on her way from school.

Getting pregnant at that age had disgraced her family and she had been cast out. On the street she had been taken in by a madam, who tried to abort the baby, but was unsuccessful. He was to live with the shame and sorrow of his father's deed forever. The huge baby grew into a huge violent boy, who terrorised the neighbouring pets and children.

When he was eleven he had bought some powder from the neighbourhood boys. They had told him it would make his mother quiet and friendly. He had watched her writhe and scream for two days before she died. He had stayed at the brothel for a few weeks before the trouble he was causing forced the madam to ask him to leave. Two days later he had returned and burnt the brothel down, killing everyone inside. He had a new family now; a gang of youths, equally as unruly and angry as himself. From them he learnt how to survive and thrive.

The pimply guard skidded to a stop outside the shed. He nervously stepped inside, carrying a bowl of ice cubes and a dirty cloth. He sneaked a quick look at the Boss, to make sure that a fist was not being aimed at his head for retrieving the wrong items.

"Hurry up, you fool. Put it on her forehead," he grunted through clenched teeth, glad that his thoughts had been interrupted.

COPING

Li ran to the hut to collect Karin. Opening the door, she heard retching noises. Karin looked up startled as the girl popped her head into the bathroom.

"So, that why you skinny," Li sighed, hands on hips looking at Karin, who had her head over the toilet hole, dribble hanging from her open mouth, eyes watery and nose red from exertion.

"I, I, don't feel very well," Karin stammered, looking up guiltily.

"Hurry up, you have work," Li said unemotionally.

Karin rose slowly and uneasily to her feet, catching hold of the wall to support herself.

"What? What do you mean work?" Karin's eyes widened with fear; they looked enormous in her shrunken face. Her hands started to shake uncontrollably at the thought of having to go and see Stefan over and over, all day.

"Other girl sick," Li stated quickly, grabbing hold of Karin's arm and pulling her to the bed to shackle her feet. This was completely unnecessary, as Karin was in no condition to run anywhere.

"What's wrong with her?" Karin's normally soft voice was raspy and barely audible.

"Sick!" Li was getting tired of these girls and their questions. They were such high maintenance, much worse than the girls before. Those girls had all become addicts very quickly, which is why they had lasted as long as they did, about ten months. All four girls had died after a particularly strong batch of heroin came through. The Boss had gone berserk, but he couldn't blame Li for that one. He had given the dose to the girls himself.

He killed the dealer though, cut his head right off with a machete. This was to show other dealers what would happen to them if they sold bad drugs to him again. It had been time to get new girls anyway. The customers didn't like to see the same ones for too long.

"I'm sick too, I can't see Stefan today," Karin babbled to the confused Li.

"Who Stefan? Client Mr. Tan, waiting. Hurry." Li had clamped the cuffs around Karin's ankles and was now helping her to her unsteady feet. The young guard lurked outside, pacing back and forth, not wanting to get too close to the white devil; the Boss had told him what these girls were capable of.

Li motioned to the guard and spoke quickly; he came into the bungalow nervously, eyes darting. He placed Karin's bony, limp arm over his shoulder to help her walk across the worn dirt path to the blue bungalow. She stumbled and tripped the whole way, mumbling and sobbing softly to herself.

Once in the bungalow, Li unlocked the cuffs and pushed Karin in the direction of the shower, no time for a bath today. Karin tripped forward, but caught herself before she fell completely. Li had the shower on and Karin's clothes off before Karin even realised. The tepid water felt wonderful on her clammy skin. Li stared at Karin's wasting figure.

"She was so beautiful when she came here. What a stupid, self-destructive girl," Li thought to herself, as she looked at the shrunken breasts, just pink nipples on sagging flaps. Every rib was visible, collar and pelvic bones jutting out. She looked like a concentration camp victim.

"I can't force her to eat, she will just throw it up. I will give her some pills to feel better." Li washed Karin quickly. Her pubic hair was still short, so there was no need to cut it again. She towelled Karin off and gave her a pretty, pink short dress to wear. Karin held it limply, just staring at it uncomprehending.

"Put on, hurry!" Li went to the door and muttered something quickly to the guard.

Li steered Karin to the bed to put the dress on over her head. It hung, ridiculous and baggy on her skeletal frame. Karin swayed while Li tugged the dress roughly into place. Li tried to brush Karin's tangle of long blonde hair, but it started to come out in the brush in large clumps. Alarmed, Li stopped immediately.

The door opened quickly and the guard came in, puffing with his effort, and handed Li a small bottle. She checked the label, opened the bottle and tipped two round white tablets out into her hand. She walked over to Karin, who had reclined back onto the bed, eyes closed. Her long legs seemed extra long, sprawled on the thick navy bed cover. Her knees looked huge and out of proportion.

"Take these, make you feel good." Li raised Karin's head up and put the tablets on her tongue, then made her drink from the bottle of water. Karin obeyed, coughed a little, but swallowed the pills, hardly aware of her surroundings at all.

"OK, bring the customer," she commanded the guard waiting outside the door. He scurried off again, to the waiting lounge.

Karin was dimly aware of Stefan mounting her and pounding away. She cast her mind back to the day they had met, two years before, in a nightclub in Stockholm. She had seen him as soon as she had walked into the place. It was dark and the music was thumping loudly, but he had stood out clearly at the bar, leaning casually against the wall, scooping the crowd. His unruly blond locks had been gelled back fashionably. He had caught her glance almost immediately. She quickly looked away, faking disinterest. This did not seem to deter him at all; he made a bee-line for her. Her heart started beating rapidly; she licked her lips nervously and tugged at the bottom of her very short, red leather skirt.

"Maybe I should have worn the black stretch pants," she fretted, waiting as he pushed his way through the throng of gyrating dancers, towards her. She pretended to look for friends in the opposite direction, all the while expecting his hand on her goose-pimpled arm. Sneaking a look at him from the corner of her eye, she saw him break into a smile and grab one of her friends in a huge bear hug. Karin was mortified. How embarrassing. She moved on quickly to the bar, to douse her parched throat. Later that night, her friend pushed through the crowd, holding the handsome stranger's hand, and came up to Karin.

"Karin, you have to meet my cousin, Stefan!", she screamed over the noise of the music.

Karin beamed. "Your cousin?" She couldn't stop smiling, she thought her face was going to crack.

"Yeah, he wanted to meet you. Stefan, my friend Karin." They spent the rest of the night shouting into each other's ears, about people they knew, where they worked, where they usually hung out. Occasionally, Karin would flirtatiously let her lips touch Stefan's ear as she talked, pretending she had been pushed, any excuse to press her body up against his. He bought her endless drinks and chatted easily, trying desperately not to look down her top. Not to be caught looking, anyway.

They had been inseparable since that night, although they still kept their own apartments. Hers was part of the family trust and he had bought his five years before, but they slept together almost every night.

Her family was happy with the relationship. Stefan was from a good family, a distant relation to the royal family through marriage. Her brothers liked him and often invited him out on horse riding and hunting expeditions. Marriage had not been spoken of yet, but it seemed inevitable.

But now, Karin couldn't stand the sight of Stefan. His erratic behaviour, coming in and out incessantly, just having sex and not even talking to her anymore, it was more than she could bear. It was like he was a different person. Didn't he love her anymore? When her father came to pick her up from this terrible place, she would tell him all about Stefan and his strange moods and behaviour. She was not used to this sort of treatment. Stefan would be sorry, that was certain.

Karin daydreamed most of that day. She didn't even notice when Li came in to bath and change her; didn't notice the endless douching and make-up. At first she had tried to please Stefan. She smiled coyly, kissed him deeply and passionately, massaged his back and front, all the things she knew he liked. Sometimes she got encouragement, sometimes he tried to talk to her, but she couldn't understand anything he said. Other times he looked annoyed and slapped her hard across the face. He had never done that before. She had cried and he left smiling. It didn't seem to matter what she did to try and please him, he was always unpredictable and distant.

Li brought some food in at one point; the disgusting meatballs, hidden in a sandwich. Karin flushed them down the toilet, but drank a little of the Coke, which bloated her stomach and made her fart and burp. Stefan hadn't liked that and had finished his business quickly.

It was late afternoon when Li came in for the final time and said she could go back to her hut and rest. Karin was showered once more and dressed in her comfortable sarong and shirt. The heat of the day was gone, but as soon as she stepped out of the navy bungalow and the cool of the fan, she felt the damp weight of humidity on her, pushing down on top of her depression. She was feeling suffocated and found it difficult to breathe.

She leaned heavily on the guard who was escorting her. Each step was an effort; the shackles chafed her paper thin skin, causing angry red welts to appear. The guard grunted his annoyance, but put a supporting arm behind Karin's back as well. He could feel how weak and close to collapsing she was, and he didn't want to be held responsible and receive the wrath of the Boss. Anything but that. The mangey dog came from out of the shadow of the bungalow, now that it was cooler. He trotted alongside Karin and the guard, keen to be a part of the action. Karin didn't even see him. There were only a few chickens now, scratching hopefully in the dust. They had eaten most of them and the Boss had been too busy to replenish the stock. The guard lowered Karin gently onto the bed.

He held out the water bottle to her. She reached for it gratefully and took a few dainty sips. He arranged the mosquito netting around the bed carefully, as instructed, and backed out of the room in a hurry, obligation fulfilled.

Karin slipped into a deep but unsatisfying sleep, filled with distorted images of family and friends, standing and laughing at her as she stumbled around blindly asking them to help her find her puppy. The puppy turned into a snarling, snapping wolf, that wanted to eat her. She tried to run away, but her heavy, fat legs couldn't move her forward. The vicious teeth were getting closer and closer.

She awoke in a cold sweat, twisted up in the bed cover. It was still night, hardly any light came in through the window. Karin felt dazed, her head cloudy. She was trying to think straight, but could not figure out where she was. She brushed her matted hair away from her wet face with the back of her bony hand. Her left arm felt strange, all pins and needles. She needed to go to the toilet, but she had no energy to leave the bed, so she urinated where she lay. It was a slight relief.

Karin sighed and rolled over, expecting someone else to be in the bed. In the dim light she could see the bed flat and empty next to her. The silence was deafening. Karin lay there, lonely and frightened. "That's strange," she thought, something nagging at the edge of her consciousness." Karin had no idea what the time was. She vaguely recalled that she was here working, but couldn't remember what the work was. She was always distracted by seeing Stefan, so she presumed she never really got any work done. Maybe that's why they were being mean and keeping her here. Karin was trying to think logically, but the harder she concentrated the more jumbled her thoughts became. She had never been an intellectual, but keeping track of day to day events had never been a problem for her before.

"It's probably those damn pills they keep giving me, I won't take them next time. I've never slept so much and felt so tired." She complained aloud to herself, needing to hear a sound, any sound. Her whole body ached. Even her bones felt too tired to move. She prodded the hard, lumpy mattress halfheartedly, trying to get comfortable. Karin was thirsty now, but she couldn't be bothered to reach out to the bedside table and retrieve the bottle of water. Everything was too hard. She closed her eyes again and tried to sleep. Rest never came, only more nightmares. One was that her hair and teeth started to fall out. She tried to push her teeth back into her mouth, but then she started choking. She woke with a start, coughing and spluttering. In a panic she quickly checked to see that her hair and teeth were still in place.

She pulled the cover up around her neck. Her sweaty body was starting to feel chilled. Karin tried to distract herself with thinking about the last fashion show she had been to, in Paris. The Spring collection. All the usual crowd had been there. Karin had not been modelling this time, she had been there as a buyer for her store. The manager of her department, a very stern, strict looking woman, accompanied her, wearing no-nonsense thick, black rimmed glasses and a black wool pants suit. Not a fashion statement at all. Karin wondered why the store would let an out of date Grandma like her dictate the next season's fashion. She had a ball being at the show, two rows from the front, waving and blowing kisses at anyone she recognised, distracting herself from the tyrant next to her. She had felt so popular; she really did belong here, with all these movers and shakers, the people who dictated what the whole of Europe, even the world, would be wearing next year.

When she had seen all the super models on the catwalk she was glad she had done the starvation diet, recommended by a co-worker. They were all so slender and beautiful. Karin felt proud that she had the will power to be able to stick to the diet and see the results. She had lost five kilograms in two weeks. Sure, she had felt sick for most of those two weeks, but it was all worth it.

"I look just as good as those girls," she had thought, vainly. She had preened and reapplied her lipstick constantly throughout the day, annoying the older woman with her incessant chatter. The day had ended with a cocktail party. Karin met, face to face, some of the high-end, top models. She had been ecstatic to see that she was even thinner than some of them. It had been one of the highlights of her life. She had put the weight back on very quickly, when Stefan had complained and her father had threatened to send her back to her counsellor. They were such over-reactors. Not in touch with the critical eye of the fashion world at all.

Karin was brought out of her reverie by the small trap door opening, a tray of food being pushed through and it slamming shut again.

"Great, again with the stinky food," she thought miserably to herself. She stayed lying down, trying to ignore the food, but she couldn't stand it being in the same room. She got up slowly from the bed, groaning with the effort. Hair tickled her arm; she went to brush it away and noticed clumps of her hair left on the bed. Frightened, she touched her head. There was still plenty of hair there, but it was much thinner than normal. She collected the fallen pieces of hair together and put them in the toilet.

Returning to the room she noticed some colourfully wrapped food bars on the tray. Was it chocolate? She bent to pick them up. They were nutrition bars, covered in carob, but she couldn't read the wrapper, so she thought it was chocolate. Chocolate was the fashion model's enemy. There was no way she could eat it. Her figure was just starting to be close to the way she wanted it. She loved her hip bones sticking out. Karin hid the bars under her pillow.

Now what was she going to do to pass time? Karin picked up one of the magazines from the floor and started flipping through the dog-eared pages. Tearing out one of the pages of a beautiful Thai model, Karin started to rip around the edges of her body, separating her from the background scenery. She ripped off the sides of her thighs as she went, making the girl look abnormally skinny.

"That's better. Why do they use such fat models, I thought Asians were slim." Karin started on another one. By mid morning she had a bed covered in mutilated skinny models and a huge smile on her face.

ANOTHER PLAN

Kelly tried to calm Laurie down.

"Come on, it's not that bad. It's all over now." She lay next to Laurie, patting her back in sympathy. "I've got some good news, anyway."

Laurie continued to sob, not really listening to Kelly, she was too miserable.

"Did you hear me? I've got some really good news," Kelly insisted, shaking Laurie slightly, to break her out of her self pitying mood.

"Leave me alone." Laurie sobbed into the pillow.

"No, really, we're going to be out of here tomorrow night." Kelly whispered close to Laurie's ear, fearful of being overheard.

Laurie looked up at Kelly. "What?" Her eyes and nose were red and watery, mouth sulky and turned down.

"I did a favour for Li and bribed her with some jewelry, so she is giving me the key to our bungalow tomorrow night," Kelly blurted excitedly.

"Are you serious?" Laurie's eyes widened with hope and disbelief.

Kelly nodded enthusiastically, smiling at her own cleverness.

"So, what are we going to do?" Laurie sat up on the bed, wiping her tear streaked face. "Just open the door and walk away? We're in the middle of the jungle, miles from anywhere."

"We're not. We're in Bangkok city. I asked one of the customers." Kelly passed a bottle of water to Laurie.

"How can you believe him? The customers wouldn't tell us the truth." Laurie took the water gratefully, drinking most of the bottle down. The paralysis drug really made her thirsty.

"Some of the customers are really nice. I've met some very educated and well travelled men and they have treated me very well". Kelly got off the bed and started pacing up and down, thinking aloud. "Li's going to give me the key after I've seen my last customer tomorrow."

"Why tomorrow?", Laurie asked.

"The sooner the better, I thought." Kelly continued to pace in the small room.

"We'll wait until it's really late, 3.00 a.m. or something like that, then check if all is quiet and clear. We'll follow the road. It should lead to the city, because that's where the customers come from."

"What about the other two girls?" Laurie watched as Kelly paced, starting to warm to the idea and get excited.

"What can we do? We can try our key in their lock, to see if it works, but I don't want to hang around here too much. We can send the Police back for them." Kelly looked at Laurie to see what she thought.

"I suppose that's the best we can do. We don't want to jeopardise our chances of escape. What will we do once we get to the city? Go straight to the nearest Police station? Can we trust them?"

"Of course we can, they're the Police," Kelly stated positively. "I wonder if we should try to find our passports. Do you think they would still have them?"

"I doubt it, they would have sold them for sure. They can make so much money," Laurie said, sitting up now, and really getting excited. Her face was lit up, her eyes focused and alert.

"Yeah, we'll just have to go to our Embassies for new passports and money. I hope it doesn't get into the papers or anything, I don't want anyone to know about this. I don't think I'll even tell my parents, how embarrassing!" Kelly's brow furrowed at the thought of her family's pity, and her face splashed all over the newspapers at home, for everybody to see. Prostitute in Thailand! She just wanted to get away and forget about this nightmare. It was her own fault for being so stupid anyway.

"I hope your customer wasn't lying about us being in the middle of the city. I wonder how far we have to run. I used to be able to run five miles in twenty minutes, but probably not now. What about you?"

"Well I don't know about miles, but I can run five kilometres in thirty five minutes, usually. Without a bra I won't be able to go too fast." Kelly held her heavy boobs for a moment.

"For fuck's sake, all you're worried about is flopping around too much? There are more important things to think about while we are running for our lives!" Laurie looked at Kelly, exasperated.

"I know that! I'm just trying to be practical." Kelly was embarrassed at her trivial comment. "Don't worry, I'll be running alright."

"I'm glad we kept fit, a little. How long do you think we have been here? A week?", Laurie asked.

"I'm not sure, it's been hard to keep track, hasn't it? When we were first drugged and taken, I don't know how long we were out for, maybe a couple of days. I think we have been in this compound for a week, so maybe it's been a little over a week. Nobody would even be looking for me yet." Kelly sat back on the edge of the bed. "So we definitely have to get away."

The trap door opened and some food was pushed through. It looked like chicken green curry again. That wasn't too bad. They both liked the green curry, it was nice and filling. They would need all the sustenance they could get before the big escape. The food tasted much sweeter, now that they had a plan for getting away. This time tomorrow, they would be free and eating roast beef at their Embassies. What a lovely thought. "Maybe I'll go with you to the American Embassy, their budget must be bigger than the Australian one, they'd have better food." Kelly and Laurie both laughed, quietly at first then uproariously. Nothing could dampen their spirits now.

Before long, Li came along to collect Laurie, to see some waiting clients. Laurie hadn't counted on that, and started to put up a bit of a fuss. Kelly glared at her and muttered, "For God's sake, it's not for long. Don't be a baby."

Laurie was ready to throw some punches, then thought better of it. Deflated she sat passively on the bed to have her feet shackled.

"Just focus on getting out of here", she tried to programme herself. It was very difficult.

The guard grabbed Laurie's arm and hauled her off the bed, saying something in Thai to himself. Kelly could see Laurie tense and was afraid she was about to forget all their plans, but then she looked at Kelly and instantly relaxed and gave a weak smile.

"See you soon," Kelly chirped cheerfully, trying to help Laurie be brave.

Laurie just looked down pitifully and was guided out of the room.

Kelly tried to catch Li's gaze, but it seemed that Li was deliberately trying to avoid her eyes.

"Am I working this afternoon?" Kelly tried to engage Li in conversation, but Li scurried out of the door after the guard and Laurie, without even answering, and slammed the door extra hard.

"What does that mean?", Kelly wondered. She decided it was better not to think too much about it, her thoughts and questions would just go in circles and she would achieve nothing but frustration. She spent the day doing stretches and limbering up, waiting for Laurie's return.

❖   ❖   ❖

Once Laurie was bathed and sitting on the beautiful bed in a flimsy gown, the Boss came lumbering into the room. Li instantly shrank back, but Laurie confidently looked him in the eye. She was imagining the look on his face when he discovered herself and Kelly missing. She almost wished she could see it.

"You need smoke," he rasped, more as a statement than a question. He came closer and held the pipe out to her.

"No thank you, I don't need it." Laurie shook her head slightly, trying to be polite.

"Smoke it!", he shouted, standing menacingly close and shoving the pipe between her tightly drawn lips, chipping one of her teeth. Laurie grimaced at the pain and opened her mouth. "I won't inhale", she thought. "I'll just pretend. I won't be able to run very far if I'm drugged".

He held the lighter above the pipe, waiting for her to draw. She sucked slightly and the flame was pulled into the small pipe, burning the Opium resin inside. The bitter taste of the smoke burned her mouth and she coughed and spluttered it all out, along with the piece of her tooth.

"Breathe in!", he instructed, slapping the side of her head, making her ears ring and her eyes water.

Laurie sucked on the pipe again and tried to inhale only a little, but could not avoid taking the lot into her lungs. Instantly she felt the euphoric feeling flow through her body, into the ends of her fingers and toes, even to the end of her hair. Every muscle relaxed and her depression lifted.

"Again!", he demanded, still holding the pipe in her mouth. This time she could think of no reason why not to inhale deeply, the feeling was so wonderful. She smiled and inhaled as much as she could.

"That's better." He smirked, and wiped a sleeve over his sweaty brow.

Laurie sank back into the lovely lush feeling of the bed. Not a care in the world. Everything outside of herself forgotten. The customer was shown in. He looked a little nervous at first, but he came over to the bed and saw the delighted smile on Laurie's face. Her eyes were heavy with desire for him, he thought. Quickly undressing and standing next to the bed, with his uncircumcised penis growing larger, he leaned forward and massaged Laurie's breasts through the see-through fabric. She seemed to enjoy the feeling and moaned thickly. This encouragement spurred his lust and he started to undo the gown, exposing her lovely freckled skin and pink nipples. He'd only ever seen freckles and pink nipples in a magazine. Hands shaking now, he fumbled with the other buttons, hungry to see all of her.

"Ohh." He moaned, the gown falling open to expose her vagina with the sparse blonde downy cover. He quickly grabbed a condom placed on the bedside dresser, pulled it onto his erection, and straddled her. Laurie writhed weakly, and let out a moan. Misinterpreting her moan as desire, he thrust his penis into her dry vagina and pounded away for the two minutes it took to reach orgasm.

Satisfied that he had proved his complete manliness to this foreign girl, he smiled and lay next to Laurie for ten minutes. He didn't want the experience to be over too quickly, not with the amount of money he had paid. Laurie fell asleep and woke up to find Li trying to drag her to the bathroom.

"Good girl, do good job, no trouble." Li praised Laurie as she led her to the shower for a rinse off, before showing the next waiting customer in.

The Boss came in after a couple of hours, and five customers later, to give Laurie another 'hit'. She half-heartily tried to refuse, but thought better of it. The more of a fight she put up the more he made her take. The drug made everything much easier to handle anyway. He took Li to one side and had a short chat with her. She looked puzzled, but nodded obediently and he left.

Laurie couldn't tell how many more customers she 'saw'. Everything was very fuzzy and unclear, but she was glad when Li rinsed her for the final time and dressed her in her sarong and shirt. The guard shackled her feet once again and she was led out, but they walked past her hut and into another bungalow. She was a little confused, but couldn't think why. She happily went into the room and lay down on the bed, exhausted.

Li and the guard went back to collect Kelly for the afternoon shift. She was waiting on the bed looking happy and relaxed. She sat up and held her feet out to be shackled. When the guard had his head lowered at her feet, she asked Li where Laurie was.

"Busy," Li responded haughtily, still not looking at Kelly.

"When is she coming back?" Kelly started to feel a little nervous. Li was acting strange.

"Too many questions. Shut up!", Li shouted, loud enough to alarm the guard, whose head jerked up as he grabbed for his machete, eyes darting from one to the other.

Kelly looked hurt and confused, but bowed her head and stood slowly. She didn't want to attract any unwanted attention, not now that everything was falling into place for her. Only another ten hours or so and she and Laurie would be free. She was a little worried about where Laurie was though. Usually they were escorted straight back to their bungalows after their work was done. Kelly tried to shrug off the lingering weight of worry, but it hung over her like a formidable black cloud, as she shuffled slowly along. She half expected to see Laurie at the bungalow, and was disappointed to see that she wasn't there. Where could she be? Kelly was even more alarmed when the Boss came in after she had showered and changed into her slinky red dress.

"You need smoke!" He was using the same intimidating tone as he had with Laurie.

"Can I have drink, alcohol?" Kelly asked demurely, trying not to raise his hackles.

"No drink! Smoke!" He lurched forward to shove the pipe into her mouth. She raised her hand to guide the pipe into her mouth herself.

"OK, OK," she murmured, lips clamped around the pipe. He raised the lighter and she inhaled slowly, exaggerating the motion as much as possible, making it look like a really deep drag on the pipe. He seemed satisfied. She held the smoke in her mouth as long as possible then exhaled.

"Another!", he instructed angrily, scowling and waving the lighter close to her face.

She repeated the performance and he seemed happy with that. Kelly had inhaled a certain amount, which was making her feel very light-headed and contented, but her mind was still clear and she went over the escape plan in her head. She didn't have an opportunity to talk with Li until the first client left and Li came back in to shower her.

"Do you have the key for me?" Kelly whispered into Li's ear, discreetly.

Li looked annoyed. "I cannot get key, only guard have key."

"You promised!" Kelly's voice was raised and high pitched with alarm.

"I tried," Li hissed in a desperate lie, trying to shut Kelly up. It was true that only the guards had the keys, and the Boss of course, but she hadn't tried to get one. It was impossible! They would know for sure, they always carried the keys on a chain at their hips.

"I did what you wanted. I can give you some beautiful jewelry, so you can escape too. You promised me." Kelly stood back, looking hard at Li, trying to work on her conscience or guilt, whatever it took.

"I'm sorry, not yet. Need more time." Li was trying anything to get Kelly off her back.

"How much time?" Kelly was still not letting her go.

"Two days, maybe three." Li tried to buy some time. How was she going to get out of this, without the girl causing trouble and maybe telling the Boss. She already knew she was in trouble over the sick girl. She was still waiting for her punishment.

"What are you going to do in two or three days?" Kelly kept persisting, hands on hips now.

"I get copy," Li said simply, not happy about being pushed around by this girl.

"How will you get a copy?", Kelly quizzed, wanting all the details of the plan, so she could see if it would work.

"I go to town for food, I get copy." Li was pleased with her quick response, she had only just thought of it. She was glad when Kelly seemed to accept it.

"OK, but not more than three days. We have to get out of here, and we will help you get out too. Also, where is Laurie?"

Li hadn't expected this question. "I don't know." But she avoided Kelly's eyes as she answered, a certain lie. Kelly decided not to push everything at once. Another couple of days were not going to kill her, as long as she laid low and didn't make any trouble.

THE SWITCH

Karin was returned to her bungalow after a long afternoon of dealing with Stefan over and over again. She really did hate him now. Stepping back into the dim room, she saw the shape of Fiona back in the bed. She felt mixed emotions over her return, pleased not to be alone anymore, but annoyed that she was stuck with such a mean person. She was too tired to care anyway.

Karin dragged herself over to her side of the bed and sat wearily. Retrieving the chocolate bar from under her pillow, she pulled the wrapper back and took a tiny bite. One bite wouldn't affect her figure too much; she needed the energy. She had a stash of ten uneaten bars under her pillow.

Fiona stirred. Karin turned around on the bed to say hello and gasped in surprise when she saw it wasn't Fiona at all. It was the curly haired, American girl, who had been injected when she tried to run away.

"Hello," Karin said happily, glad it wasn't Fiona.

Laurie jumped off the bed quickly, backing up against the wall, staring at Karin.

"Sorry, I scared you. My name's Karin, what's yours?" Karin gave a happy smile.

Laurie relaxed. She vaguely remembered this girl from the dining room, when they first met. She had lost a lot of weight; she looked very sick now, white and skeletal.

"Sorry, I got a fright. My name's Laurie, how are you?" Laurie held out her hand to shake. Karin took it in her bony one and gave a limp shake.

"What's happened to Fiona?", Karin asked, sitting back on the bed and stuffing the chocolate bar back under her pillow, careful to put her sarong over her withered legs and only chew on the left side of her mouth twenty times, all part of her eating ritual.

"Is Fiona that other girl?", Laurie asked, clarifying who Karin was talking about.

"Yes, the redhead, sour face." Karin gave a soft giggle at her small attempt at humour.

"I dunno, I haven't seen her. Did she do something wrong?" Laurie sat back on the bed and tried to get comfortable. It was too muggy to put the cover on, so she lay on top of it.

"I don't think she did anything major, she was always complaining though." Karin frowned, trying to think of something bad that Fiona had done. She shook her head and stray strands of hair flopped around her shrinking skull.

"Maybe she tried to escape, like I did." Laurie sighed and picked absently at the bed cover, recalling the betrayal by the local people she had stumbled across.

"You escaped?" Karin's mouth hung open in awe. "When?"

"About four days ago I think. It's hard to keep track of time."

"What happened, how'd you do it?" Karin crossed her thin knobby legs and leaned forward, interested in getting all the details.

Laurie told her the story, while Karin listened and held her hand over her mouth, eyes wide with disbelief at certain parts.

"My God, that's terrible. That wasn't very nice of those people to turn you in to the big Boss. Maybe they're friends of his." Karin was mesmerised by this new girl's bravery. "I don't think Fiona would have the energy or the inclination to run away, she's pretty drugged up most of the time," Karin continued, matter-of-factly.

"Why do they drug her all the time?" Laurie was curious; maybe this girl, Fiona, was even more aggressive and dangerous than her.

"She asks for the drugs, I think she is an addict. She was like that right from the start. Really foul mood all the time too. I'm glad she's gone." Karin decided that this girl was much nicer than Fiona. "Do you want a chocolate bar? I have lots of them," Karin offered generously, reaching behind her pillow and holding one out to Laurie.

"Yeah, thanks. We haven't been given these. Are you special?" Laurie took the offered bar gratefully, managing a small smile.

"I couldn't eat any of the other food, I have a very delicate stomach," Karin answered, in her soft sing-song voice.

"Yeah, you look pretty skinny. Are you OK now?", Laurie asked with genuine concern.

Karin bristled slightly at the skinny comment, but decided to let it go.

"Yes, I'm perfectly alright." Karin wanted to change the subject. "I'm looking forward to my father coming and getting me."

"Your father's coming?" Laurie asked incredulously. "When?"

"He shouldn't be too far away. He would never leave me in a place like this for long." Karin tucked her hair behind her ears and looked very smug, as if her father had left her at a strict health farm.

"How does he know you're here?", Laurie continued, baffled at Karin's casual manner.

"He's very clever and powerful. He'll find me," Karin assured her.

"Wow, that's great. I hope he hurries. Does he live in Thailand?"

"No, he lives in Sweden."

"Does anyone know you are here?" Laurie was confused.

"My boyfriend does." Karin seemed to get more and more distant with every question.

"Your boyfriend?" Laurie was trying to piece it all together. "How did he find you?" Laurie wondered if this girl was friends with the big Boss.

"I'm not sure." Karin's voice faded, and she turned her head away.

"Do you have contacts here?", Laurie persisted.

"My father knows an old Swedish couple, who I stayed with when I first came to Thailand."

"Did they send you here?"

"I'm not sure." Karin was starting to look uncomfortable under all this scrutiny. It had all made perfect sense in her head.

Laurie tried a different tack. Appearing calm and solemn, she asked, "How do you cope with having to see all those men?"

"What men?", Karin asked, looking confused.

"The customers, the reason we are here!" Laurie was starting to look just as confused.

"I just see my boyfriend. He visits all the time, everyday." Karin went into the bathroom to wash her hands thoroughly and rinse her mouth of any taste of food or scraps in her teeth.

"Your boyfriend? Who's he?", Laurie shouted out to her in the bathroom. She was not following this strange, skinny girl.

"Stefan. He used to be really nice, but recently he has been terrible and I hate him now. I told him not to visit me anymore, but he keeps coming back, and the big Thai guy keeps making me see him."

"Is he a client?", Laurie asked, trying to figure the whole thing out. Maybe her boyfriend was one of the Thai or Japanese clients.

"No, he works in his family's property development business. I know he still loves me, but he has a strange way of showing it sometimes." Karin returned from the bathroom and stood at the door, looking dreamily off into space.

Laurie was getting exasperated with the conversation. It wasn't making any sense.

"Would your boyfriend help us escape?"

"I've already asked him. He acted a bit strange, as if he didn't understand what I was saying. I ask him to get my father every time I see him, but he never really answers," Karin said softly.

"What kind of boyfriend is he? How can he visit you here and not help? Does he know about us other girls?" Laurie was firing the questions out thick and fast.

Karin said something in Swedish.

"What?", Laurie asked puzzled.

"What?" Karin was dumfounded, not looking at Laurie anymore.

"You said something in another language. What was it?"

"No, I didn't. Look, I'm tired, can we have this conversation in the morning, I desperately need some sleep." Karin pulled the cover up and turned her back to Laurie. Conversation over. Laurie couldn't believe it.

"What's wrong with her, she doesn't make any sense," Laurie thought. Her mind was racing, not tired at all. "God, I hope Kelly makes it out tonight. She is probably wondering where I am. Will Li tell her? The Police had better get back here quickly, the big Boss is not going to be happy at all. I'll talk to Karin again in the morning. Maybe she'll make some sense then. She's a bit of a scatterbrain. Maybe because she isn't a native English speaker. I should give her a break."

Laurie rehashed Kelly's plan of escape over and over, keeping a sharp ear for any shouts or unusual noises, hoping that the mangey dog didn't know how to bark. She awoke with a start, still in a sitting position. Had something woken her? Had something gone wrong with Kelly? She stood on the bed and tried to look out of the window, but she couldn't reach from the bed and it was too dark outside to see anything anyway. She moved to the door and put her ear up against it, straining for any sound. Nothing! She stood like that as the minutes dragged by. Everything was quiet and still. She shivered involuntarily, went back to bed and slipped under the covers. She thought she would never be able to sleep with worry and stress, but it wasn't long before she was dreaming strange, disjointed images.

ALARM RAISED

Meanwhile, in a seedy suburb of London the drug boss put the phone down wearily. He stuffed a cigarette between his droopy lips, lit it and drew in deeply before squinting through the cloud of exhaled smoke to look at Stubby.

"Well, looks as though the fuckin' little bitch has disappeared into thin air. Who would 'ave thought she'd 'ave the nouse to give us the slip. Even the Police over there don't know nothing 'bout her." He leaned back in his fake leather recliner and put his feet up on the desk.

"Fuckin' little whore. Wait 'til she tries to come back, then we can nab her." Stubby sneered. "What did your contact over there say? Didn't they pick her up at the airport?"

"They said she never arrived. But the airline says she did, so does Thailand immigration. Someone is not telling the truth." The boss looked thoughtful as he blew more smoke into the stale air.

"What ya gonna do?" Stubby was curious, he wasn't sure how much was riding on this deal. The boss was being very secretive.

"Fuck it! Let's look for another courier. What about that blonde tart who works at the service station on Fleming Street, how much does she owe us now?"

Fiona was forgotten. Her family weren't even aware that she was missing.

❖   ❖   ❖

Karin's father, Hans Johannsen, picked up the ringing phone on his monstrous desk. His back was turned on the fantastic view over the factory floor and a hundred or so of his diligent workers. His brow was creased with concern and the amalgamation of years of stress. He was a very tall, lean man, with a balding head and a large, sharp pointed nose. Karin had always teased him about his nose and remarked that she was very glad she hadn't inherited it. He rubbed the side of his nose absently thinking about his late wife's delicate nose, most relieved that Karin had taken after her.

"Hans?" An older woman's shaking voice jerked Hans from his reverie.

"Annika? Have you heard something? Has Karin contacted you?", he blurted.

"Hans! Oh, Hans." Annika began to sob.

Hans felt his heart skip a beat. No, not bad news! "Annika, what is it?" His voice wavered, he was afraid of what she would say, but knew he had to hear it.

"I have just heard from the man in charge of Karin's case. They have found a body matching Karin's description." Annika broke down sobbing and couldn't continue.

"A body! She can't be dead." Hans choked back a yelp of pain, squeezing his eyes tightly shut, trying to block out the thought of his poor baby girl lying cold and lonely in some morgue in a foreign city.

Annika recovered slightly and continued. "They asked me and Stefan to go and identify the body, Hans." She blew her nose loudly.

The shock was too much. Hans couldn't believe this was happening to him. Not his beautiful, precious Karin.

"Oh Hans, I am so sorry." Annika didn't know what else to say, she couldn't help but feel partly responsible and guilty.

"It might not be her," Hans croaked, with wavering conviction.

"That's right," Annika agreed, hoping to sound positive. "When Stefan arrived last week, saying he still hadn't heard from her, I was so worried." She chewed on her lip nervously. "We have been going to the Police and the Swedish Embassy every day, but this is the first we have heard anything back."

While standing in the Police waiting room, she and Stefan had stared in open-mouthed horror at the notice board. It had been covered in photographs of smiling faces of young women, and a few men, from all over the world, all reported missing. So many young travellers missing and unaccounted for. Was anything being done about it? They had come away disappointed and depressed.

She just couldn't believe that all of these young people were drug addicts who had come to Thailand for a cheap fix and then lost track of time and the fact that they had family and friends worried and waiting for them. Stefan had pulled out a copy of a photo of Karin he was carrying around to show people at all the popular tourist areas he had been searching, and they pinned it on the board with all of the others.

"The case worker at the Police station said that young people were always going off by themselves on holidays here, and one week was not long enough to start worrying," Annika continued.

"Yes, Stefan and the Police told me the same thing." Hans' voice was gruff with emotion.

Annika wiped at her tears. She sometimes regretted not having children, but it was at times like this that she was relieved; they were just too much worry.

"I know she likes going off by herself, but she usually calls after a day or two. It's been two weeks since she left your place to go to that island." Hans pressed a handkerchief to his welling eyes.

"Yes. Stefan told me that Karin made up the story about having friends on Koh Sammet Island. She was getting a little bored in the city and wanted to go to a beach by herself. I'm so sorry Hans. I should never have let her go." Annika began to sob softly. The guilt was unbearable and she was desperately worried that Hans would blame her for losing his precious daughter.

"No, I'm sorry, Annika. Please don't blame yourself; it is Karin's fault, most irresponsible of her." His voice sounded weary and heavy with grief.

He would never forgive himself now. She was a sensitive child and needed him.

"I thought it was a little strange that she took off so quickly without leaving a phone number." Annika didn't feel annoyed with Karin's deception, only a little relieved that Hans wasn't angry with her. "Still, I shouldn't have let her go."

"Please, Annika, I'm sorry to have put you in this situation. I'll come to Thailand immediately."

"Yes, I think that is a good idea." Annika sat heavily on the chair nearby, all the strain was finally taking its toll. There was no way she was capable of identifying dear Karin's body.

"I'll call and charter a plane, and head out as soon as I can," Hans replied slowly. He started logging out of his computer as he spoke, trying to remember anything else he needed to do before going off for an indefinite period.

"Hans you know you are welcome to stay with Tim and I for as long as you like. Stefan is staying here." Annika knew he would refuse, but she had to make the offer anyway.

"Thank you for all your kindness. I will phone you from my hotel when I arrive, if it's not too late."

He placed the phone back in the cradle and sat staring for a moment. Was he prepared for what he might find in Thailand? What if the body was Karin's? He shook his head, trying to rid his mind of any negative thoughts. He would find his precious girl, even if it was the last thing he did.

❖   ❖   ❖

Laurie's parents looked at each other over the dining table in their sunny kitchen, smiling happily. A postcard had arrived from Laurie today. It was of an Asian temple, the towering walls clad in gold leaf, making it sparkle richly in the sunlight, while orange robed monks walked serenely in front of it, shaved heads bowed. It had been sent three days after her arrival in Bangkok.

"She sounds as if she is having the time of her life. I'm so glad she is enjoying it," her father beamed, tears in his eyes.

"I guess it was all meant to happen." Her mother walked over to the fridge and stuck the postcard to it. "If she was still in the Military she would never have experienced all these amazing things. Isn't it funny how life works?"

"I wish she would phone us," one of her sisters complained, looking up from her homework. "She is so independent. I could never be like that."

"You will be, in time," her mother reassured, smiling as she checked a pot bubbling on the stove and giving the contents a brief stir.

"She's probably conserving her money, that's why she hasn't called. We'll have to wait another couple of weeks for the next postcard I suppose." Her father sighed and turned back to the newspaper he had been reading.

❖   ❖   ❖

Kelly's mother was flicking back through the family diary, which sat on the kitchen bench, next to the phone.

"I'm not sure when Kelly last phoned," she was saying to a family friend who had just rung and asked how Kelly's trip was going.

"Here it is, she phoned two Sundays ago, when she had first arrived in Bangkok. She was supposed to be meeting friends, but some of them were running late, coming from other countries, or something. She was going to wait for them, then they were all going on to Japan. I suppose she will call when she gets to Japan, in a week or so. Yes, she was having a great time, loves the food and culture. I don't know where she gets that from." Her mother laughed and was soon talking about other matters.

HANGING IN THE BALANCE

Li stepped into the darkened shed. She could smell Fiona, even before her eyes adjusted to the dim light and she saw the motionless body under the sweat soaked covers. Li slowly edged closer, not wanting to get too close. Malaria wasn't infectious, but Li didn't want to take any chances. One of her young brothers had died of Malaria, her father had written in one of his letters, so she had sent some extra money, to pay for the funeral. She was very afraid of sickness, it was so random and harsh. She prayed every night not to be struck down with an illness. The guards refused to administer medicine, only punishment, so it was up to Li to give Fiona the vitamin and antibiotic shots, to help her body fight the infection. The Boss had rigged up a basic drip, to keep Fiona hydrated. Dehydration was the biggest problem with Malaria. Her arm had to be strapped down, to ensure the needle wasn't constantly pulled out with her thrashing, so her arm was black and blue from the bruising. Fiona was having all the typical reactions to the disease; swinging between raging fevers of over thirty four degrees that made her thrash and drip with sweat, and freezing chills, that would plunge her into fits of shivering and teeth chattering, no matter that the shed was warm and humid. Her bones ached and she had thrown-up and defecated where she lay. It was very taxing on the body.

Li wished that they could just call a doctor, but the Boss didn't want to attract any unwanted attention. He had plenty of people on his payroll, and more than one was probably a doctor, but the fewer people who knew about this enterprise the better. People had big mouths, especially when it wasn't them making the big money. Li held the bottle up, took the syringe out of her pocket and sucked the medicine into it. Stepping up to the lifeless Fiona, she wasn't shocked to see the dull yellow complexion, sunken eyes and white, chapped lips. She had seen the results of the sickness many times. Fiona had kicked off the covers, exposing the puss filled sores on her red, blotchy legs. The smell, the muggy room and now the poxy sores combined to make Li's head spin with revulsion. She hurriedly administered the shot and quickly changed the soiled bedding. She would have to just throw it away. "I must put some antibiotic powder on those sores too", Li thought, making a mental note to come back, as soon as she had finished some of the most pressing chores, maybe in a couple of hours.

Usually the girls lasted for six months or so, depending on how addicted they got, or how susceptible they were to disease. Fiona had only lasted two weeks, a very weak girl.

Li hurried back to the customers waiting in the lounge and served tea, begging them for a moment's more patience, then she was off to collect Kelly for the red room, and Laurie for the navy room. Li scurried from one task to another like a chicken with its head cut off, as the arrogant guards sauntered along beside her, cigarettes a permanent fixture, dangling from their stained lips. She was still walking on egg shells, waiting for the Boss to dish out the punishment he had promised her. He never forgot anything. Li opened the door to Kelly's bungalow.

"Customers waiting, hurry," Li said firmly.

"Good morning to you too. Yes, I'm fine thanks and you?" Kelly was being a smart mouth.

Li wasn't sure how to react, she didn't know if this girl was being funny or not. She usually didn't mind Kelly, but today she was just not in the mood for it. Li stepped aside, without even cracking a smile and the guards both came in. One fastened Kelly's ankles, while the other stood watching, holding his machete casually over his shoulder. Kelly could feel Li's sober mood, so just sat quietly while they cuffed her legs. Once in the red bungalow Kelly went through the usual motions of bathing and putting on a nice dress and make-up. This was her only chance to be alone with Li, so she didn't want to say the wrong thing and upset her. Li was her only chance at escape.

"Are you OK? You seem upset," Kelly ventured, while dabbing on some gaudy lipstick.

"I very busy, very busy." Li fussed with straightening the bed and hanging up towels, deliberately not looking at Kelly.

"Where's Laurie?" Kelly was feeling bolder.

"Run away again," Li said, looking Kelly squarely in the eyes now.

"What?" Kelly stood suddenly and all the make-up spilled onto the floor.

Li's mouth twitched into a faint smile at the reaction. "Yes, she run away. Boss very angry."

"Why, how did, when?", Kelly stammered, unable to form a complete sentence. She couldn't believe Laurie would run away without telling her, especially since they had made a plan to run away together last night. It didn't make sense.

"After customer, she attack guard and run away, very fast." Li was starting to enjoy the lie. The reaction from Kelly was hilarious. This might make her think twice about trying to escape herself.

"Yesterday? I didn't hear anything." Kelly bent to collect the spilled make-up, a dazed look on her face. How could Laurie do this to her?

Just then, the Boss burst into the room. Li jumped in fright and quickly busied herself in the bathroom, while Kelly sat on the bed, like a stunned mullet, still trying to digest Li's information.

"Smoke!" He strode over to Kelly and held the pipe out. She took it numbly and he lit it. As she inhaled deeply the thoughts of confusion and betrayal started to slip away, replaced by warm happy feelings of nothingness.

Li couldn't help but smile at her own handiwork. She was surprised that Kelly had believed her so easily. For the first time in days she almost forgot about her impending punishment.

The Boss shot a warning look at her. "What are you smirking at, stupid?", he snapped. "More customers will be arriving, hurry up and greet them, you lazy, good for nothing."

He gave her a quick cuff around the ear, enough to make her ear ring loudly, but not bleed, as she scurried past him to greet the customers. No sooner had she entered the waiting lounge than two customers stood up and started shouting at the same time.

"Please, please, one at a time. What is the problem?" Li held her hands up at the onslaught of angry voices.

"I have an appointment to see the girl called Kelly, I always see her, I have to see her, I won't see anyone else!", Mr. James jabbered, hysterically.

"I have an appointment to see Kelly. I will not see anyone else, either", the other customer said stubbornly.

Li usually double booked the girls; it wasn't normally a problem, except in a situation like this, when two regular clients of the same girl met. The guards should have known better than to have these two wait together. They should have been separated as soon as possible.

"Yes, yes. Of course, you can both see the girl you want. Please come this way Mr. James." Li tried to defuse the situation. She knew how important this customer was to the Boss, so hurriedly led Mr. James to the red bungalow. Kelly was sprawled on the bed, eyes glazed. Li hurried back to the other customer, who was still fuming, pacing up and down the room.

"I'm terribly sorry to keep you waiting, Sir. Kelly has gone into town shopping today, but she said that you would love her best friend. She is also very beautiful, from America." Li was giving the usual spiel.

"Really? America?" His eyes sparkled.

"Yes, she's stunning. Beautiful blonde hair, lovely white body, only sixteen years old," Li encouraged. "Let's settle the business side and I will show you to her, she's waiting for you."

He pulled the required amount from his wallet and passed it willingly to Li, excitement already flushing his sallow face.

"This way Sir." Li led him off to the navy bungalow, where Laurie was ready and waiting. The Boss had already paid her a visit with the pipe, so everything was calm and orderly. Laurie smiled as they entered, eyes half-closed and dreamy, limbs heavy and unmovable. Li closed the door behind him and raced back to the lounge to greet more clients and hopefully put a couple of loads of washing on, and prepare some dinner for everyone. It was never ending. She completely forgot to go back and put antiseptic powder on Fiona's sores.

THE LIE
CONTINUES

Mr. James stood smugly at the door, his fatty face and hanging jowls making him look more like a bull dog than ever. When Kelly didn't look up or greet him he walked over to the bed.

"Mummy, can I have titty?", he said in a high pitched baby's voice, slipping straight into his role.

Kelly barely heard him through the fog. She tried to move her hand in response, but found that it was too heavy. He sat next to her on the bed and started to undo the buttons on her dress, to expose her generous bust. He loved this part; the unveiling. He was breathing heavily and his fingers trembled in anticipation. Kelly's mind was somewhere else, but she vaguely felt his fingers tugging at her top. He lay down next to her and started sucking and biting at her nipples, moaning with pleasure and rubbing his stiff little penis with his free hand.

When Kelly came around again, she had no idea how long she had been out. Mr. James was still sucking on her nipples, like an over-grown infant, groaning every now and then. Suddenly his legs went stiff, he jerked, then went limp with the relief of release.

"I'm a bad boy," he mumbled into her bosom, ashamed, his mind in another place and time.

She didn't have the energy to reply, and she couldn't understand what was happening. Following Kelly's lead, he continued to lie next to her and even had a nap. All the while Kelly was in her dream world, oblivious to the perverted man next to her. Eventually he pulled himself off the bed slowly and dressed, pulling a couple of extra notes out of his pocket and leaving them on the dresser for her. He bent and kissed her forehead.

"See you again in a couple of days." He gave his cheesey grin and left.

More customers visited Kelly over the rest of the day, most of them clients she had seen before. One regular client liked to talk with her, but he left very quickly today, after only staying ten minutes. Kelly hadn't spoken to him at all, just stared unseeing, mumbling once in a while. He was very disappointed; it was hard to find beautiful white women to talk with.

Kelly was eventually bathed for the last time that day and escorted back to her bungalow. She had to be half carried by the guard, who was not happy with the close contact. She was dumped unceremoniously onto her bed. Kelly awoke sometime in the night with a splitting headache and cravings for more of the pipe the big Boss offered so generously. She gulped some water instead and tried to go back to sleep. The bed seemed big and empty, but she couldn't figure out why. Thoughts and ideas raced at the edge of her hazy mind, but she was unable to make them form properly. There was definitely something she was supposed to remember, but just couldn't grasp. She had forgotten all about Laurie and their plan to escape.

Morning came again, too quickly. Li was shaking Kelly out of her exhausted sleep.

"Wake up, lazy girl. Hurry, wake up. Customer come soon." Li was all business again.

"No, I can't, I'm too tired, I didn't sleep at all last night. Please Li, leave me alone."

Li pulled the covers off Kelly with one hard tug. Kelly curled up with the sudden cold and moaned in complaint. Li then started to slap her legs, careful not to hit too hard and leave bruises.

"Come on, hurry." Li grabbed one of Kelly's arms and was pulling her off the bed and trying to stand her up.

"No! Stop it. I'm too tired today."

"You need smoke. Make you feel better. OK?" Li held out the pipe invitingly in front of Kelly's face.

"Just a little, to make my headache go away," Kelly agreed, reaching for the pipe unsteadily. Li held the light to the pipe, while Kelly sucked the opiate down. Instantly a smile came to her face and she started to giggle.

"Feel better? Work now?" Li questioned, looking at Kelly's eyes droop and her head start to wobble.

"Mmmm, very good," Kelly sighed breathlessly, the euphoria completely enveloping her.

The guards didn't bother to cuff her ankles this time; they could tell by looking at her that she would be unable to run anywhere. She was very passive and obedient after having a couple of tokes on the pipe, all the girls were.

Finally things were starting to run like clockwork, now that the girls were addicted to the drug. Except for the sick one; she had finally died last night, after battling the illness for the last four days.

In the end, they were pretty sure that it was the blood poisoning from the infected bites that eventually killed her, not the Malaria. She was too much bother anyway, these three girls worked much better.

Sometimes Kelly would have flashes of people she half recognised, her family and friends from home, but, recently, there was another face that came into her thoughts and dreams at night. A pretty girl, with shoulder length, curly blonde hair and a defiant expression. She wasn't sure how she knew this girl, but she seemed important and familiar. If only she could remember why. As soon as she thought she was getting close to solving the puzzle, the image would slide away. Kelly didn't like the pipe, but the pain each morning when she woke and the drudgery of the day became too much and to have a toke or two didn't seem to be a very big deal. She just wished that she could remember things a little better. Why was she at this place anyway? Before long she ceased to even wonder.

Kelly slipped into the routine very easily. Li would wake her in the morning, she wasn't sure what time, but the sun was up and it was hot and humid already. She would have a terrible headache or sore limbs or find it hard to breathe, but as soon as she got to the beautiful red bungalow and had a puff on the pipe the rest of the day flew in a fabulous rollercoaster ride of adventures and happy faces.

She would feel lethargic and fat sometimes, but she just didn't have any energy for exercise. They were still operating the two bungalows with three girls, so the girls would work two half days and then a full day of work. When they were not working they would sleep or lie around in their bungalows. Time slipped by.

THE
INVESTIGATION

Stefan couldn't help but feel responsible for Karin's disappearance. He had scoured the streets of Bangkok with her photo every day since he had arrived in the city. He should never have let her go alone. He admonished himself as he traipsed unsuccessfully from one restaurant, guesthouse or money exchange to another. He should never have let her go off to the island by herself, or lie to her hosts. The guilt was heavy and unrelenting. Hans Johannsen had arrived in Bangkok two days ago and had been met by Stefan and Annika. All three had gone directly to the morgue to identify the body, the most difficult task any parent, friend or lover could ever go through.

Thankfully it had not been Karin. Some other poor family had lost a child and was not even aware of it yet. They would probably never know; if the body went unclaimed for one month then it was cremated and stored in the 'unknown' area of a cemetery, abandoned for the rest of eternity.

Now, Hans and Stefan were both waiting outside the Swedish Embassy. Hans had managed to wield his influence and they had finally been granted an appointment to see the Ambassador first thing this morning.

"Thank you for seeing me, Ambassador. I know you are a very busy man." Hans could barely be bothered with the protocol of greeting, but knew it was all necessary, to expedite the recovery of his daughter; these bureaucrats loved to feel important and respected.

"No problem Mr. Johannsen, it is a pleasure to meet you, Sir. Please take a seat." He waved Hans and Stefan into large antique chairs facing his massive desk. "I am sorry we have to meet under these circumstances. Please know I will do everything in my power to help you find your daughter."

"Thank you, Sir. Have you been in touch with the Police, Mr. Ambassador?" Hans hoped his impatience was not obvious in his tone.

"Yes, indeed we have. We filed a report with them after I first spoke with you, um, two weeks ago." He shuffled some papers, in a file on his desk, to confirm this date.

"Have you done any follow-up since then? I am afraid I received no help, whenever I called the Police from Sweden or even when Stefan here went to see them." Hans rubbed a big hand over his face wearily.

"I filed the report with the Police after I first spoke with you, and they told me that they would put her picture and details around other Police stations, but no real investigation would be done on the case until she had been missing for a month." The Ambassador was about to continue, when he was cut off by Hans and Stefan both shouting,

"What? A month?" Their mouths hung open in disbelief. "That is outrageous! Why would they leave it so long?" Hans pushed himself to the front of the chair, gripping the edge of the massive desk. "I, I just don't understand."

Stefan was shaking his head, incredulous and bursting with frustration. He felt like running out of the building and screaming. No one seemed to be doing anything to help. Was this a city of heartless monsters?

"I, I sympathise with your frustration, Mr. Johannsen." The Ambassador held up his hands to calm Hans down. "But we get a lot of these cases every few months or so. I have gone through this procedure many times before, you must trust me."

"You mean there are girls going missing all the time?" He couldn't believe this man's attitude. "What are you doing about it?"

"Please, Mr. Johannsen, calm down. Thailand is a beautiful country, with many fantastic places to visit, lovely beaches and scenery. Many fun opportunities that may not be readily available in Sweden."

"What do you mean 'fun opportunities'? What are you implying?" It was Stefan's turn to be indignant.

"Please, gentlemen!" The Ambassador tried to regain control of the situation. "Many Europeans come here for holidays, expecting cheap food and entertainment, pristine beaches and exotic jungles. Thailand has all these things, and it is a fabulous place to relax and have a good time. But some people get caught up in the more flamboyant side of a city, far away from home. They indulge in things that they wouldn't necessarily try at home." The Ambassador was trying his damnedest to be subtle. None of the parents of missing girls that he had met so far were thrilled to hear some home truths about their perfect children.

"You mean she was caught up in something illegal? Like what?" Hans couldn't believe that he was being spoken to like this.

"Well the most common cause for girls going missing here, is that they want to be independent and experiment with life a little. Your daughter is young. She probably met up with a young man and is off having a lovely time on a beach somewhere, drinking and smoking dope."

Hans had to stop himself from leaping up and punching the Ambassador! Who did this fat, lazy upstart think he was dealing with?

"I'm afraid I do not appreciate the implication you are making, Sir!", Hans bellowed, rising from his chair again. Stefan jumped to his feet as well, uncertain if Hans would be able to control himself, even though he was not known as a violent man.

The Ambassador remained seated, lowering his eyes and breathing deeply, before addressing them both with a quiet, even voice.

"Look Mr. Johannsen, I have seen this many times over. I am not saying that your daughter is involved with anything illegal, necessarily. The point is, many Western people come to Thailand for a good time and end up disappearing for a short while, but resurface within a month or two, after they sober up or become homesick, or most commonly run out of money. The Police have all of your daughter's information posted throughout the city and outlying regions. Someone will spot her soon and report it. But until she has not been seen for one month, the Police will not do anything more. I'm sorry. That is their policy, not ours, but we are still guests in their country."

Hans felt hollow and deflated. Was that it? They had to wait for another two weeks before anyone would do anything to help them? It didn't seem right. There must be something they could do. Surely the longer they waited the more difficult it would become.

"I will be in touch." Hans turned and marched out the door, back rigid, fists clenched. Stefan muttered a quick thank you, before scurrying after him. He didn't want to completely alienate the Ambassador.

They sat silently in the back of the limousine. Hans was too angry to talk, Stefan too scared. The driver just stared at them in the rear vision mirror, awaiting instructions. They both jumped when Hans' mobile phone suddenly rang.

"Hello?" Hans rasped.

"Hans, it's Annika. I hope I'm not interrupting."

"No, no, it's fine. We have just left the Embassy. They refuse to help until Karin has been missing for a month."

"I know. That is the same answer Tim and I have been getting. I'm so sorry, Hans."

"I think I'll go to the Police now. I just have to see and hear it for myself, that there is nothing they can do for another two weeks."

The Police station was modern, but dirty and raucous. People rushed this way and that, jostling and looking important, carrying an armful of files or dragging surly, cuffed prisoners behind them. There seemed to be a lot of peasant like people just milling around and talking loudly, drinking tea from large jars and squatting on the floor.

Stefan had been here many times and led the way up to the appropriate floor and office. It was quieter in this back office, and a smartly dressed Thai woman sat at the front desk to greet them.

Stefan had never received much attention or help before, but once Hans explained he was Karin's father and demanded to see someone in authority, they were ushered through to meet the senior officer and Karin's case worker.

His name was Captain Thay Pok. He was of average height, with a heavy droopy face and a portly figure. His thick glasses and nicely greased back hair gave him a very soft, pampered look. They followed him to his small, cluttered office. The walls of his office were covered entirely with newspaper clippings and photographs. A large picture of elephants working in the jungle hung precariously on the wall, looking ready to fall at any moment. His desk was piled high with bulging files, books and newspapers. As he sat down he moved some files over to get a better view of his visitors.

"Please sit down." Captain Thay Pok indicated two rickety wooden chairs, facing his desk. Hans and Stefan lowered themselves carefully.

"First, I would like to say how sorry I am, that your daughter is missing. I have been working in this position for six years and I would like to inform you that ninety five percent of missing foreigners in Thailand are found safe and well. I'm sure your daughter is fine and we will find her very quickly." He smiled reassuringly.

Hans started to breath again; he hadn't realised that he had been holding his breath. This man seemed to be a lot more helpful. His spirits started to rise a little.

"I am very pleased to hear that, Sir," Hans responded respectfully, wanting to start off on the right foot. "May I ask what has been done, so far, to find my daughter?"

"We have a set protocol in place for this situation," the officer continued with authority. "As soon as someone is reported missing, their photo and details are entered into our national computer. Police stations throughout Thailand have access to this information and street Police are informed immediately."

"So you are actively looking for my daughter as we speak then?" Hans was starting to feel some hope at last. That Ambassador was a moron. He made a mental note to make a complaint against him.

"Yes, the Police keep an eye out, while on their usual rounds," the officer replied, punching some keys on his computer.

"So, what about an investigation?" Hans relaxed back in his chair a little, but still gripped the armrests tightly.

"Please look at this information that we have on your daughter and confirm that everything is correct." The officer ignored the question, as he turned his computer screen around to face Hans and Stefan.

The photo on the screen was Karin's passport photo. Hans had to choke back a sob as he looked at his happily smiling daughter on the flickering screen. Would he ever see that lovely face again? He rubbed his handkerchief quickly over his face and cleared his throat. Reading over the birth date, height and colouring descriptions Hans continued down. She was last seen at Annika and Tim's address, she was on her way to Koh Sammet Island. The information was quite brief.

"Yes, that all seems to be correct. Now, is there any investigation under way?" Hans was not a man who would tolerate being ignored.

"Yes, we have a highly trained investigative team working around the clock on this case." The officer turned his computer screen back and typed some more.

"Really?" Hans was surprised with this positive response. "So, we don't have to wait for a month or anything like that?"

"No, Sir. We are working on the case right now. We have a couple of leads that we are pursuing, and feel very optimistic that we will be seeing results shortly." The officer smiled at his own cunning. Parents were always happy as long as they heard what they wanted to hear. This was going very well and he breathed a sigh of relief. Hans and Stefan both smiled back. At last progress!

"What are the leads you have?" Hans was excited to hear more, maybe he could help.

"I'm afraid I cannot discuss the case. You must understand, we take it very seriously when tourists go missing here and we cannot speak to the public about our sources or methods." The officer stared intently at Hans, polite but unwavering.

"Yes, I appreciate it is a very serious matter, but surely you can tell me about any leads or information you have about my own daughter. I would never jeopardise this case." Hans tried not to be argumentative, but he was not satisfied with just sitting back and waiting, not knowing what information they had.

"The Police in northern Thailand sent a fax yesterday, confirming that a young woman matching Karin's description has been seen in a small village," the officer confided to them.

"Really? Which village?"

"Please, let me do my job. We are following up all the leads and we predict that this will all be solved very quickly."

The officer's phone rang. He rose to his feet and started to hurry them out of the office, muttering excuses and assurances that all efforts were being made and he would keep in touch. He jotted down Hans' mobile number on a stray piece of paper and waved them goodbye.

They were happy that finally someone seemed to be taking the whole matter seriously, but they still felt a little unsettled and dissatisfied.

Captain Thay Pok rushed out of the Police station and to a pay phone in a nearby alley. The Boss answered on the first ring.

"Listen, I'm getting a lot of heat about this Swedish girl, Karin," Thay Pok whispered into the phone. He didn't like making contact with this maniac, especially so close to the station.

"You worry too much," the Boss growled. "Just do exactly what I told you and everything will go according to plan." He ground his back teeth, frustrated with how weak Thay Pok had become. The addicts always were.

"Maybe we should just let her go," Thay Pok continued. "I told them that she had been seen up north. Let's dump her and we can find another one that is less trouble. We should have just stuck to the junkies, anyway," he added under his breath.

"No!", the Boss bellowed into the phone. Thay Pok snatched the receiver away from his ringing ear.

"I am making too much money off this one to just let her go. How do you think you are getting double your usual fee, you moron?" He was so sick of putting up with this snivelling, bureaucratic paper-shuffling idiot. "If it wasn't for my contacts you would never have got that promotion to Captain. So you'd better just shut up and follow the agreement." The Boss' voice had risen to a scream again.

"OK. OK. There's no need to shout," Thay Pok whined. "I just want you to know that we have to be careful with this one. Her father has a lot of influence and the Swedish Embassy is going to start their own enquiry soon."

"Well, if you do your job, then we have nothing to worry about, do we?" The big Boss slammed the receiver down with a crash; he had more pressing chores to attend to.

❖   ❖   ❖

Hans and Stefan arrived at Annika and Tim's for dinner. The mood was relaxed but sombre, long silences broken by uneasy small talk and furtive glances. Eventually Annika rose from the table to help the maid take the dishes to the kitchen. The Thai maid looked nervous and distracted, opening her mouth to say something, then closing it quickly, deciding otherwise. Annika noticed this unusual behaviour.

"For God's sake, Tina, what's the matter?"

Tina almost dropped the plate she was loading into the dishwasher.

"Sorry Madam, very sorry." Tina ducked her head in shame, cheeks hot and red.

"Tina, is there something you want to tell me? Did you forget the ice-cream for dessert?" Annika frowned in annoyance, she could always tell when her maid had done something wrong, she was so transparent and child-like.

"No Madam, I didn't forget ice-cream." Tina hurried to the freezer to produce the evidence.

"Well, what is it? Something is on your mind."

"Um, Madam I am very sorry. I was not listening to your conversation, but is that Miss Karin's father?", Tina stammered hesitantly.

"Yes. Her father Hans and boyfriend Stefan. Why?" Annika looked up at the fidgeting maid.

"Well, Madam, I wanted to tell you before, but I was afraid you would be too angry with me. Mr. Hans looks so sad and..."

"What are you trying to tell me? Spit it out." Annika stood there holding the melting dessert, waiting expectantly. Tina looked ready to burst into tears.

"Let's talk about this later, shall we? I'm busy now." Annika turned and marched back to the dining table, where conversation was still slow.

In the kitchen, Tina couldn't stand the guilt any longer. She thought she would probably be fired for keeping this information to herself for so long, but she felt too terrible looking at Karin's poor father's tragic face. She was a mother, so she could understand the pain he must be going through. She decided to face up to her responsibility.

As they all sat in silence eating the ice-cream, Tina approached the table. Clearing her throat timidly she continued.

"Please Madam, I must tell Mr. Hans about his daughter."

All heads swung around to face the small, shy Thai girl.

"What? What about my daughter?" Hans turned to face Annika questioningly.

Annika looked alarmed. "What is it Tina, do you know something about where Karin is?"

Hans jumped up from the table, sending his chair skidding backwards. He strode over to the petrified girl and grabbed her by the shoulders.

"Please, what do you know about my daughter?"

Tears escaped her reddened eyes and slid silently down her smooth face. "I was watching her very carefully, but, she..."

"Watching her when?" Hans barked, trying to be calm, but not managing very well.

"When we went to the market, to get the food for the party. I was taking care of her, but she was very quick," Tina sobbed.

"What happened?", Hans encouraged, releasing her from his grasp, but still standing over her.

"The bad man at the market was talking to her, he gave her brochure and she put it in her pocket," Tina continued. Her tears had ceased and she was talking a bit more freely.

"A brochure, what brochure?", Hans queried, confused as to how this would help.

"This bad man have reputation. He work for very bad man. They always asking about young foreign women, they pay big money if you introduce one to them." Tina looked up at Hans and then over to her employer. "I'm sorry Madam, I should have told you before. I told Karin not to talk to him, but she didn't listen."

"So, why do they pay money to be introduced to foreign women?" Hans still didn't understand.

"This bad man own many brothels in Bangkok, he very powerful man." Tina tried to make it clearer.

"So, they are looking for foreign women to work in his brothels? Karin would never do that! She has a good job at home and plenty of money." Hans was angry and disappointed; this was no help at all.

"They give the girl drugs, they keep her." This had all been explained to Tina, in her regular visits to the markets, by the gossiping women stall owners. The bad men were not always there, they moved around a lot looking for young foreign travellers.

"Karin doesn't take drugs!" Hans retrieved his chair and sat back down, heavily, at the table.

"She has taken drugs before," Stefan's quiet voice piped up. He didn't dare look at Hans.

"What? What kind of drugs?", he fumed, glaring at Stefan, angry and embarrassed. Did he even know his daughter?

"She experimented with a few, just socially though." Stefan regretted even opening his mouth, but he was prepared to do anything to get Karin back.

"Look, all young people experiment a little with different things. I'm sure she isn't a regular drug taker." Tim tried to diffuse the conversation before it got too heated.

"Tina, can you take me to this market and point out the bad man to me, tomorrow?" Hans addressed the young maid, still standing awkwardly to one side. She looked at Annika.

"Of course she can go with you tomorrow," Annika assured. "Thank you for helping us, Tina."

The next morning Hans and Stefan met Tina outside the apartment and went together to the market. They strode up and down the aisles, peering expectantly this way and that, hoping for a glimpse of this 'bad man'. Tina explained to the stall owners why they were there. No one spoke to them or was helpful after that. Their spirits had reached a new low by the end of the day. There had been no sight of the bad man and there probably never would be. One of the stall owners would have warned him of their presence by now. The next day they took the maid to three other markets, desperately searching for the bad man. Hans called the Police station and asked to speak to the case worker. Captain Thay Pok was out of the office, so he left a message.

The next day they took the maid to four other markets, desperately searching for the bad man. The case officer had still not returned his phone calls, so Hans kept leaving messages. Eventually he went back to the Police station, only to be turned away by the smartly dressed woman at the front counter. The case officer was out following up an important lead. He left another message and replaced the missing photo of Karin on the notice-board.

Hans and Stefan decided that the authority's progress was too slow; they would do a little investigating of their own. Stefan remembered that Karin had wanted to go to Northern Thailand to ride the elephants, so he caught a bus up to the biggest city, Chang Mai. He called into all the popular and out of the way guesthouses, restaurants and tour companies, handing out Karin's photo and asking questions. No one had seen her. He went to the Police station, repeating the information that Karin had been spotted in a small village in the north, but none of the slightly confused Policeman knew anything about it. She wasn't even listed on their computer. As a last resort Stefan began visiting all of the brothels in the area. At first, he was greeted with open arms and welcoming smiles, until he began asking questions about Karin. The frosty response was rapidly followed by a request for him to leave and never come back. Soon he was not welcome anywhere, word was out, so he returned to Bangkok, where Hans had been getting the same results.

They were all confused and disheartened. Karin had been missing for a month now. Hans was receiving more and more pressure to return to work, to over-see the staff and fulfill orders.

They agreed that Hans would return to Sweden and Stefan would stay, to continue the search. Hans felt guilty at giving up and returning home, but he had huge responsibilities that couldn't be ignored any longer.

They would keep in touch by phone every day. Stefan moved to a cheap guesthouse, close to the district where all the foreigners hung out, Khao San Road. Maybe Karin would just turn up, as the Ambassador had predicted. Hans had given him some extra money to spend on bribes for information from local people. Stefan started his own little private investigation force, made up of local people, keen to earn extra cash from this very generous foreign man.

Hans was back in Sweden for less than a week before he decided that Karin was more important to him than the family company. He brought his sons in to take care of everything. It was about time they took responsibility; he was returning to Thailand and not giving up until he knew what had happened to Karin, whether it was good or bad news. He couldn't live with just not knowing. He needed closure.

THE BREAK

About a month after the girls were first taken, the Boss went to pick up some supplies, and to follow up a lead from one of the locals about a new young foreign girl travelling alone. He was quite confident leaving Li and the guards to handle everything at the camp, especially now that the girls were beyond resistance.

Li was busy and stressed, as usual, having to do the bulk of the work, all the washing and cooking and organising of the girls. She raced madly from one task to the next, getting more and more behind. Her punishment for not looking after the fire haired girl properly and therefore causing her death and the loss of so much revenue, was another five years labour. Her hopes of being reunited with her family were dashed. She guessed now that she may never be freed. The Boss would find a way to keep her forever. Li was furious and sullen.

The guards did as little as they could get away with, but it was a relief for everyone when the big Boss left for a while, even if it was only one night.

One of the regular clients didn't want to see his usual girl, Kelly, so Li hurriedly prepared Karin for the job. Running out of time, she asked one of the guards to give Kelly her afternoon fix, other clients would be along shortly. The guard she asked was a particularly lazy man, and a liar. He told Li he had given Kelly the dope, but instead he had pocketed it for himself, to sell later. As the afternoon wore on, Kelly, waiting in the red bungalow for another client, started to feel withdrawal symptoms. Her head hurt, her bones ached and her skin was crawling. Luckily, her last client cancelled, so she was shown to her hut early. After nightfall the withdrawals kept Kelly awake. Nauseous and wracked with pain she tossed and turned in her bed, soaked in sweat. The next morning she was rostered off. Food was shoved through her slot but she was left alone in her bungalow without any smoke until she was needed for work that afternoon. By mid-morning her mind was starting to clear. She sat up in bed and her thoughts were slowly coming together. She started to remember Laurie, that she had managed to escape, and the purpose for them all being here.

"How long have I been out of it?", she wondered, eating a little of the food and drinking all the water. "It's not like me to get sucked into taking drugs and having no control. I have to get out of here. Li was going to help, I wonder what happened to that? I guess I can't count on her, after all. If Laurie had got away, she would have sent help back, she mustn't have made it." Kelly hugged her knees to her chest, feeling very sad and depressed about what might have happened to Laurie.

Thinking about her own plans for escape again, Kelly suddenly remembered her stash of jewelry. She jumped off the bed and checked under the mattress. Not a very original hiding place, but there were not many places to choose from. Her fingers touched the small black velvet bag and she pulled it free. All the pieces were still in there. Thankfully, Li was too busy to check their beds. Kelly stuffed the bag back in its hiding place and relaxed on the bed.

"Now, how do I get out of here? I can't get back into smoking that damn pipe, it fries my brain and I will end up rotting here. I'll have to fake it."

Sometime in the early afternoon one of the guards came to Kelly's hut to give her the afternoon fix, before she was taken to her first job. Li was too busy with the other girls to accompany him, and now that the girls were so passive, it didn't take two guards and Li to escort them anymore.

The guard strolled casually into the hut, holding a machete in one hand and reached out with his other to pass Kelly the pipe, no longer worried about staying as far back from her as possible. Now that Kelly was out of her daze she noticed that the guard didn't look so scarey. He was actually quite small and skinny. Kelly took the pipe obediently and put it in her mouth, waiting for him to light it. He pulled a lighter out of his dirty pants and held it to the pipe. Instead of sucking Kelly blew out lightly with her nose, which extinguished the lighter flame. The guard flicked it on again, she blew it out again. Thinking there must be a draft, he pushed the hut door closed with his foot and put the machete against it, then stepped up to Kelly holding the lighter with one hand and protecting the flame with the other. Kelly felt that this was a chance, now or never. She jumped up suddenly from the bed and pushed the guard back, with all her might, against the wall. He stumbled crazily backwards, caught totally unawares, and fell against the block wall with great force, his head snapping back and banging with a mighty thud against the blocks. It was a sickening sound, like a melon dropped onto concrete. His eyes closed and he slumped down onto the floor, leaving a dark crimson stain on the wall. Kelly stood back from him, not really knowing what to do, but now that she had started, she couldn't go back. Her mind raced but her thoughts were slowed somewhat by weeks of Opium.

"Should I just run for it?" She slowly inched the door open. The compound was quiet, no sign of anyone. "I can't fight another guard, Li and the Boss. I need better odds." Suddenly an idea hit her, it was a gamble, but it might work. Li would probably come and see what was taking the guard so long. When she stepped into the room, Kelly would threaten her with the machete and Li would help her and let her go. It seemed feasible. Kelly grabbed the unconscious guard under the arms and tried to haul him onto the bed. She would cover him and when Li looked in, she would think it was Kelly and come into the bungalow. The guard was much heavier than he looked. Kelly heaved and pulled, finally getting his upper body on the bed. Then she swung his legs up and quickly covered him with the blanket.

"God, I hope he doesn't wake up too soon." Kelly was sweating and heaving with the exertion. She stepped to the door and picked up the machete, then took another peek out. She couldn't believe her eyes. There was Li and the other guard leading Laurie, with her head hanging and feet dragging, towards one of the working bungalows.

"So she is still here." Kelly's heart leaped with joy. "That's great." She didn't look in very good condition, but at least she was still alive and here, not dead and buried in the jungle.

The machete was heavy in her hand. She hefted the blade higher, wondering if she would be able to use it if confronted. It shone in the dim bungalow light and was as sharp as a chef's vegetable knife. Sharpening it was probably the only work he did all day. Kelly peeked out of the door again. Still nothing. "Maybe I should run for it." Kelly was still dithering over the decision when she saw the other guard heading in her direction.

"Oh no! Not the guard! It was supposed to be Li," Kelly thought in alarm, hopping from one foot to the other not knowing what to do. She wanted to hit him over the head with something heavy, but there was nothing like that in the room, all she had was the machete. Kelly jumped behind the door as the guard pushed it open and stepped inside. He took a couple of steps into the room and stopped, looking at the body in the bed. The machete hung loosely at his side, he wasn't expecting any trouble. Kelly had a split second, she knew she had to make a move. If he turned he would see her and the alarm would be raised. She had to have the advantage of surprise. She didn't know what to do with the machete, one wrong move and all she would do was wound him, but she wasn't too keen on killing him either. She just wanted to knock him out like the other one, much cleaner and easier. He stepped closer to the bed and put his hand on the leg under the cover and shook it, saying something in Thai. After a moment he pulled the cover back, revealing the guard.

Kelly panicked, lunged forward and pointed the machete at the guard's back. She meant to give him a fright so he would drop his weapon, but the razor sharp blade sliced through the soft skin and meat much more easily than Kelly could have imagined. She felt sick, but the adrenaline was pumping, it was either him or her. The guard stiffened in surprise, a gurgling moan escaping his open mouth. Kelly was afraid he would scream, so pushed the blade in even further. It slipped through all the way to the handle, and she felt the sticky warmth of his blood as it drained out onto the fabric of his shirt, the red stain spreading quickly. He fell face forward onto the bed and the blade was pushed back out of his body by the hard mattress, slicing his torso and making the wound even bigger. He shook on the bed and made more gurgling sounds, but was soon still.

Kelly's heart was pounding in her ears, she thought she was going to throw up or faint. She staggered back against the wall, unable to believe what she had just done, it had happened so quickly, one moment he had been a threat, the next, dead. It had been so easy. The blood was pouring out of him and all over the bed, so much blood. She had to run now. Dropping to her knees by the bed Kelly reached her arm in under the mattress to retrieve the jewelry bag. It took a lot more effort now, with the weight of the two bodies, but finally she grabbed the velvet package and pulled it free. Fear and panic were fighting inside her, making her stomach churn.

"I'm in big trouble now, this is really serious." She tied the jewels into the sash of her sarong, went to the door and looked out. All was quiet. Sweat was running down her face and she wiped it quickly with the back of her arm. She went back to the side of the bed and picked up the machete that had dropped out of the second guard's hand. The guard's blood on her hands was sticky and beginning to dry. She darted out of the hut and ran to the side of the next building, waiting to see if there was any shouting or commotion. She could barely hear anything over the pounding of her heart and gasping breath.

"Now, breathe, just breathe." Kelly tried to slow her breathing and calm herself. Then, she remembered that the guards had the keys to the bungalows. She forced herself to return to her hut to take a set of keys from one of the bodies. The sight was revolting, blood everywhere. She saw the keys hanging at the dead guard's waist and quickly twisted them off. Leaving her hut again, she closed the door and locked it behind her. She ran to the next hut where she had seen the other two girls being taken on the very first night. She tried three different keys before the door gave way. It took a moment for her eyes to adjust to the dim interior light. She stepped in and closed the door. The mosquito net was spread apart, revealing the tall, skinny girl lying on the bed. The bed cover was scrunched up at the foot of the bed and her sarong lay open, exposing her painfully thin legs covered with nasty red spots.

At first Kelly thought she was dead, she was so still and the room smelt stuffy and unclean. She leaned over the girl's face; her breathing was shallow and her breath stank. Kelly shook her gently. The girl's arm was like a stick.

"Wake up, hey, wake up."

Karin started to stir lazily. She rolled onto her side and pulled her legs up to her chest. Kelly shook her again, a little more firmly. "Hey, let's get out of here."

"Umm, go away Stefan," Karin moaned softly.

Kelly slapped her face lightly. "Hey, wake up." She grabbed Karin's skeletal arm and pulled her up.

Karin opened her eyes slowly. "Stefan, leave me alone." Karin was speaking Swedish, so Kelly didn't understand a word.

"C'mon, we're escaping, get up." Kelly was trying to pull Karin up off the bed.

Karin tried to yank her arm from Kelly, believing it was Stefan taking her to the horrible place again, but she was too weak to break Kelly's hold.

Kelly tried to support Karin's weight by pulling the spindly arm over her shoulders; it was very awkward with Karin's height and lack of co-operation. They made a couple of staggering steps to the door which was suddenly pushed open by Li.

Li gasped in surprise at seeing Kelly helping the other girl. Kelly flung Karin back on to the bed, then jumped forward, grabbed Li and pulled her into the room, quickly slamming the door shut and picking up the machete. Li sat on the bed next to the sprawled Karin, her mouth still open in amazement.

"What on earth is this girl doing?", Li wondered, not panicking or feeling worried. It was only Kelly after all. "Where the guards?", Li asked, coming out of her initial shock.

Kelly was getting desperate now. Things were not going as planned. She worried that at any moment the huge Boss would come thundering through the door. She had no idea that he was away for the day and night. Kelly was feeling braver with the machete now, and held it dangerously close to Li's face.

"What's wrong with her?", Kelly asked Li, waving the machete slightly in Karin's direction.

Li looked at the desperation in Kelly's face and a nagging worry started to set in. People did strange things when they were desperate and cornered.

"She never eat, and little funny." Li tapped the side of her head, indicating Karin had mental problems.

"Help her up. We're leaving," Kelly instructed, a little optimistically, since Li was a good head and shoulders shorter than Karin.

Li started to shake Karin's limp body. "Get up, girl." Li shook her a little more.

Karin didn't move or even make a sound. Li shook her harder and pinched her arm.

"Hey, girl. Get up." Li said loudly into Karin's ear.

Kelly looked from Li to Karin to the door, waiting for the Boss to come bursting in, or maybe another guard. Kelly didn't know how many there were. Fighting panic she hissed at to Li, "Throw some water on her face."

Li went to the bedside table, picked up the bottle of water and tipped it slowly onto Karin's chalk white face. No reaction. This was not right, what was wrong with her?

Kelly leaned forward and grabbed one of Karin's wrists. Still holding the machete up and watching Li she felt for Karin's pulse. She couldn't find it. She then pushed her fingers into the side of Karin's throat, trying to find the jugular. Still nothing. A great depression was starting to descend over Kelly. Karin was dead. Her heart had finally given up. It was already weak from the years of anorexia when she was a teenager, and after the last month of starvation, Opium and stress, it had finally had enough.

"I think she's dead." Kelly was numb with shock.

"Really? Second one." Li moved away from Karin on the bed, not wanting to be too close to death.

"Second what?", Kelly asked, confused, not bothering to hold the machete to Li's face now.

"Other girl dead," Li said calmly. There had been a lot of death and sickness in her short life so far. It wasn't anything special, just a fact of life.

"What other girl?" Kelly panicked. "Do you mean Laurie? You told me she had run away, and I saw you with her just now. You're a liar!" Kelly raised the machete again and thrust viciously towards Li.

"No, other, fire hair girl," She shimmied backwards on the bed, away from the sharp blade.

"The one with the English accent?"

"Yes, yes," Li confirmed, not knowing what an English accent sounded like, but wanting to say anything to calm this crazy girl down.

"So, where is Laurie?", she asked Li.

"Laurie?" Li didn't know their names.

"The other girl in my bungalow, the one who ran away." Kelly was starting to get agitated again.

"Hair, like this?" Li was making swirls with her fingers on her head.

"Yes, the curly haired one, Laurie."

"She OK, she good," Li reassured, nodding furiously and smiling.

Kelly didn't trust her. "Where is she?"

"She working, client here." Li was trying to buy some time and confuse Kelly into making a mistake and letting her guard down.

Kelly continued to pace. "How many guards are there here?"

"Many guard, many," Li lied.

"I have killed two, so how many others are there." Kelly stopped and looked hard at Li. "Don't lie, if I find out you are lying, I will kill you too."

This took the smile off Li's face. "You kill two guard?"

"Yes, and I will kill you too, no problem. Where's the big Boss?", Kelly asked, gaining control of the situation again.

"He no here, he go town." Li decided to be helpful, to save her own skin now. If this girl really had killed the only two guards, then Li had no protection and when the Boss came back and found no girls and no guards, she didn't want to be around to see it, or feel the punishment. He would probably kill her this time.

"Who's here? How many guards?", Kelly asked again, hoping for the truth this time.

"No guard, only client here, waiting for other girl."

"Where is he waiting?", Kelly barked.

"Big bungalow." Li answered quickly, fearing Kelly's desperation.

"Where is Laurie?"

"Blue bungalow."

"Take me to Laurie." Kelly indicated with the machete for Li to get off the bed and show the way. Li scurried out of the hut with Kelly fast behind her.

When they arrived at the bungalow Li said, "No key, guard have key."

Kelly pulled the ring of keys from her waistband. "No problem, I have the keys."

Li hurriedly opened the door and went in, then screamed. Kelly looked on in horror.

"How could this happen?"

ONE WAY OUT

Laurie had tried to talk with Karin again in the morning, but Karin had been in the bathroom from the time she woke up until Li and the guards came to collect Laurie for work. Laurie was feeling a bit slow and headachey from the drugs the day before, so when she was forced to take another hit on the pipe, she didn't really mind. It made things so much better. She passively went to the navy bungalow and the morning passed in a whirl of different people coming and going and broken conversations that she couldn't keep track of. At first, she had tried to think about what Kelly had said about escaping, but as the days wore on and the Opium had its effect, Laurie couldn't remember what was real and what she had dreamed. It was all mixing together, until eventually she couldn't even remember who Kelly was.

In the mornings Laurie would wake feeling very low and depressed. She allowed all the different men to mount her and do what they liked, with no trouble or resistance, but deep down she loathed it. She couldn't remember why, but she just knew that she didn't like it. Life became a series of being woken up by the guards and Li, being taken to the beautiful navy bungalow, having shower after shower, man after man, pipe after pipe, all blurring into a day. Laurie couldn't keep track of time and didn't even try to after a while. She slept in the same bed as Karin, but they hardly spoke. Mainly because they were always so tired, but also because every time Laurie tried to make conversation Karin could not understand or would answer in another language or just refuse to look at her, calling Laurie 'Stefan' and starting to cry. Eventually Laurie just gave up and slept.

Sometimes when she was woken in the mornings her body was so heavy that the guards had to literally pull her out of bed. Her moods became darker and she couldn't remember life before coming to this place of darkness. She could see no end to it, no hope of ever feeling good. Only when she sucked on the pipe did she feel great, but that lasted for a very short time and then the darkness was even worse.

"I need more smoke," Laurie said with a thick tongue, as soon as Li came into the bungalow to shower her, ready for the next client.

"I just give you some," Li answered, annoyed.

"I need more, I don't feel good, everything hurts." Laurie held her head in her hands, looking miserable.

"OK, OK, I bring some." Li was pulling her to the bathroom.

"I really need something now. I feel terrible. Please, anything." Laurie was white and desperate looking. Li had seen this before, some of the girls got very depressed on the Opium. Maybe pills were better.

"Here, have these." Li tipped a couple of valium out of a small bottle she had in her pocket. Laurie snatched them up and swallowed them quickly. She couldn't stand this feeling any longer, anything to get rid of it.

"I need smoke," Laurie continued, after the shower, having forgotten about the pills she had taken a few minutes beforehand. She stood naked in front of the fan, trying to cool down. She wished she could sit in front of it with her legs spread, her pussy felt like it was on fire. It had been itchy last night, but now it was burning, especially when she peed.

When she had the smoke and the pills she couldn't feel the pain, everything was wonderful, but as soon as they started to wear off, the black cloud would descend over her and her pussy would burn. She had forgotten how many days had passed, when Li was showering her and asked, "What that smell?"

Laurie just shrugged, eyes half closed, enjoying the tepid water on her hot skin. Li put her nose close to Laurie and was sniffing different parts of her body, until she came close to her vagina, and Li screwed her nose up.

"That bad smell. You have infection."

Laurie didn't even bother answering. She used to really enjoy her vagina. It was her friend and companion. But, now she felt like it was responsible for all this pain and suffering.

"If I didn't have a vagina, I wouldn't be in this mess," Laurie thought. She felt that her vagina had betrayed her, and now, it had got sick and was making her sick.

She hadn't slept well last night. She noticed that Karin hadn't slept well either. She had been moaning and holding her left arm, her face twisted in pain most of the night.

Li straightened and said, "I get medicine. Client here soon."

Laurie just shuffled back to the fan and stood there. As soon as Li left the bungalow Laurie felt alone and deserted. It was a terrible dark feeling, worse than any she had had so far. She wanted to end it, end all the pain, end the procession of men, end her painful pussy. Laurie looked at the floor, at her discarded sarong lying there, looking like a snake. Laurie bent and picked the sarong up, twisting it to make it long and tight, like a rope. Trance like, she walked to the door jamb, between the bathroom and the room. She made a noose of one end of the sarong and slipped it over her head, and put a big knot in the other end.

"I'm ready to go, ready to end this pain. I can't stand it anymore." She mumbled softly to herself. She started to feel amazingly clear and focused. "I have a plan." She spoke aloud to the friends she could see sitting on the bed, smiling their approval.

She pulled the door closed with the knotted end of the sarong caught in the door jamb. She relaxed and let herself slide down the door, the sarong tightening around her neck. It hurt at first, but she was so used to pain now that it felt kind of nice. She could see her Military buddies, smiling and congratulating her on doing the honourable thing. She smiled and slipped away, free at last.

31

THE GETAWAY

Kelly pushed past Li, who was just standing, with mouth open, gawking at Laurie's limp body hanging from the door frame. Kelly grabbed Laurie around the waist and opened the door. They both fell heavily to the ground. Kelly started to cry, holding Laurie and rocking back and forth.

"How could she do this? We were just about to get away." She sobbed into Laurie's hair.

Li was the first to come to her senses. "We have to get out. Big trouble now."

Kelly looked up at Li through her tears. "How can we get out of here? Will you help me?"

"We both in trouble now. I have to leave too. He will kill me." Li was looking desperate now too, rubbing her rough hand over her mouth.

"You said there was a customer waiting. Has he got a car?", Kelly asked eagerly, getting up from Laurie's side. There was nothing more she could do now, she had to look after herself and mourn later, when she had the luxury of freedom and time.

"Yes, he has car." Li replied, looking hopeful.

"Can you drive?" Kelly asked Li.

"No."

"That's OK, I can. Where are the keys?" Kelly was getting excited again. Maybe they would get away.

"I dunno." Li shrugged.

"OK, you ask the customer to wait a bit longer, but you need his keys to move his car to another parking place. I'll meet you at the car." Kelly grabbed Li on both shoulders and looked at her closely. "Can you do that?"

"Yes, yes, I do," Li responded, twisting away from Kelly's grip.

"OK, let's go." Kelly pushed Li ahead of her, and watched as Li raced across the dirt path to the big bungalow. She was still not completely convinced that she could trust her. Li had betrayed her before.

Kelly waited until Li was in the other bungalow before she darted out herself. She saw the big black Mercedes immediately, with a man sitting in the driver's seat. Kelly stopped dead, shocked, then dived behind one of the buildings between her and the car.

"It must be the driver. Stupid Li, didn't she know he had a driver?" Kelly groaned with frustration.

Just then the mangey dog came around the corner and started barking furiously at her. Alarmed she crouched down and held her hand out to it.

"Here boy, c'mon, come here, be quiet," Kelly coaxed with her voice. The dog started wagging his tail furiously. He had never got this much attention before. He ran to Kelly eagerly, lying on the ground for a tummy scratch. Kelly scratched his dirty belly, not particularly keen on touching the animal. She peeked around the bungalow and watched the driver get out of the car, stretch and spit on the ground noisily. He picked his nose and then lit a cigarette, while leaning against the car.

Li came out of the big bungalow and saw Kelly crouched out of sight of the driver. She continued over to the driver, said something quickly and he took a last hurried drag on the smoke then stamped it out on the ground. He followed her directions to go into the bungalow and see his boss.

Kelly saw what Li was up to and went around to the back of the bungalow, just in case the driver looked her way. He didn't. Kelly raced to the car. Li was already in the passenger seat, holding a small bag on her lap, so tightly that her knuckles were white. Kelly jumped in the driver's seat. Her legs couldn't reach the pedals, so she had to fuss around for a moment, trying to find the lever to adjust it.

"Hurry, hurry, no time," Li said loudly.

"Shut up! I'm hurrying." Kelly's hands were shaking and the seat tipped back. She righted it and tried another button. Finally, she found it, then tried to start the car.

Li screamed, her eyes wide with fright as she watched the driver come out of the bungalow, hurrying back to the car. "He coming, hurry."

"Lock your door!" Kelly finally started the car and locked her side, as the driver banged on her door, shouting and trying the door handle. Li kept screaming. The car lurched forward, sending the driver backwards onto the dirt. Kelly swung the big steering wheel. Her feet were barely touching the pedals and the car lurched forward again, in the wrong direction. She was a good driver, but she wasn't familiar with this type of car. They zoomed past the big bungalow and into the clearing. It was a dead end. The customer came out of the bungalow and took a second to understand what was going on. Then he too started to chase the car. Kelly thrust the gear into reverse and went screaming backwards at full speed. The men both jumped out of the way, only just avoiding being hit by the huge car roaring by. Kelly managed to turn the car around, with the driver banging on the car the whole time, shouting and screaming. Moments later, they were roaring down the small dirt road, away from the compound, to freedom.

After their breathing had calmed down Kelly asked Li, "Do you know where to go?"

"Where you want to go?" Li smiled back, still not grasping what freedom involved. All she was focusing on was getting away from the Boss, and not letting him find her. She had to contact her family.

"The Police, or maybe the Embassy would be better." Kelly was thinking aloud.

"Police no good, they customer." Li looked at Kelly, worry crinkling her brow. She was starting to get quite scared now. The Boss had great influence in many circles.

"OK, we have to find the Australian Embassy then," Kelly asserted. It was mid afternoon, they had plenty of time. Suddenly, the dirt path ended, it was a T-intersection at a tar-sealed road.

"OK, which way?"

Li looked a bit nervous. "Not sure, where Embassy?"

"I don't know. Are we in Bangkok or what?" Kelly's nerves were frazzled.

"Yes, yes, Bangkok. But city very big," Li retorted, arms flying around angrily.

"OK, OK, we have to ask somebody." Kelly turned right onto the road and continued driving slowly, gaining confidence. She stopped outside a house that was fifty metres up the road. "OK, ask these people."

"No, too close. Boss pay these people, drive more," Li said anxiously.

Kelly put the car back in gear and started off again. The road joined a bigger one, the traffic became heavier and before they knew it they were caught up in the usual afternoon rush hour traffic jam.

"This is ridiculous! Of course I have to go to the Police." Kelly convinced herself.

"I haven't done anything wrong. I'm the victim here." She was feeling so tired, all she wanted to do was lie down and sleep.

"The Police will believe me. You can tell them your story as well, to back me up." She turned to glance at Li, who didn't look convinced at all.

They pulled up at a red light. "OK, ask those people where the main Police station is." Kelly nodded to the people in a car next to them.

"Maybe not good idea, Police no good".

"Hurry up!" Kelly screamed, making Li jump with fright.

Kelly lowered Li's window and gave her a push. Li leaned out and indicated to the driver of the next car to lower the window. She spoke quickly in Thai. The driver seemed unsure, shrugging her shoulders.

Li pulled her head back in. "She don't know."

It took them several more stops before they eventually found someone who was able to give them fairly precise directions. It was another hour, and a few more stops, before they managed to find the impressive modern building which housed the central Police station. Li looked ashen and scared to death as they drove by the many Police cars and men in uniform; she slid down in her seat, so she was barely able to see out.

"Don't be stupid, they will help us." Kelly assured her, happy to be in safe territory and near help.

It was difficult to find somewhere to park, every space seemed to be taken up, and the afternoon traffic was still thick. Kelly pulled into a back alley, about a block away, and stopped the car.

"It doesn't matter if we get a parking ticket, I suppose." Kelly smiled to herself, the tension starting to ease, now that she was so close to salvation.

Li stayed in her seat, silent and brooding.

"C'mon." Kelly persuaded. "We'll tell them our story and they will find that big Boss and put him in jail. We'll be safe."

Li shook her head. "Police no good, they no believe us," she insisted.

Kelly shrugged her shoulders. She didn't have the energy for this, but she needed Li to corroborate her story.

"I'm going to the Police to tell them everything. If you don't come, you are on your own." Kelly knew Li couldn't stand being by herself, and thought this would make her come. Li was afraid of being alone, but was more afraid of the Police. "No!" She folded her arms defiantly, and looked determined not to move from her seat.

"Fine!" Kelly shouted, slamming the car door she strode off to the Police station.

Li started to feel nervous in the silence of the car by herself. She turned around to see if Kelly had stopped to wait for her, but she was nowhere to be seen.

Suddenly, the phone in the console started to ring. Li jumped with fright, she hadn't noticed it before. It rang and rang. When it stopped, it was only for a moment, and then it started ringing again. Li picked up the phone and answered quietly, then dropped it with a squeal of alarm. It was the Boss! Li quickly slammed the handset back into the cradle. It immediately rang again. Her heart was beating uncontrollable as she opened the car door, ready to run. Then she realised he didn't know where she was. The phone kept ringing.

Li knew she would never be able to escape on her own, maybe she should beg forgiveness and he would not kill her. She slowly picked up the phone.

"Hello?" The Boss's voice was very calm.

"Li, you are a silly girl, how did the white girl kidnap you?" His voice was smooth and convincing.

Li couldn't believe he thought that she had been taken against her will. That wasn't so bad; maybe he wouldn't be angry with her then.

"I know it's not your fault, the white devil tricked you," he continued. "Bring her back and you won't get in any trouble, none at all."

Li was relieved, maybe she should go back, she only had another five years and she would have paid her debt and be free. It was tempting.

"I, I don't know," Li stammered, nervous of the Boss and his silky voice.

"… and if you come back and bring the girl, you won't be in any trouble. I know it was the girl's fault, not yours. You are a good worker, I need you." He was a very convincing liar.

Li was thinking now. "Yes, it wasn't my fault," she replied in a childish voice.

"I have reported her to the Police, you know I have connections there, and they have gone to her Embassy. They are waiting for her. They know she is a junkie and a drug smuggler and she has killed local people and those other three white girls. She will be arrested and never seen again. But you are a good girl. Where are you? I'll come and pick you up. Where are you?"

"But, she didn't kill those other girls." Li was confused.

"It doesn't matter, she will get the blame for it, and you too, if you don't hurry up and tell me where you are, you stupid bitch!" He was losing his temper, this girl was so slow.

Li suddenly realised that he would never forgive her for this; he would kill her for sure. She hung up the phone with a bang. What should she do? Kelly was walking into a trap!

The phone started to ring loudly. Li couldn't stand it, so jumped out of the car.

"I'd better help Kelly. She helped me get out of the compound, so I should help her now. We are more likely to survive together than apart".

She ran towards the Police station to warn Kelly.

BETRAYED

Kelly dragged her weary legs up the carefully washed stone steps of the impressive Police station. Suddenly shy and embarrassed about her shabby appearance, bloodied hands and bare feet, she stepped nervously through the huge rotating door and into the noisy chaos. Uniformed men marched stiffly down endless hallways heading off in all directions; men and women in smart suits carried overflowing briefcases into private rooms; local people milled around on the floor, some sleeping, while others sat noisily chatting on wooden benches, all waiting their turn.

Kelly felt completely overwhelmed, but relieved. Finally she was safe and with people who would help her get home to her family.

She looked around, unsure where to go first. There was a front desk, with three uniformed Police behind it, helping a disorderly crowd of people. Kelly pushed her way to the front. The jostling locals took one look at her matted hair and blood stained hands and quickly stepped aside, but closed in again so they could eavesdrop.

A fat Policeman looked up at her with tired, bored eyes.

"Please help me!" Kelly spoke hurriedly. "I have been kidnapped and held against my will, for I don't know how long. I just escaped!" She looked at him expectantly as he ran his eyes over her clothes, hair and hands.

"Just a junkie looking for a free meal and place to sleep", he thought, but knew that the protocol for dealing with foreigners was to contact the 'Tourist Police' division upstairs.

"One moment please madam." He replied in perfect English. "I will call upstairs to see who can help you. Please wait over there." He pointed to where everyone was waiting on wooden benches. Kelly moved aside to wait.

On the wall was a notice board filled with scraps of paper and photographs, announcing the most wanted terrorists and drug dealers, stolen property and missing persons. Kelly was shocked to see a photo of the smiling, beautiful face of the Swedish girl, Karin. She almost didn't recognise her, she looked nothing like this photo the last time Kelly had seen her, starved to a skeleton and delirious.

Kelly reached up and took the photograph down. It was definitely Karin.

Just then, Li ran in and spotted Kelly. She hurried over to her, eyes darting in all directions. "We have to go, you big trouble." Li grabbed Kelly's arm and started to pull her towards the exit. Kelly tried to shake her off.

"Boss man tell Police and your government people you are drug smuggler and you kill local people and the other girls. They waiting for you."

Kelly looked at Li in disbelief.

"That's not true." Kelly replied angrily. "I'm not a smuggler and I didn't kill those other girls."

Li continued to plead, desperately pulling Kelly towards the exit. They collided with a dumpy, older blonde woman and a tall skinny white man, as they stepped from the elevator; Annika and Hans.

"I beg your pardon," Hans stammered, catching Kelly tightly around the shoulders before she fell completely.

Li screamed terror and ran like a wild rabbit out of the building.

"Let me go!" Kelly screamed with fear, not thinking that Hans could maybe help her. She couldn't trust anyone now.

"I'm sorry." Hans quickly let her go, apologising profusely, revolted by her smell and appearance. Then he noticed the photo of Karin in her hand. He grabbed her wrist before she could run any further.

"Why do you have that photo of my daughter?", he insisted angrily, pulling her closer.

Kelly looked up at him shocked and disbelieving. "Your daughter?"

"Yes. My daughter, she's missing." Hans glared at Kelly's scruffy clothes and bare feet.

"Why are you stealing her picture?" They had been wondering why Karin's photo always seemed to disappear from the board.

Suddenly they heard boots pounding on the stairs and voices shouting. "Stop that girl!" Their heads jerked around to see a group of uniformed Police streaming in their direction, led by a small man with thick black glasses and dark suit, Captain Thay Pok.

Kelly couldn't believe her eyes. Her client, Baby, Mr. James, worked here! They would never believe her story now. She had to get away!

"He knows where Karin is. He's a customer", Kelly blurted to Hans and pointed directly at the Captain.

"Captain Thay Pok?", Hans gasped in disbelief.

The Police were almost upon them.

Kelly tugged her wrist free and slammed through the revolving door, down the steps and away.

Finally some hope, someone knew about his daughter. Hans and Annika blocked the entrance to the revolving doors.

"Out of the way! Move!", shouted the Police in panic. They could not let this girl get away; orders had come from the top, she was very dangerous.

"She knows my daughter, they have been kidnapped!", Hans screamed over the noise.

"She said she knew you!", he yelled into Captain Thay Pok's stricken face.

"That girl is a junkie murderer, a known criminal." The Captain pushed past Hans and out the door, but Kelly had already disappeared. There would be trouble, now that Kelly had seen his face. "Damn that girl", he fumed, shouting instructions to his men.

Kelly ran down the maze of small side streets and back yards, finally making it back to the car, thankful to find it still there. Li popped up from behind some rubbish bins nearby and jumped in the car, just as Kelly started the engine and roared off up the alley.

They didn't speak for a while, both breathing heavily, their hearts pounding. Sirens blared, but they couldn't see any lights or Police following. Kelly twisted in and out of traffic, down small streets and alleys. Finally stopping at a dead end, she put her head in her hands and started to cry. Li sat there, numb and silent.

"What am I going to do?", Kelly wailed in despair. "Mr. James works for the Police. They will never believe me now."

Li explained in her faulty English about the Boss calling on the car phone and that it was not safe for Kelly to go to the Police or the government people.

Kelly started to calm down and think, she blew her nose on her sarong and wiped her eyes.

"Thank you for coming to warn me." Kelly looked bleary eyed at Li. Could she be trusted? Maybe Li was going to set her up somewhere else, and take her back to the Boss?

"I have to get a passport and get out of here. I have jewelry. Can you help me sell it?" Kelly looked weary and old, dark circles under her eyes and spotty skin. She really did look like a junkie.

"I can't help you, don't know where to go," Li said bluntly, shrugging her shoulders and looking hopeless.

"OK, get out then!" Kelly leaned across her and opened her door. "Out! I don't need you." Kelly tried to push Li out of the car.

Li squirmed and held on to the inside of the car. "No, I stay, I help you," she said hurriedly. "I help you."

Kelly stopped pushing her. "How can you help me?" She was tired of all these mind games and not knowing if Li was telling the truth.

"I help sell jewelry. I help." Li would have said anything to stop Kelly from pushing her out onto the street in the middle of the city. Li had no idea where to go or how to find her family, and she certainly could not go to the Police now.

"OK, where can we sell it?", Kelly insisted, testing Li.

"We drive, I see shop, I ask," Li answered energetically, nodding her head and smiling, trying to convince Kelly that she could be of help.

Kelly pulled the car back into the stream of traffic. A Police car pulled up alongside of them and looked over. Kelly's hands started to sweat and slip off the wheel, she was terrified. She wondered if she could outrun them. Kelly didn't realise that she looked like any ex-patriot out with her maid. The Police just kept going and they both started to breathe again. They drove around the streets for another hour, before Li shouted, "Stop. That shop buy jewelry. I ask. Give me jewelry." Li held out her hand.

There was no way that Kelly was giving the jewelry to Li; she might just walk off with it.

"No. I will park the car and come with you." Kelly steered into the parking space behind the shop. Luckily she spied a tap, where she quickly washed her blood stained hands. She didn't want a shop keeper to raise the alarm just because she had dirty, bloodied hands. They both walked casually into the shop and were greeted by a very happy, smiling Indian, with a bright red turban wrapped around his head. His English was perfect. He was less friendly when he found that they wanted to sell and not buy, but he looked at the jewels anyway.

"I'll give you fifty dollars U.S.", he offered, smiling generously, after inspecting all the items with his eye piece.

"What? You must be joking. They're worth much more than that," Kelly insisted indignantly.

The Indian shopkeeper snorted his disbelief. "How much do you think then?", he asked.

Kelly hadn't thought about it too much, but had presumed all the pieces were quite valuable. "One thousand dollars U.S. These are diamonds and emeralds you know."

"I'm afraid that they are not, Madam. They are plastic." He was constantly flabbergasted at how people could be fooled by cheap, fake imitations.

"What? They are not, you're trying to cheat me!", Kelly shouted, making the Indian step back in fright. All the commotion brought a couple of older Indian gentlemen from the back room.

"What is the problem here, Madam?", the older one asked calmly.

"Your man here says that my jewelry is fake and plastic, and not worth anything." Kelly pointed accusingly at the first man. The older Indian stepped over to the jewels spread out on a black velvet mat and asked for an eye piece. He assessed the jewels and said to Kelly, "I'm afraid, Madam, that he is right. These are fake. I am very sorry."

Kelly was furious. She grabbed all her jewels and marched out of the shop, shouting over her shoulder that she would find another shop. Li scurried after her, looking scared. They both got back in the car and drove off, with a squeal of tyres, to look for another shop. They stopped at four other jewelry shops, and received the same response from all of them. It was starting to get dark by this time and Kelly was exhausted from the whole day's stress. They stopped at another flashy jewelry store, hoping for an ignorant shop keeper. They went inside, and were offered sixty dollars U.S. Kelly had been offered eighty dollars at the last store, but had no idea how to get back there again, so decided she would take the sixty dollars. As the clerk was writing up the paperwork Kelly walked around the shop, browsing. A TV was playing in the corner. There was a news broadcast, and to her horror, her passport photo was plastered all over the screen. She grabbed Li. "What are they saying?", she whispered, checking over her shoulder to see that the shop keeper wasn't watching them.

Li leaned closer to hear. "They say you are drug addict and you kill two local people and two foreign people. Everyone looking for you."

Kelly was horrified. Li had been telling the truth at the Police station.

"The Boss know many people. He big man." Li was glad to see that her picture was not on TV and there had been no mention of her.

Kelly quickly took the money and fled the shop, back to the car. Then she had an idea. "Li, go back and ask the shop man how to get to Khao San Road. Get proper directions."

Li nodded and went back into the shop. She came out a short time later, holding a piece of paper with scribbles all over it. Kelly snatched it from Li.

"I can't read this mess."

"I can", chimed Li happily and jumped into the car.

Kelly hoped that Li wasn't setting her up. She would just have to watch her carefully.

They drove for another hour or so, in circles Kelly thought, but she said nothing. Finally, she saw shops and restaurants that she recognised from when she first arrived. They had found it! Kelly parked in a back street and started off towards the busy main shopping street.

"What are we doing here?", Li asked, trying to keep up with Kelly's quickened pace.

"I have to find someone who looks like me and steal their passport. That's the only way I'll be able to get out of the country." Suddenly, Kelly had a thought.

"Do you have any pills left?"

"Yes." Li nodded and fished the small valium bottle out of her pocket.

"You want some?"

"Not for me, for the person whose passport I will steal."

They hit the busy road and Kelly relaxed a little. There were so many people here, from all over the world, she felt a little less conspicuous. She could blend with all the other blondes.

"I'm hungry," Li complained, holding her stomach.

"Do you have any money?" She was not about to buy Li anything with her precious little money.

"A little." Li clasped her little bag closer.

"Well, buy your own food then." Kelly's stomach was in knots from withdrawal pains. She could think of nothing worse than food at that moment. They strolled from bar to restaurant looking for someone who looked like Kelly. It was harder than they expected.

Suddenly Kelly spotted two Policemen moving towards them on the street. The smartly uniformed cops were scanning the faces in the restaurants and on the street. Kelly grabbed Li and ducked into the nearest shop; a travel agency. It was a small shop, crammed with many different people booking fares and making enquiries. Kelly moved quickly to the end of the store and sat on a stool, craning her neck nervously, watching out for the Police, praying that they would not come into the shop.

Li hovered nearby, twisting her little bag tightly between her fingers and jiggling from one foot to the other. Being on the run was so stressful, maybe she should go back. Li spotted a water dispenser in the corner and went to fetch a drink. While pouring the water she heard a group of young men booking tickets to go up to Chang Mai. She looked at them casually, then froze. One of them was so similar to Kelly, the same features, same mouth. Li hurried back to Kelly and hissed in her ear.

"Him, he look like you." Li pointed in the youth's direction. Kelly snorted, annoyed.

"He's a guy, I'm a girl, not to mention that he has black hair and is bigger than me. For God's sake, Li, could you try and be a little more helpful please." Kelly turned back to face the door, still waiting for the cops to burst in and drag her away. Li tapped her on the shoulder.

"Police look for blonde girl. If you black hair boy, no problem."

Kelly looked at her, and slowly started to smile.

"You're right, I'm sorry, I wasn't even thinking. Being a guy would be perfect cover." Kelly looked at the youth with new appreciation.

The group of young men had finished their transaction and moved out of the shop. Li had overheard that they had bought tickets to Chang Mai, leaving at midnight on the overnight bus.

"Let's follow them. Hurry up! I don't want to lose them." Kelly motioned to Li, then slipped out the door after the group, and as nonchalantly as possible followed them back to their guesthouse.

There was a restaurant at the front of the boys' guesthouse, overlooking the street, and the young men sat down noisily, pushing and joking with one another, excited with their imminent departure on a new adventure.

"Beers please!" One of the youths shouted out to the waitress, who scurried away to get their order. She knew by now what beer they liked. They chatted amongst themselves happily, totally unaware of Kelly and Li watching them.

"I think they are American," Kelly said to Li.

"That good, American passport good." Li smiled.

"OK, this is the plan." Kelly spoke to Li, without taking her eyes off the boys across the street. "I will go and introduce myself to them and try and crack on to the one I want, and convince him to take me to his room. You follow us and find out which room number he takes me to, then go and buy some black hair dye and meet me at his room with it, thirty minutes later. OK?"

Li looked serious and nodded. "OK, but what about me?"

Kelly rolled her eyes. "I just told you what to do!"

"Yes, I know. All this help you, but after you out of Thailand, what about me?" Li was looking at Kelly defiantly, but, shaking with fear inside, afraid of being left alone. She had never been alone before.

Kelly softened. "I'm sorry, I have been selfish. What about friends or family? Where do you want to go? You haven't got a passport, so you can't leave the country with me."

"I need money," Li said flatly.

Kelly quickly checked that the youths were still happily drinking. They were laughing and joking, shouting out for more beers. That was great. Kelly wanted the young man a little tipsy before she went over.

"I don't have much money, you know that, it was all taken off me by your mates." Kelly was getting pissed off with all this hassle.

"He have money." Li inclined her head towards the group they were watching.

"OK, OK. I will give you half of the money I steal off him, but that is all. OK?" Kelly held out her hand to shake on the agreement. Shaking didn't mean anything to Li, but she shook Kelly's hand and said. "OK."

They waited for another fifteen minutes or so, before Kelly got up the courage to approach the group. As she was going to the restaurant she noticed one of the guys in the group coming back from the toilet. She decided it would be better to talk with the one she wanted alone first, so she went straight out the back, to the toilets, to wait for him. She didn't have to wait long. Peeking from her hiding place in the ladies' toilet, she timed it so that when he came out of the toilet she did too. Pretending to almost collide with him, she grabbed his arm to steady herself and laughed.

"Oh, sorry. I'm sorry about that," he stuttered, alarmed that he had almost knocked her over, and was relieved when she smiled.

"That's alright, it was my fault. I wasn't looking where I was going." Kelly kept holding him, and gazed into his eyes seductively. He smiled nervously.

"I saw you at the travel agency just before, didn't I?" Kelly tried to guide the conversation.

"Umm, I don't know. I was at the travel agent, buying a ticket to Chang Mai. Were you there?" His eyes were flicking from her to his friends and back again.

"Yes, I was buying a ticket to Europe, I'm leaving in a couple of days."

"Yeah? We're leaving tonight." His dark hair flopped into his eyes and he flicked it back self-consciously with his hand. Kelly tried to look at him without making it too obvious that she was analysing his features. He was quite similar to her, same eyes and mouth. His nose was straighter than hers, but hopefully on a passport photo, that wouldn't show. He wasn't that much taller than her, a bit short for a guy, but perfect for what she wanted.

"Leaving tonight, that's a shame. I would have liked to spend some time with you." Kelly lowered her eyes and then raised them slowly, flirting outrageously.

He laughed and put his hands in his pockets, then took them out again and folded his arms. He had never met such a forward woman before, it was a little intimidating.

"Yeah? What do you mean?", he asked, not sure if he was getting the signals right.

"It's just that I am really homesick. I'm from Australia, and I saw you and you seem really nice, and I find you really attractive and ..." Kelly's voiced tailed off and she just looked at him, with big round eyes.

"Umm, really? Umm, do you want to join us for a drink or something?" He pointed towards his friends, who were starting to look his way, jostling each other and sniggering.

"Yeah, that would be great. I have to meet my friends a little later, they're shopping at the moment," Kelly lied, standing close to him, so he could feel her body warmth.

"Cool, maybe they can join us later?" He was getting excited, the beer, a beautiful girl hitting on him and more of her friends to come for his buddies. This was a great holiday. They both returned to the group and he introduced Kelly.

"This is, umm..."

"Hi, I'm Sarah. Nice to meet you all." Kelly shook their hands. She loved Americans, they were so friendly. The one she was interested in was called Andrew.

"Would you like a drink?", Andrew volunteered immediately, a total gentleman.

"Thanks, just an orange juice please." Kelly beamed and sat down on the chair Andrew offered. Kelly could see Li across the street, watching them. She felt a brief pang of guilt for what she intended to do, but it was soon gone. After all she had been through, she was lucky to be alive and if she didn't get out of the country soon, she probably wouldn't be for long. She shuddered at the thought of going into a Thai jail for murder and drug smuggling.

She smiled at Andrew and chatted mainly to him. His mates were looking on in disbelief. Why was this girl so into Andrew? He never pulled the babes, it was usually Tom or Chad. These two both looked on jealously, as Kelly and Andrew giggled and whispered to one another.

Suddenly Kelly saw two Policemen come into the restaurant and scan the faces of the patrons. She quickly ducked her head behind Andrew and started whispering into his ear about how attracted she was to him, and how little time they had together.

Two more beers and Andrew's eyes were starting to narrow, he was slurring his words and leaning heavily on Kelly. Kelly decided to make her move, before he collapsed completely.

"Let's go to your room and have some fun, before you have to leave." She made her voice husky and alluring, her lips brushing his ear. Kelly could already see the erection in his pants. She grabbed his hand and stood up, not even giving him the option of answering. All the others cheered and Andrew smiled a sheepish grin as Kelly led him away.

"See you at 10.30 out the front here, Andrew," Tom shouted after him.

"Absolutely!" Andrew shouted back happily, following after Kelly and winking at his buddies.

"Have you got any drink in your room, sweety?", Kelly asked, her mind reeling.

"Nah, nothing, babe. You want some beers? We can get some to go." Andrew swayed over to the waitress and asked for four beers. She was back in a flash, and they went to his room. Kelly hadn't noticed if Li was following them, she prayed that the girl hadn't just taken off and left her, or worse, been caught!

They entered his tiny room. His pack was open on the single bed, with his clothes and crap scattered everywhere.

"Uh, sorry, I wasn't expecting company." Embarrassed he tried to clear the bed, so they had somewhere to sit. It was just a small room with a bed, a chair and nothing else. Kelly was disappointed. She had been hoping that at least he would have his own bathroom.

"Where's the toilet?" Kelly remained standing by the door.

"Umm, just at the end of the corridor, I'll show you." He moved towards the door.

"It's OK, I'll find it. I'll be right back, open the beers, I'm thirsty." Kelly quickly ducked out. Li was hovering in the corridor and jumped when she saw Kelly. It took Kelly a moment to even recognise her. Li had different clothes on and was wearing a cap with all her hair tucked up into it. She looked like a boy.

"OK, thirty minutes and be back here with the hair dye. See if you can get some scissors too. Watch out for the Police, they are everywhere." Kelly whispered to Li.

"I need money, no have money," Li whispered back, looking over her shoulder nervously.

Kelly was afraid to give Li any of her precious funds, in case she never saw Li again, but she had no choice.

"OK, but you have to come back in thirty minutes, don't let me down." Kelly held Li's hand firmly as she handed over the money.

Li pulled her hand away. "I come back." She turned and hurried away.

Kelly took a couple of deep breaths and went back to Andrew's room. He was lying on the bed with shoes off and chest bare.

"Come here beautiful." His voice was low and his eyes half closed.

Kelly laughed. "Give me a sip." She went to take his drink.

"I opened one for you." He leaned over the side of the bed, reaching for the other beer.

"I want to share yours, lover." Kelly sat on the bed and started to kiss him deeply. He responded immediately and kissed her back, using lots of tongue and slobbering around Kelly's mouth. Kelly moaned her encouragement, trying not to think about his hopeless technique. He held her tightly and rolled her over so she was underneath him. Kelly was squirming and rubbing his back with one hand and trying to reach the valium with the other.

"Hang on, hang on, let's slow down a bit. I need some more drink." Kelly laughed, throwing her head back to get a breather from his out of control slippery tongue.

Andrew jumped up and started to undo his belt feverishly.

"Do we have any romantic lighting? A candle or something?"

"I have a torch," he volunteered happily, and started rummaging through his pack to find it. While he was distracted Kelly retrieved the little bottle of pills from her waist band and sat up so he couldn't see them. She tipped four tablets out, unsure how many it would take. She didn't want him to wake up, but she didn't want to kill him either. She reached for the bottle of beer and kept chatting innocently, asking about his travel plans. He was head down and bum up when Kelly popped the four pills into his drink, crushing them to powder against the rim of the bottle, and wiping off the remaining evidence.

"Here, babe. Can I help?" Kelly offered him the beer and started lifting up clothes indiscriminately.

"Thanks." He took a huge swig, then burped loudly. He covered his mouth, embarrassed, but Kelly just laughed. "What a gentleman!"

He relaxed and took another drink. He offered it back, but Kelly had already picked up the other opened bottle.

"Here it is!" Andrew held the torch up in triumph. Kelly clapped her hands together in mock glee. Andrew turned it on and placed it on the chair next to the bed, then turned the main light off. "How's that for romantic lighting?" He chuckled at his own ingeniousness.

"Fabulous. Now get your butt over here." Kelly got up and guided him onto the bed, while she stood next to it and started to do an erotic strip.

He smiled from ear to ear as he watched her slowly take off her top and reveal her braless breasts. They were magnificent. He loved big tits. She rubbed her hands over them slowly and tweaked her nipples, making them stand out immediately. Andrew groaned and started to rub his penis through his pants. Kelly bent and unbuttoned his jeans and pulled them down. He was wearing boxers, so she played with the waistband briefly, then, pulled them down as well, exposing his surprisingly big erection. It was always the nondescript skinny guys that gave you a surprise.

"Wow, look at that. Very impressive," Kelly murmured. She held his beer to his smiling lips and he drank deeply, before she continued with her strip.

She undid the sarong and slowly unraveled it from her body, turning as she went. He had his hand wrapped around his large penis and was jerking it wildly.

"Come and sit on it, baby," he moaned, as he wanked furiously.

Kelly straddled him and started to rub her breasts on his body. He moaned in ecstasy. Kissing his chest, his stomach, working her way slowly down, then she took his big cock into her mouth and started sucking up and down rapidly, flicking her tongue over the head, then plunging her mouth down towards the base. He was close to orgasm; she could feel it in his movements and his breathing. He grabbed her hair and groaned loudly.

"Oh, yeah! Oh yeah!" He gave a couple of quick thrusts then came in her mouth. Kelly held it in her mouth for a moment, then spat it out onto the bed. His eyes were still closed in pleasure.

She reached for her beer and rinsed her mouth, swallowing quickly. He went to take the beer off her and have a drink, but she held it back and handed him his beer, safely waiting under the bed. He didn't make a comment, he was still reeling. Kelly lay next to him and stroked his chest affectionately.

"Mmm, that was great, just what I needed. How do you feel?", Kelly breathed into his ear.

"Man, that was fantastic, you wiped me out!" He tipped the beer up and drained the last drop.

Moments later Andrew just managed to grunt, "I'm wrecked!" His speech was slow and his breathing was starting to even out. Kelly lay still for another five minutes or so, until his breathing was deep and he started to snore a little.

"Hey, lover. Are you awake?" Kelly propped herself up on one elbow to look at him.

In the dim torchlight she could see his mouth slightly open and he looked completely asleep. She shook him, softly at first then more vigorously. He didn't even stop snoring. Kelly smiled and jumped up off the bed.

She quickly dressed in some of his clothes. His jeans were a bit tight on her hips, but they were comfortable enough. She put on three t-shirts, trying to cover her breasts, but they still showed, she would have to wear a jacket when she was at the airport and going through customs and immigration.

It didn't take her long to find his money bag. It was under the bed, with the shirt and shoes he had taken off. Kelly opened it to find two thousand dollars in American travellers cheques, three credit cards, five hundred American dollars in cash and some Thai money.

"Jackpot!", she whispered to herself. The passport was there too. Nice and new and fresh looking. Kelly quickly checked the photo. Maybe with coloured short hair she would look like that. She hoped that the officials at the airport wouldn't look too closely. "Maybe we all look the same to them," she thought hopefully.

She started to pack his bag with all the clothes that she wanted. Mainly pants and T-shirts. She left the underwear, she wasn't going to bother with boxers. As she packed some of his toilet gear, there was a soft tap on the door. At last, Li was back. Kelly went to the door and was about to open it when a man's voice said.

"Hey, Andrew, you there man?" Kelly froze.

"Andrew, dude, are you there?", he repeated, more loudly this time, and tried the door handle. Kelly stood stock still, sweat broke out on her brow.

"He's a little busy at the moment, go away!" Kelly shouted out bravely.

The friend laughed and replied, "We leave in one hour, man."

Kelly could hear his steps retreating. She didn't have much time, where was Li? Kelly finished packing and then didn't know what to do. She had hoped that Li would be back here and that she would have time to colour her hair in the bathroom at the end of the corridor. It was not working out. She paced up and down the room impatiently, stealing a glance at her victim regularly, to make sure there was no sign of him stirring. Eventually there was a soft tap at the door. Kelly kept quiet.

"Hello, Kelly?" Li's voice carried through the door. Kelly hurried to open it, and she pulled Li into the room and quickly closed the door.

"Did you get the stuff?" Kelly asked nervously, in a hoarse whisper.

"Did you get money?" Li asked back, determined not to be pushed around.

Kelly sighed heavily. "Look we don't have much time, we have to get out of here, his friends are coming back."

"I know, they at front desk." Li said flushed.

"What? No! We have to leave." Kelly grabbed the pack and money bag and went to the door. Li grabbed her arm violently and swung her back around.

"You give me money." Li was shaking and her eyes were wide, but she meant business.

"Look, we don't have time here, wait 'til we are safely out of here." Kelly tried to reason with her.

"No! Now."

Kelly didn't want to waste anymore time. She pulled the cash out of the money bag and gave Li two hundred of the American dollars and all of the Thai money.

"OK? That's all the cash. Travellers cheques are no good to you without ID." Kelly stuffed the money bag into the pack and slipped out of the door, with Li close behind.

"Is there another way out? If his friends are at reception, we can't go that way, they will recognise me." Kelly was starting to panic. She felt terrible drugging and ripping off that poor boy. He looked like he could afford it, but that didn't make her feel any better.

"Yes, this way." Li led Kelly past the toilets to a back exit. They ran out and never looked back.

"I have to quickly cash these travellers cheques, before they are reported stolen, but I have to cut and colour my hair before that, so I look like the passport photo. Where can we do that?" Kelly breathed heavily as she and Li ran down the alley.

"We go another guesthouse," Li said, slowing down to catch her breath. Kelly saw a sign for a guesthouse twenty metres up the street. It was quiet in the back streets here, not many people at all.

"Let's go there." Kelly strode off with Li close behind.

They both went into the front reception area. Kelly walked up to the desk and smiled, as much as she could through the strain, and asked for a room. The young, nicely dressed Thai man beamed.

"Yes, Madam, how many nights please?"

"One night please."

"You want private bathroom or share bathroom, Madam?"

"Private, please. How much is it?" Kelly wiped her top lip. She was sweating with the three T-shirts on.

"How do you want to pay, Madam?" He continued his spiel politely.

"Umm, cash, American dollars, OK?

"Yes, no problem, Madam. That will be forty-five dollars."

Kelly handed him the hundred dollar note. He sucked on his teeth, not happy at getting such a big note. He held it up to the light to check authenticity then meandered to the back office to get change.

"I'm in a bit of a hurry. Can I go to the room and get my change later, please?" Kelly was wondering if this man had seen her photo on the news and was going to the back room to call the Police. He smiled, obligingly, and came back to the desk.

"Of course, Madam. Now, please fill out this registration form." He slid the sheet of paper over the counter to her. "May I see your passport please? By the way, locals are not allowed into the room with you." He was looking at Li with a hostile air, presuming she was a prostitute.

Kelly wasn't sure what to do, she looked at Li. Li gestured with her hands for Kelly to come over to her and talk.

"Excuse me a moment, please," Kelly said to the man. He gave a quick, bored smile.

"What should we do?" Kelly tried to keep her panicked voice down.

"We go another place, here too small." Li whispered. "Let's go."

Kelly collected her $100 note back, much to the man's disappointment and they ran off to find another guesthouse. This area of Khao San Road was full of them; it wouldn't be a problem to find one with looser security.

They soon found a bigger guesthouse and entered the café in front. As they approached the reception desk Kelly noticed a couple of young Thai men looking straight at her and they started to head in her direction. Panicking, she turned around to run, but the entrance was already blocked by some more rough looking men, intently staring at her. She screamed at Li to run and turned back, desperately searching for an escape route. The men were almost upon her when she jumped up on one of the tables and tried to run across other tables to an open window over the street. Diners leaped out of the way as she sent plates and glasses smashing to the floor in her effort to get away. But the men were quick, and as she jumped from the window they were upon her and pinned her to the ground in seconds. People in the café looked on with concern, but no one seemed to want to involve themselves in what was happening. Li was being held on the café floor by three men, with one arm bent painfully up her back, her face a mask of horror and disbelief.

"Help! Let me go!", Kelly screamed, twisting and writhing to get free. The men held them both tightly, there was no escape. Workers at the café started shouting at the men, words shot back and forth, words she couldn't understand. Li had her eyes shut and was rocking back and forth whimpering. They were hauled to their feet and marched to a waiting van. The door slammed shut with a bang, and they were driven away. Kelly sat hunched with her head in her hands; she couldn't believe they had been caught so easily. What was going to happen to them now?

"I suppose we are being taken back." She looked over at Li, curled up on the seat, moaning.

"He will kill us." Li's voice was barely a whisper, her eyes red.

Kelly shivered as sweat ran down her face. Would it be a quick death or would the big Boss make an example of her and drag out her suffering for as long as possible?

It wasn't long before the van stopped and they heard voices. The lock scraped and the door was flung open. A handsome blonde man stood there, a worried frown on his face.

"Kelly?", he asked cautiously, squinting into the darkened van.

Kelly's heart jumped in her chest at hearing this stranger speak her name, she didn't recognise him.

"It's Kelly, isn't it?" He was standing closer now.

"Who are you? What do you want?" Kelly asked warily.

"You don't know me. My name is Stefan", the handsome young man said with a thick accent.

"I recognise you from your photo at the Police station. You have been reported missing, and you met Hans at the Police station today."

"I don't know any Hans."

"Hans is Karin's father. You told him today that you had been kidnapped and held with Karin. She is my girlfriend, she went missing over a month ago." Stefan wasn't sure if this was the right girl. She didn't look very much like the photo.

"Yes, I am Kelly. I was with Karin."

Stefan beamed, his relief obvious. Kelly felt guilty about the news she would have to break to him.

"I'm sorry about all this." He waved in the direction of the men who had brought them here. "I've been looking all over for you since this afternoon."

"Have you seen today's news?", she asked fearfully.

"Yes. Was that you? Did you really kill those people?" The names of the foreigners had not been released, so Stefan still didn't know about Karin.

His face was creased with worry and the strain of weeks of fruitless searching in Bangkok definitely showed.

"I have to call Hans and tell him we found you. We have hundreds of people out looking for you." He quickly made the call.

"Come, we will go to a safe place." He pulled a huge wad of cash from his pocket and handed it to the Thai men standing around, waiting expectantly.

Holding Kelly's arm securely, he raced out onto the street to hail a taxi. Li followed, blindly, not really knowing if she should go with them. She was lost by herself.

"Have you seen Karin recently?", Stefan asked, as soon as they were settled in the taxi. He was not sure if he could trust these girls, after all, he had seen on the news today that Kelly was an experienced drug smuggler, responsible for four murders. Maybe it was a mistake inviting them back to Annika and Tim's, where Hans was waiting. She didn't look like a junkie murderer, a bit rough maybe, but not a murderer. But then again, what does a murderer look like?

"Yes, I've seen her." Kelly looked straight into Stefan's eyes, and he could tell that she was telling the truth, but there was not good news to follow.

"Please, is she OK?" Stefan's voice caught in his throat as he stared at Kelly.

"No, she is dead." Kelly didn't know how to say it any other way. How do you lessen the blow of someone's death?

Stefan chocked back a sob and rocked his head in his hands. They were all quiet for a moment, until he raised his head and asked, "What happened?" Tears blurred his vision, but he had to know.

"She was abducted. So was I, and another two girls. We have been kept on a compound, near the city, and prostituted to wealthy Asian men. I'm not sure how long for, we were drugged." Kelly felt so much better after saying it. It was like a huge weight had been lifted.

Stefan started to cry freely, his body convulsed with savage sobbing. Kelly and Li sat quietly, allowing him a moment of privacy for his grief.

"I can't believe it. How can this happen?", Stefan stammered, continuing to weep.

Kelly didn't know what to say.

"Who is this then?" Stefan had composed himself slightly and was pointing to Li.

"She is Thai, she was a slave of theirs too and she helped me escape. We tried to get Karin out as well, but she was very sick, I'm not sure what was wrong with her," Kelly replied.

"She never eat. She make herself sick." Li spoke up, looking directly at Stefan.

He just nodded, understanding how Karin would have been unable to cope with the horrendous situation and just given up. He felt so sad for her, that he had been unable to protect and save her.

"How long have you been here, looking for her?", Kelly asked, wanting to break the depressing silence.

"Over three weeks. I arrived two weeks after she left a friend's house here." Stefan was wiping his face with a large white handkerchief and blew his nose loudly.

"So, we must have been there for over five weeks. Didn't you go to the Police here?" Kelly was confused.

"Of course I did, along with Karin's father, who is very influential and has some good friends here, but the Police and Embassy officials said they were doing everything they could. They said they had people scouring the streets for Karin. Sure, they went through the motions, but after checking hospitals and jails they had more or less said that hundreds of people were going missing every year, and that they were usually found high on drugs on the beach somewhere, enjoying themselves. I knew that Karin would never do that, but no one would help us. So I started my own investigation about a week ago, paying local people for information and surveillance. I saw your picture at the Police station, so your family has probably reported you missing as well. You should call them." Stefan handed her his mobile phone.

Kelly was shocked to realise that she hadn't thought about her family in ages, she had been focusing so much on surviving and getting away.

"I would love to call my family. Thanks." Kelly knew that they would be worried sick about her. No one answered and the answer phone did not click on. She hung up, disappointed, but also a little relieved. She had no idea what she was going to tell them.

"The whole Police force is probably looking for me by now," Kelly said miserably, handing the phone back. "I need to follow through on my plan."

"What is your plan?" Stefan asked. "Maybe, I can help."

Kelly quickly explained her plan to Stefan as he listened intently. He was sceptical about it working, but stayed silent.

❖　　　❖　　　❖

It was a little after 10.00 p.m. when they arrived at Annika's and Tim's apartment. They were quickly buzzed into the building. The security guard at the entrance looked up at them questioningly, as they ran past to the elevators. He wasn't too alarmed, he had seen Stefan many times before; his phone had started to ring so he let them go by.

Tim, Annika and Hans greeted them at the door. Tina, the maid, brought tea, and the story was hastily retold to Hans by Stefan. Hans' face went ashen as he sat hunched at the table. Annika looked sick and sat crying softly. Tim quickly put a comforting arm around her, looking close to tears himself. The couple felt guilty for having invited Karin to stay with them. Would they ever be forgiven? Tim wished he could do something to make it up to their grieving friend, but what could replace a child?

They sat around in silence for a long time, all engrossed in their own misery.

"How did you know Captain Thay Pok at the Police station today?" Hans suddenly looked over at Kelly.

"He was a customer, he would come and see me at the compound every couple of days," Kelly replied. She told them how he had bought her jewelry, but it had been fake and how she had asked him to help her when she was first taken and he had become angry and threatened to tell the big Boss.

"That bastard! He knew where Karin was the whole time. I can't believe we trusted him!" Hans bowed his head in sorrow once again.

"Unfortunately there is a lot of corruption within the Police here, especially the tourist Police," Tim agreed.

Hans asked Kelly more about the compound and Karin, but it was Li who was better able to answer. Annika sobbed softly into her handkerchief as the horrific story was retold.

"You help protect me from big Boss, I show you compound where Karin is." Li spoke solemnly to Hans. If they were going to help Kelly, then she wanted help as well. She couldn't survive by herself and she had a lot of incriminating evidence against the Boss. He would definitely not let her live after this fiasco. Hans agreed to help Li. He wanted to see for himself if Karin was really gone. He would hold out hope until then.

A sudden banging on the front door startled them all out of their depression. Li let out a small whimper and Kelly looked ready to pass out.

"Police! Let us in!", a loud man's voice barked from behind the door.

"Oh my God! Don't let them in!", Kelly whispered in alarm.

"We know you have criminals in there! Let us in!" The Police pounded against the door.

"Quick, into the kitchen, there is a back door." Annika grabbed both of the panicked girls' arms and dragged them to the kitchen. Off the kitchen was a small room for Tina, who stayed over three nights a week, and another door that led into the stair well. They all ran out, tumbling and jostling against each other as they stumbled down the eighteen flights of stairs. Tim was in the lead and stopped suddenly when he reached the bottom holding his hand up for the others to be quiet. Annika puffed heavily, holding her heaving chest, her face bright red. They listened intently. Footsteps were racing down from the top floor after them.

"They're coming!", Kelly squawked unnecessarily, grabbing Stefan's arm for reassurance.

"Listen, I have an idea!" Tim quickly spoke in Swedish to Hans who nodded agreement. He hurriedly whispered further instructions to them all. It sounded like it just might work. They split into two groups and ran out of the fire door, down the side alley and into the night.

FREE

Stefan and the two women hailed a taxi. Diving into the backseat he asked the young Thai girl to tell the driver to take them to the international airport, quickly! The taxi swerved back into the onslaught of traffic and they were off, to freedom!

Hans was busy now, distracted for a short time from his grief. He had thirty minutes to organise a charter plane out of Bangkok for Stefan and the other two. Twenty minutes later Stefan's phone rang and he answered on the first ring.

"Stefan. It's all organised." Hans' voice was steady and efficient. "Go to Hangar 8 at the private end of the airport and a charter plane will be waiting there for you. The pilot's name is Jim McGinty. He will fly you to Shanghai. It is the closest airport that is safe and has no extradition laws with Thailand."

"Thanks, I'll call you when we get there." Stefan rang off. Was this going to work? He looked at the worried faces of the women as they tore through the incessant Bangkok traffic.

They didn't have much difficulty finding Hangar 8. As they approached they saw the huge shed brightly lit, and a stocky redheaded man racing around, checking the exterior of the craft, a corporate gulf-stream jet. They were going to go out in style! They piled out from the taxi and ran over to the plane.

"Jim McGinty?", Stefan called out as he approached the man.

"Certainly is." The redheaded man grinned and looked over at Stefan, then the women, one white and one Thai. He wasn't about to start asking questions, there was too much money in it for him. He loved this cloak and dagger stuff anyway, it reminded him of the fun days running illegal arms in the Middle East.

"How long until we can take off, Jim?" Stefan didn't know how much longer he could take all this waiting. They had been standing around for thirty minutes now. He was getting nervous.

Jim had just hung up the phone. "Not much longer, our flight-plan has just been accepted. Let's get in the plane. We'll start off in about ten minutes."

Stefan rounded up the two others and they hurriedly boarded the plane.

The engine roared, but was barely audible, as the three sat back in the huge, lush leather seats of the luxury aircraft. They all grinned at each other. The plane taxied slowly out of the hangar and along the clearly lit side road, which met up with the main runway taxi area. It seemed to be taking forever, as Jim moved slowly into his position, waiting for final clearance. Then, without warning, they saw masses of lights flashing; red, blue and white. The Police!

Stefan jumped up and ran to the cock-pit. "Go, just go!", he screamed at Jim, arms waving desperately.

"I can't, man! They haven't given me clearance! I have been instructed to stay put. I'm sorry." He pulled the throttle back and the engines whined to a soft idle.

Stefan ran back to the others, all they could do now was wait.

The Police entered the cabin with guns drawn. They had no idea how dangerous these people were, or what they had done, but orders from the top were to keep them until the boss arrived. They must have done something pretty bad to get the Police Commissioner out of bed at this time of night. They were cuffed and led single file into a waiting room inside the main terminal. There they sat morosely, not talking. Footsteps echoed and voiced rapped back and forth as the three heard people approaching. The door opened. The small, very well dressed Captain Thay Pok entered and behind him came a huge hulk of a man. He was very scary looking with a large, sweaty head and a grimace for a smile, which soon disappeared when he looked at the miserable three seated in the room.

"What? Who are these people?", the huge man bellowed, looking back at the uniformed Policeman who had opened the door.

"The prisoners, Sir," he answered nervously, unsure what was happening.

"These are not the people I want! Who are they?" The huge man glared at the prisoners, then back at Captain Thay Pok, barely containing his fury.

"You said 'A white male, a white female and one female local', Sir. They were in the chartered plane you asked us to stop." The Policeman's voice was shakey and he glanced nervously at his superior.

The big Boss stared in disbelief at Stefan, Annika and the maid Tina.

❖   ❖   ❖

Tim and Hans had taken Kelly and Li, dropping Li at a friend's house, where she could lay low until all this mess was sorted out. Kelly hugged her quickly with tears in her eyes,

"Thank you for helping me. Good luck!"

Li smiled back, "No, you help me. Thank you." She quickly ducked into the house, she hated good-byes.

They continued on to the wharf. The plan had hit Tim as they were escaping down the stairs. He had several container loads of furniture ready to depart by ship tonight from the international wharf. Hopefully the Police would be distracted by Stefan and two women chartering a plane and that would leave the coast clear for Kelly to board a ship and get away safely.

The ship was scheduled to leave at 1.00 a.m., as costs were cheaper after midnight, and it was headed for Tokyo.

"How ironic", Kelly thought, "That was where I had originally planned to go. Is this a sign that I'm going to make it after all?"

They arrived at the wharf about midnight and entered the main office. Tim had been sending container loads of furniture from this wharf for many years, so it was no problem to be shown straight through to the night manager's office.

"Mr. Tim! What a surprise, nice to see you." Mr. Jook, the manager, jumped to his feet and greeted Tim happily. Mr. Tim was a very good customer; he always paid his bills on time and was very generous. Not to mention the letter of introduction he had written to help secure a place for his daughter in a French University. He was one of the few white men who understood how to grease the wheels of business.

"Mr. Jook, nice to see you. How is your family? Your daughter doing well at her studies?" Tim shook his hand warmly.

"Yes, yes. She very clever girl, not like her father at all!" Mr. Jook laughed loudly at his own joke. "Please take a seat, and your friends." Mr. Jook raced around from behind his desk to pull up another chair. "Would you like some tea?"

"Thank you. That would be lovely." Tim settled back in his seat looking most relaxed, as Mr. Jook picked up his phone to order tea. "I have to handle this very carefully", he thought. "I don't know if Mr. Jook has seen the news or not. I'd better stick as close to the truth as possible."

Kelly jiggled in her chair nervously, anxious about the time it was taking to get to the point.

Mr. Jook politely ignored the scruffy girl and turned his attention back to Tim. "So, how is business?"

"Business is very good, thank you. I have a couple of containers going to Japan tonight." Tim looked like he had all the time in the world for a chat.

"Yes. I saw that on the manifest." Mr. Jook nodded, flashing a casual glance at Kelly as she wriggled in her seat. Something about her looked very familiar.

"Actually, I've come to ask a bit of a favour, Mr. Jook." Tim kept his face calm, although his heart was thumping in his chest. He had a good working relationship with Mr. Jook and he did not want to jeopardise that, but he wanted to do everything in his power to help this girl out of her dreadful situation. It was the least they could do, since they had been unable to save Karin. He was happy in the knowledge that Kelly's family wouldn't have to go through the pain Hans was experiencing right now. That would be reward enough.

"These are my friends, Mr. Hans Johannsen and his wife, Kelly. Mr Johannsen works for me and he came to me this afternoon to ask for some help." Tim took a deep breath, hoping that his exterior still looked calm. "His wife has got herself into a little bit of trouble. Unfortunately she has become addicted to the poppy and indebted to the wrong crowd of people."

Mr. Jook nodded his head, turning towards Kelly with a look of sympathy and understanding. He had many friends who were slaves to the opiate.

"Yes, most unfortunate." Mr. Jook agreed. Suddenly he realised where he had seen her face. "I saw her on the TV tonight! She is a smuggler and has killed people!"

Kelly looked up in alarm. "I am not a smuggler," she yelled.

The door opened and the office girl entered with a tray laden with cups and a tea pot.

Tim held up his hand for Kelly to be quiet. Everyone was quiet until the office girl departed.

"Please, Mr. Jook, look at her. Do you think a young girl like this could possibly kill all those people? It's a bit far-fetched."

Mr. Jook started to look a bit doubtful, but kept a keen eye on Kelly.

"She needs to get away for a bit, to wean herself off the drug and get her health back. Mr. Johannsen knows of an excellent hospital in Japan where she can get the treatment that she so desperately needs." Tim wasn't sure if Mr. Jook believed any of the story; his poker face was unreadable. "The people she has become indebted to are in the Police and have made up this nonsense about her being a drug smuggler, so she cannot expose their corruption," Tim continued.

Mr. Jook waved his hand. "You do not have to explain any more to me, Mr. Tim. You have helped my family immeasurably and I owe you." He guessed that this story was not entirely true, but he was grateful to be able to return the favour and so fulfill his obligation. This was a relatively small price to pay for his daughter's education.

"Do you want both of them on the boat?", Mr. Jook asked, reaching for the phone.

"No, just Kelly. Hans will fly to Japan and meet her there in four days," Tim lied.

Mr. Jook shouted some instructions into the phone. "OK. It is all organised. She has a private room on the top deck, next to the rest of the crew." Mr. Jook's face became very serious. "I trust that she will not be taking any of her bad habit with her onto the boat. I do not want any trouble with customs in Japan."

"Yes, of course. She has nothing with her", Tim assured him.

"Well, you better hurry, the boat is leaving soon." Mr. Jook stood up and followed them out of his office. "I will drive you to the boat."

Kelly was weak with relief, she could hardly believe that these people were going to so much trouble and risking their own future to help her and Li, without even knowing them. She vowed to herself that if she got to safety, she would never forget what they had done for her and she would pay them back, everything. Tim and Hans walked with her onto the ship and took her to her cabin.

"Now, when you get to Tokyo port, you have to go to Immigration," Tim explained.

"But I don't have a passport!", Kelly exclaimed, eyes wide with fear.

"It's OK," Tim calmed her. "Just tell them that you lost it overboard. You fill out some papers and your Embassy will issue you with a new one. No problem." Tim beamed his reassurance.

"I don't know what to say. You have been so kind to me. I will pay everything back, when I can." Kelly looked earnestly at Tim and Hans.

"That is not necessary, I am happy that I was able to help. I only wish that Karin could have escaped with you." Hans smiled, but his eyes gleamed with unshed tears. "And the other girls as well. I have a feeling that there will be a lot of trouble over this. I am certain that there will be no more girls disappearing in the future."

"Yes. So do I." Kelly looked at her feet, guiltily. "I feel bad that I was the only one to get away."

"It is not your fault." Hans held Kelly in a tight hug. "You were strong and you survived. The others have their own reasons for what happened to them." He hoped they were not being premature, this girl deserved to get out of here.

Kelly could barely tear herself away from his embrace. It felt so safe and secure. She never thought she would feel that from human contact ever again, after all that she had been through over the last five weeks. She was glad that she hadn't been affected too adversely. Maybe she would be able to go on with a normal life after this.

"You'd better get on the ship. You are not safe until you are two hundred kilometres out to sea and in international waters."

Kelly took Hans' business card. "I will be in touch." She smiled and walked with them back to the gang plank. They watched from the shore as the ship readied itself for departure. Hans' phone rang and he answered with trepidation.

"Hans, it's me." Stefan's voice sounded small and tired.

"Yes, Stefan, everything has gone well here, are you OK?" Hans was starting to feel tired now too.

"Your friend is fine, Mr Johannsen, but I'm afraid you are required to join us for questioning. You are all accomplices in a very serious crime." The male voice sounded very serious.

"I would be happy to join you Captain. I have a lot of my own questions to ask you, and I'm sure your superiors would be interested in the answers as well."

AUTHOR'S NOTE

In the early 1980s tourists from all over the world started flocking to Thailand for its beautiful tranquil beaches, exotic jungles, cheap products and friendly people.

Asia, as a whole, was just starting to open up to Westerners and Thailand became very popular as a cheap holiday destination. It was especially attractive to young backpackers, who were drawn to the lifestyle, food and affordable prices, not to mention the easy access to cheap drugs, like hash, heroin and hallucinogenic mushrooms.

It was not long before the demand for cheap sex also led to the supply. Thailand earned a reputation as the sex capital of the world. Tours were organised from many countries to travel to Thailand for experiences which were illegal in their own home states.

Foreign funds poured into the country, giving a massive injection to the flagging Thai economy. Unfortunately some local people begrudged the invasion of their quiet lives by raucous foreigners looking for cheap drugs and quick sexual fixes. Soon foreigners began complaining of poor service, below standard products and outright thievery. Many innocent and not so innocent youngsters were targeted as couriers for illegal drugs to pay for their habits. Sometimes, without their knowledge, packages were planted in their luggage or clothing.

Travellers started disappearing without a trace. They were mainly females, but men also. Often they were found dead from drug overdoses or in jail or hospital, but many were never seen again.

The Thailand Tourist Police force was founded in 1986, to provide security and help for the huge increase in foreign tourists complaining about stolen property, bad behaviour and other grievances against local people. These Tourist Police were very harsh to any Thai person caught jeopardising the tourist dollar, but there was also a lot of bribery and corruption within their ranks.

It wasn't until 1990, when with extra funding authorised by the Thai Government and mounting pressure from foreign Embassies, that the Tourist Police force was restructured. The majority of corruption was cleared out and Thailand has been a much safer place to travel as a tourist since then.